# FATE WEAVER

By

Brian Tripp

ISBN: 978-1-945567-261
Library of Congress: 2020922789
Cover Design: Designs by Emily
Cover Illustration: Designs by Emily
Interior Design: Ruth A. Souther
Published by Crystal Heart Imprints
Springfield, IL
www.crystalheartimprints.com

# Dedication

To Joey Pacay, for teaching me from a young age to never be afraid of adventure and creativity.

To Mr. Strait, the first teacher to work one on one with and encourage me with my writing rather than saying "wasting potential" on my report cards.

# ACKNOWLEDGMENTS

And of course, to my family, who never stopped believing in me and supporting me every step of the way.

Special thanks to Mallory, Gary and Rosy for all of their editing help, and to Ruth for guiding me along this journey.

# Prologue

Master Talius stood on the balcony of his quarters, enjoying the warm breeze as he watched his three pupils spar in the yard below. He'd been overseeing their training, unbeknownst to them, since they were nothing more than children, ignorant to the world's horrors they would someday come to face.

Talius had been in charge of the Citadel, nestled deep in the capital of Stormhaven, for many years now, turning green young men into soldiers and sending them to the front lines to die for the sake of humanity. The children of prophecy had needed time to develop their skills.

"They have grown," a woman spoke, walking up to him. She made no sound as she moved save for the muffled slaps of her bare feet as they made contact with the cool stone of the balcony floor. Power radiated from her beautiful amber eyes.

"They have," Talius agreed. "But not enough."

"Whether or not you believe it to be enough no longer matters. There is a storm approaching; one that your people are not nearly prepared for. Even now, my brother gathers his forces hoping to break back into your realm. Without the tower in your control, you will have no hope."

Talius turned on her, anger in his eyes. "I locked their power away deep in my vaults on your orders. I've sent thousands of my people to their deaths on YOUR ORDERS, and I've left thousands more unprotected to the monsters at their doorsteps so that your prophecy could come to fruition. And now you're telling me that all of that was for nothing?"

"Of course not," the woman replied calmly, leaning against the balcony railing. "You have bought yourself valuable time; time enough for the three children to blossom into the warriors they need to be. You fight against the power of the gods, Talius. You may slow them down, but you cannot keep them out of your realm forever. Eventually they will break through, and when they do you will need fate on your side."

Talius looked back down at the young adults he had come to

love, as if they were his own children. “They are not ready,” he whispered.

“Time has run out Talius,” the woman replied, not unkindly. She rested her hand on the sleeve of his orange robes; a soothing gesture. “Send them to me and leave this place until matters are settled. Your guidance will be necessary in what is to come.”

He sighed, turning his attention back to the small woman in front of him. “As you wish, Lady Hestia.”

# Part One

# CHAPTER 1: The Heroes

The three stood before the darkness of the cavern buried deep within the Arholm Peaks. The cavern was merely a fable used to draw adventurers from around the world to the little mountainside village of Gall in an attempt to boost trade; or at least that's what the villagers believed. But the three knew better than that.

They had been brought up on the stories and myths of ages past. Their training to take the throne had begun from a very early age. The tower had existed in this world for little over a century now, and the war that came with it had reached a fever pitch.

Mortals fought an endless battle against the hordes surrounding the tower to take the throne from the fading powers of old. The villagers had warned these three that the mountains were crawling with monsters now, and that everybody who had gone looking for the cavern had disappeared.

They begged them not to leave the safety of their walls chasing after a legend. After all, they were only in their early twenties and it wasn't worth the waste of life. But the three knew there was a weapon hidden deep within the earth that could turn the tides of the war.

It was their mission to retrieve it so that mankind could claim the throne. And so, they'd set off from the little village, much to its residents' dismay.

~~~

Levy, Ashe and Quinn stood at the entrance of the cavern, staring deep into the blackness. The wind had stopped nearly a mile ago causing the air in the valley to become stagnant and hot. The villagers warned them about the vast number of monsters prowling around the mountains, and they had been right. Their clothes clung tight to their bodies, drenched in sweat and ichor.

"Are we sure this is the place?" Ashe asked, shielding her viridescent eyes from the sun. She turned her nose up at the smell of her ruined shirt. "I was expecting something worse than rabid harpies."

Tearing a strip of fabric from a gouged shred of her vest, she tied her long, platinum hair back into a ponytail. The heat was stifling, and she was hoping to feel any kind of breeze on the back of her neck. Thanks to the ridiculous number of harpies they'd had to fight off to reach this cavern, the black fabric of her tunic clung tight to her body.

"This is definitely the right place," said Quinn, brushing his lengthy, black hair from his eyes. "I can sense something with an absurd amount of energy coming from within."

Levy shrugged. "Maybe we got lucky and the guardian is nocturnal."

The sleeveless tunic he wore was also soaked, showing off his broad, muscular frame. His normally coiffed hair was damp with sweat; causing it to hang limply to the side.

"I don't believe in luck when it comes to monsters," Ashe squinted into the darkness. "Something feels off."

Quinn pursed his lips. She was right of course. When it came to anything relating to the old legends, those who relied on luck didn't live long. But what choice did they have?
~~~

Humanity was on the verge of extinction, fighting a losing battle. There wasn't a lot they could do against monsters with their limited weaponry. Humans were flesh and blood.

Anything hard enough could kill them. But monsters were made from essence and ichor and mortal weapons just didn't affect them. There were a few essence engraved weapons in their ranks that could hurt them - in fact, each of them had one - but they were spread so thin that it was like swinging a stick at a cloud of hornets.

Sure, they might kill a few, but what's one stick against a swarm? That's why their duty was to track down myths and stories across the land. The more weapons they could find that would help them against the hordes the tower attracted, the more likely they would find themselves victorious.

"Well, we won't know until we try, and I don't want to wait around until something else notices we're here," Levy said. "Wait outside if you want, but I'm going in."

Quinn rolled his eyes as Levy made his way towards the mouth of the cave. "What a hero," he muttered and looked back to Ashe, entranced by the light smattering of freckles across the bridge of her nose. "Shall we?"

Ashe smiled and took his hand, meeting his crimson eyes with her own, as he led her into the darkness.

Their ears popped upon entering the cavern, and they had to fight down a wave of nausea. From what their training had taught them, it was a clear sign that they had entered somebody else's dominion. The air became cool, and a slight gust blew deeper into the cavern, beckoning them forward.

"Okay," Ashe bit her lip, "now I really don't like this."

Quinn tightened his grip on her hand, reassuring her. "Don't worry, if anything happens, our lord and savior Levy will protect us, right Mr. Hero?" He batted his eyelashes in the man's direction.

Levy smiled a wolfish grin. "Don't worry princess, I'll save you from the bad guys. You too Ashe."

"That's gonna be kind of hard with my foot up your ass," Quinn fired back.

"Now boys, let's not get sidetracked. You can have your little lover's quarrel once we get back."

They walked deeper into the murky cavern, until the light from the entrance finally faded, leaving them in complete darkness.

*"Illumino,"* Quinn whispered, pulling the flow of natural energy in the air toward himself.

A soft red light sprang forth from the burgundy crystal he wore around his neck, illuminating the cave. The air thickened as they descended deeper into the earth.

Sharp stalactites dotted the ceiling, causing a slight unease to begin building in Quinn's stomach. He didn't like their chances in the event of even a slight tremor. Though the floor they walked upon was rock, a path of stones formed down the center, splitting into three separate gateways before them. Above each gateway a symbol was carved into the stone.

Levy looked back at Quinn. "Which way is the energy coming from?"

Quinn closed his eyes, concentrating on each gateway. He shook his head. "Either the energy is coming from all three paths equally, or it's so immense that I can't pinpoint its exact location."

"You're right on both accounts actually." A soft, female voice drifted through the air. "All three paths lead to the flame, though each path can only be walked by one of the three."

The air in the room grew heavy with the presence of this new voice. If the pressure built any further, Quinn was certain his ears would have popped again. The smell of burning coals lingered in his nose.

"What's to keep us all from going down the same path?" Ashe asked the empty cavern, feeling slightly foolish to be speaking to air.

"Why, I am of course!" The voice responded with mirth.

"And who are you?" Quinn asked.

"Pass the test, and we'll meet soon enough. Or disobey the rules and we'll meet even sooner," the voice challenged.

The air grew significantly warmer, as if daring them to disobey. Quinn looked over and saw a slight sneer resting on Levy's face. Gods he hated that look. It always led to trouble.

"Suppose I don't feel like following a faceless voice into an unknown darkness, what then?"

"Well," came the voice again, in an unpleasant tone, akin to a dull knife trying to saw through metal, "You could certainly *try* to disobey."

Levy looked over at Quinn. "C'mon buddy," he smiled. "Let's go down this center path and see what's in store for us."

Quinn sighed. He knew better than to argue with his friend when he got like this. The last time he'd tried to reason with him, they'd accidentally let half of the Master's prized horses back at the Citadel free, resulting in hours of hunting and herding.

It was a long story that ended in months of extra duties. Together they made their way to the center archway. Quinn closed his eyes wishing silently that nothing bad happened. Of course, he didn't get his way. Things were never so simple.

No sooner had they stepped beyond the threshold, the voice, dripping with honey, said, "Don't take this personally, but rules are rules."

The air in front of them pressurized immensely creating what felt like a solid barrier. With a sound like the crack of a whip, Levy and Quinn were launched back out into the opening. They hit the ground hard, rolling to a stop next to where Ashe stood, a look of complete shock upon her face.

Levy got to his feet first and coughed, dusting off his clothes. He quirked his eyebrow, "Well, I never was one for tests, but I get the feeling we don't have a choice this time, guys."

Ashe swallowed. "Ya think?"

The hall echoed with a beautiful, melodic laugh. All around the cavern, tiny flames of every color imaginable sprang forth, lighting up the darkness and dancing to the voice.

Quinn had finally caught his breath and was struggling back to his feet when the voice spoke again. "Choose your paths wisely."

Quinn took a few deep breaths and looked up at the symbols over each archway. Carved into the rock above the left gate was a hand with small orb of flame in its center. Over the center, a bear was carved and over the right was a circle with eight arrows pointing outward.

"Before we choose, can you tell us what the symbols mean?" Quinn asked.

"Ah," the voice answered, amusement ringing in her voice. "Clever of you to ask. Very well, I will reward it. The left is the symbol of fire. It stands for the loyalty and devotion that burns within us all. In the center is the bear, a symbol of strength.

"Above the right gate is the symbol of Chaos. It is the wild element of the three. This gate will bring many twists and turns. Choices will be made, though not always for the right reasons."

Levy walked up to the center gate, "Looks like this gate was meant for me. I'll see you guys on the other side."

Before anyone could protest, he turned and was gone. Ashe looked over at Quinn. "I'm going to choose fire. I think you would know better than anyone how devoted I am to something I love."

Quinn gave her a nervous smile. "Luck," he said.

She winked and gave him a quick kiss before walking through the gate. He watched her until he could no longer see her outline in the darkness before walking up to the gate of Chaos.

"Why do you hesitate? Is this not what you came for?" the voice asked.

"What awaits us down these paths?" Quinn took a deep breath.

"Each path contains a guardian of the flame. You must defeat your guardian to prove your worth."

"That's not what I meant, and you know it. When you were explaining my path you said, 'choices will be made'. What did you mean?"

"Clever, clever," the voice smiled again. "Alas, I cannot answer your questions at this time. Walk your path, defeat your guardian and come speak to me."

With that said, he could feel the presence leave the room.

Quinn looked up at the symbol of Chaos over his gate, and walked through it, feeling as though something had changed, and would never be the same again.

# CHAPTER 2: Quinn

The first thing Quinn noticed as he walked down the dimly lit stone path was that the atmosphere of the cave had completely changed. The air here was cold, almost frigid. The slight breeze he'd felt before had turned into bouts of irregular gusts and he had to brace himself against each one in order to continue on.

It was as if the cave didn't want him here or was warning him to turn back. For a second, he was tempted to do just that. But he continued forward, if for nothing else than to meet his friends on the other side.

"I wonder how they are doing against their "guardians" whatever that was supposed to mean," he muttered.

Before him, a white light beamed through a cracked stone archway. He tucked the crystal away in his shirt, no longer needing the light it was providing. As he reached the archway, he had to convince himself what he was seeing was real.

The cavern ended right there, and opened up into a misty, grey sky. Snow swirled off of the ground into the gusts of wind. The clearing was shaped into a giant circle, reminding him of an arena. The sides dropped down into what looked like an endless abyss.

Scattered around the arena were stone statues, all with faces twisted into grotesque forms. Across the way lay another cavern entrance. He made it halfway to the opening before a figure rose up from the snow, blocking his path.

"Hero, stop there and listen if you wish to keep your life." The man walked forward through the swirling snow, meeting Quinn in the center. "Do you know who I am?"

Quinn looked at the ancient leather armor the man wore and the short bronze Xiphos at his side. He was about to offer up a comment on how his skirt brought out the blue in his eyes when he noticed the head in the warrior's hand, covered in writhing snakes.

He decided he'd better not.

"You're Perseus," Quinn responded, taking a step back and reaching for the blade strapped to his back.

"That is correct. I am Perseus, the hero who slayed the Gorgon, Medusa." At this he drew his bronze sword and pointed it at Quinn. "Many false heroes have tried to reach the flame. If you wish to live, turn back now. Do not become one of them."

Quinn had heard enough. He didn't particularly hate Perseus. Though he was an ancient hero, which meant he was filled to the brim with hubris, growing up with Levy had numbed him to it.

He'd been putting up with hubris his entire life. That being said, Quinn wasn't a fan of being threatened. He drew his sword and rested it against Perseus' outstretched blade, whose eyes widened in recognition of the sword.

"An engraved blade," Perseus noted. "That is impressive. But do not believe that just because you have a blade filled with the essence of the gods, you are able to win this fight. Your fate was sealed the moment you drew your sword."

Both warriors jumped back and lifted their weapons. Quinn knew that while Perseus' sword was dangerous, the real threat would be the head of Medusa. One wrong glance would turn him into a statue, cursed to spend the rest of eternity welcoming other "false heroes."

Perseus lunged at him, whipping his sword across Quinn's body. Quinn met the blade with his own, showering them both in white-hot sparks. It was immediately obvious that Quinn was not his match in strength. But that was expected.

Quinn wasn't like Levy. Whereas Levy was broad chested, muscular and built solid as an oak, Quinn was lean and built with whipcord muscle. He had never intended to win this fight with his might. His strength was in his speed.

He waited until Perseus began to push both of their blades toward his neck and then ducked down low, sweeping his leg out in an attempt to take Perseus off of his feet. Perseus reacted quickly, jumping in the air and sent a thrust down at Quinn's face.

*Perfect.*

Quinn rolled underneath the blow and leapt back to his feet, spinning a kick at the hand that held Medusa's head. Perseus, realizing his mistake, whipped the head back behind his body, taking the kick full in the chest.

Though his leathers absorbed some of the blow, it was enough to knock him off balance. Quinn swept his blade upward across Perseus' chest, slicing the armor in twain and opening a thin cut along his body.

Perseus jumped back with a fierce smile, a fire building behind his eyes. "Excellent," he said, as he let a laugh escape his lips. "It has been quite some time since I have been met with an able challenger."

Quinn couldn't help but smile as he felt the adrenaline coursing through his body.

"Yeah," he said through his grin. "But don't feel bad. Nobody beats old age."

Perseus let out a booming laugh, echoing through the nothingness around them. "You're a cocky one, aren't you?"

"You think I'm bad," Quinn smiled back. "You should meet my friend Levy."

"Unfortunately," Perseus said, sobering up, "I don't think either of you will be around much longer for introductions."

Perseus let out a snarl and flung his blade out again. Quinn saw the move for what it was and chose to dodge it rather than parry. As the blade swept down, Perseus thrust out the head of Medusa. Her eyes flew open, releasing a bright white light.

Quinn hadn't been expecting the flash of light and nearly looked toward it purely by reflex. Instead he caught himself and swiftly turned his head away. But that was exactly what Perseus had been waiting for. As soon as Quinn's head had turned, Perseus struck.

Realizing his mistake, Quinn lifted his blade up to try and deflect the blow. However, there was no momentum behind the swing, and Perseus' blade struck true, slicing a vertical cut down the right side of Quinn's face, running from his eyebrow down to the bone in his cheek. He felt the warm blood run down his face, forcing his right eye closed.

Quinn cried out in pain and jumped back, attempting to buy some time to wipe the blood from his eye. Perseus pressed on, like a shark smelling blood in the water. Quinn backed his way to the edge of the arena, constantly deflecting Perseus' sword.

Small cuts continued to open up along his body as he could only do so much to deflect the swipes on his blind side. He took another step back and his left foot felt the edge of the abyss reach out to him.

*Vlakas*. He had gotten himself pinned between a mad warrior and an endless drop. *Come on Quinn, think.*

For a split second he considered jumping into the abyss. He was sick of always fighting a losing battle. Humanity was on their last legs, after all. If he could jump into that blackness and end the suffering now, why shouldn't he? Better this way than being eaten by some monster or trapped in stone by Medusa.

*Yes, jump. Let me end your suffering,* whispered the wind.

Quinn's eyes began to feel heavy, and the urge to jump became overwhelming. Then he saw Ashe's face flicker across his mind. Quinn began to feel his body warming up, until a fierce fire was burning through his blood.

*Don't you dare,* she scolded.

He snapped back to reality, pausing, his foot stretched out over the abyss. Was the Abyss sentient? He was sure he had heard it calling to him, and the urge to jump had been so strong. He thought back to the legends of Perseus and was struck with inspiration. A fierce smile spread across his face.

He knew how to win this fight. He recalled the myths he had spent hour after grueling hour studying back at the Citadel where he had been trained. There was one thing above all else Perseus had fought to protect when he was alive. He looked Perseus in the eye and said, "your mother was a whore."

Perseus stopped in his tracks; a look of absolute shock frozen on his face. A moment of sadness followed as if Quinn had hurt his feelings, before just as swiftly changing to rage. As the insult finally sunk in, Perseus roared at him, tensing his legs and pouncing.

The move was a good one, and had Quinn been attempting to block it, he surely would have died. Perseus feinted a strike toward Quinn's head and then lunged forward, stabbing his sword at Quinn's heart. But Quinn had no intentions of blocking. Instead, he threw himself backwards over the abyss and grabbed onto the edge.

Perseus's eyes widened as he realized his mistake.

*Too late*, Quinn thought, and he watched the momentum of Perseus's strike carry him over the ledge. For a second, he thought he had misjudged the speed of Perseus' strike, as he reached out seeking to grab Quinn's leg.

Feeling a moment of guilt, Quinn stretched out his hand in an attempt to save the demigod from the abyss below but felt only air as he watched Perseus flail into the darkness.

Quinn dragged himself back over the edge of the cliff as the fire within him began to die down. For a while he lay on his back in the cold snow thinking of Ashe. Had he just imagined her voice? That had to be it. She wasn't here with him. She had her own trials to face. Still, something about it had felt so real.

A familiar presence filled the air and a lady's voice sang, "Well done. You have defeated the guardian and passed the first trial."

"The first?" Quinn questioned with a hint of despair. He knew he was strong, but he didn't know if he could survive another fight of that intensity so soon after the first.

"Have no fear," the voice reassured him, "The fighting is done. All that remains is to determine your strengths and to confront your weaknesses."

Quinn pushed himself up off the ground, shaking. His shirt was soaked with sweat and blood, making the wind bite harder than it should. He wiped his wounded eye with the collar of his shirt, noticing his vision blur before returning to normal.

The cut along his face stung, but it wasn't as deep as he had first thought. It was certain to scar, but at least his eye hadn't been damaged. He breathed a sigh of relief and began staggering towards the exit.

Inky blackness filled the tunnel before him. As he stepped inside, he realized how pleasant it was to be out of the snow. With his adrenaline pumping, he hadn't noticed how bitterly cold the wind had been, and he became suddenly aware that his hands were completely numb.

"Illumino," he spoke, relighting the crystal around his neck, hoping to catch a peek at what lay ahead of him. About fifty feet before him, the path split off into two separate directions. The path on the left seemed to have a sharp incline, while the path on the right led further down into the mountain.

Quinn felt the pressure lingering in the air and asked, "Well?"

The voice responded, sounding amused. "Well what?"

He couldn't help but feel a little irked. "I don't appreciate you toying with me. I can feel your presence when you're in a room with me, and that only happens when you have something to say. I'm assuming this isn't a test of how lucky I am which means you clearly want to give me some kind of cryptic information on where each of these paths lead."

"And how is it you can feel my presence, when I am not physically in the room with you?" the voice mused.

Quinn didn't really feel like playing this game, but if it's what it took to continue on, he figured he'd play along. "Each of the three of us were given special training based on a unique skill we possessed. Levy was able to take a hit like a champ…."

"So, I've noticed." the voice interrupted.

"…so, he was trained to enhance his stamina. Ashe is good at tuning in to the emotions someone is feeling and to play off of them to her advantage."

"And you?" the voice asked, though Quinn was fairly certain they already knew the answer.

Maybe this was a test of his honesty, or perhaps the voice wanted to test if he was stupid enough to reveal this kind of information to a strange voice pushing him deeper into its lair.

*Whatever. At least this way I can venture on*. But if this was a game the voice wanted to play, he could at least try to get some information out of it too.

“Do you know why my eyes are red?” He asked. The voice took the bait.

“I would assume that there is Abyssal blood running through your veins.”

The Abyssillians were a unique type of human whose lineage could be traced all the way back to ancient times. People had always claimed that trace amounts of monster ichor ran through their veins as a way to excuse the strange traits that Abyssillians inherit. Because of that, they had been shunned by humanity, becoming reclusive, and taking refuge in the uninhabited Wastes.

Quinn’s parents had been Abyssillian.

“Am I wrong?” the voice asked.

“No,” he answered. “What do you know of my people?”

Though he asked this in order to gain insight on just how much the speaker knew of the outside world, he was also genuinely curious. The truth was, Abyssillian culture was never a large part of his training at the Citadel. Whenever it came up, the Masters would quickly change the topic as though they were afraid it might taint his growth.

“Ages ago, your ancestors mated with the Echidna, allowing mortals born with ichor flowing through them. Though in this day it's been so tainted with mortal blood that it's practically nonexistent.”

That was news to him. Quinn had always thought the monster thing was a myth. He thought back on his knowledge of the ancient legends. The Echidna was a monster with the top half of a woman and the bottom half of a snake. Which means if his ancestors had….

He stopped that thought before it could begin. He didn't even want to know how that worked.

The voice continued, “I also know that in order to survive the harsh environment of the wastelands, they had to find ways to adapt to the dangers. Which I am guessing is where your skill comes into place, no?”

She had hit the nail on the head, which made Quinn even more confident that the owner of the voice was no fool.

“That's right,” he said. “Due to the severe dust storms that kick up in the wastelands, our senses became useless.”

His people had had to find a new way to see, a new way to feel. Over time their bodies became sensitive to their surroundings, though some had even stronger gifts than that. Quinn's instructors at the Citadel found a way to finely tune that to fit humanity's needs.

Long story short, he could sense her power when it was near. It was how Quinn and his friends had found this cavern in the first place.

The strength of their bloodlines played a role in their gifts as well, though Quinn hadn't noticed any special gifts of his own outside of his increased senses.

"Now then," Quinn continued before the voice could inquire further. "Shall we get back to the two paths and where they do and do not lead?"

"Very well," the voice responded. "What is it you fear most?"

"Do you mean mentally and emotionally? Or are we talking physical substance? Because honestly, I'm not overly fond of spiders." When the voice didn't respond he continued, "Fine, I'm afraid of choices."

"Choices?" the voice asked with genuine confusion.

"Yes, choices," Quinn replied. "The idea that I might make a choice that will affect anyone other than me. If I fail to choose correctly, someone might suffer for it. That's why Levy makes a better leader than me. So, you can imagine my pleasure to not have to choose a path, and my chagrin in receiving the Path of Chaos."

"Ah," the voice said in understanding. "In that case allow me to make this choice for you."

A loud snap reverberated through the chamber. The walls began to shake, causing dust to rain down upon him. When he looked back at the doors, the path leading up had collapsed in upon itself, completely blocking off the entrance. When the voice spoke again, it was no more than a whisper, directly in Quinn's ear.

*"Time to face your fears, my hero."*

Quinn's face paled, as he set off down the path, leading him deeper into the darkness.

It wasn't long before Quinn could hear the sound of rushing water. The tunnel widened around him the further down he travelled, allowing him more room to move laterally should the need arise. A little deeper in and the ground leveled out.

The stone floor turned into something much softer, and each

step squelched beneath his feet. Tiny, luminescent mushrooms sprung to life with each step, leading him toward an exit he could just make out in the distance.

*Time to face your fears...*

Not knowing what waited for him beyond, he realized he would rather fight Perseus again than face what was ahead. At least then his instincts could take over and he wouldn't have to think about what was to come.

He reached the end long before he was ready, but there was nothing more to do about it. With a deep breath, he did his best to clear his mind, and stepped through the doorway.

His ears popped again. *Another dimension.*

Quinn found himself standing in a grassy meadow. A gentle breeze blew through the air, ruffling his hair and calming his nerves. On the other side of the meadow stood lean man dressed in light grey finery. He had piercing brown eyes, matching his light hair. As soon as Quinn met his eyes, the breeze dissipated, and chills crawled down his spine.

“Welcome! I've been awaiting your arrival, hero.”

“And to whom do I owe the pleasure?” Quinn gave a quick nod.

“Oh,” the man gasped. “This little hero is so polite! It's so rare that we come across a hero with manners.”

Quinn forced a smile. He was in a hurry, but he’d learned from the multitude of myths he had been forced to study that when dealing with strange forces, rudeness tended to lead to unfortunate consequences.

“Where am I?”

“You're in a meadow,” the man happily responded.

Quinn bit back a sigh. “Ok, and why am I here?”

“Why indeed?” The man’s tone was cheerful.

“Oh, would you just tell him already.” A gruff, heavily accented voice shouted from behind him.

Quinn peered around the man but couldn't see anybody.

“Come now,” the man chided. “You will have your time with him, just keep your mouth shut for now.” The cheerfulness was still there, though now it felt much more forced.

“Nonsense,” the angry voice yelled back. “I'm sure the lad is already sick of you. Just let me take a look.”

The man noticed Quinn shuffle a few steps back and said "Now look what you've done! You've spooked him."

"Well that wouldn't have happened if you'd have just let me talk to him in the first place. Now turn these cheeks around and let me have a proper look at him."

With a sigh that felt all too practiced, the man turned around. On the back of his head was another head identical to the first, but with a bushy brown beard.

"Scrawny one, ain't ya lad?" The bearded head laughed. "Don't make heroes like they used to, I suppose. Then again, maybe that's a good thing. Easier to take down if need be. I had to blow up a volcano in order to take care of that bastard Romulus. The man was all muscle and no brain."

Quinn's face had gone stone white.

"I-I know who you are," he stammered, his eyes transfixed upon the god's second face. Curse that voice to Hades for sending him here.

"Good," the head boomed. "Makes this a lot easier if I don't have to make introductions."

"You're Janus, god of choices."

"Guess you're gonna make 'em anyways," Janus grumbled. "Listen now lad, we both know why you're here. That silly goddess has decided that I was the right one for your second trial and I have just the thing."

Quinn calmed himself, though it took a bit of effort. *A goddess, eh? First Perseus, then Janus, and now a goddess that controls fire.* Quinn was fairly certain he knew who was pulling the strings.

"Now then lad, if you'll just follow me, we'll get this show on the road." Janus set off deeper into the meadow, not even bothering to see if Quinn had decided to follow. Ironically, for now, Quinn had no choice to bare.

They walked through a field covered in bright blue flowers for what felt like a lifetime. The scents mingled with a soft breeze that played with Quinn's hair. All the while, the rush of water continued to grow.

The air around them grew heavy with mist, and it was only after they came over the crest of a hill that Quinn saw the waterfall in front of him. He turned to speak with Janus, but he was no longer anywhere to be seen.

"Boy!" called the cheerful half. Quinn looked up to the top of the waterfall. There on the very edge of it stood Janus, waving at him enthusiastically. Quinn walked to the edge of a cliff on the other side of where the water fell.

To his surprise, it was not a lake or river that it fell into, but instead another large abyss. Quinn looked up and studied the waterfall, careful to take in as much detail as he could since it was apparent it would be involved in whatever this next trial would be.

The water was a deep green. Though it was fairly large in size, the volume of water that spilled over the edge was not immense. It was enough to apply pressure should one choose to stand in it, but not enough to push said person down into the abyss waiting below.

Looking through the waterfall Quinn saw what appeared to be the outline of yet another cave entrance. He didn't really like where this was going.

"Alright lad, you've had your time to study, now look up here and listen, for I'll only be saying this once."

As soon as he finished speaking he split himself in two, and the cheerful Janus he had first met leapt over the river and landed on the other side, staring down at him.

"This trial is fairly simple," The bearded Janus continued. "Each of us are going to drop something down the waterfall. All you have to do is catch one."

"Or." The other Janus chimed in, merrily. "Fail to catch one, plummet into the abyss, and never be heard from again! Isn't this exciting, Janus?"

"For Jupiter's sake, will you just keep your mouth shut for once," the intense Janus shouted back.

"What's to keep me from just jumping now and not playing this little game?" Quinn interrupted.

"Ha," The bearded Janus yelled back. "She said you'd say that."

"You'll play this 'little game'," he mimicked making air quotes, which was quite impressive to Quinn, considering he only had one arm left. "Because if you don't, the barrier over the entrance won't open and you'll fall."

Quinn's body ached with exhaustion. He was ready to be done

with this and meet up with his friends. "Let's get on with it then, shall we?"

"Wonderful," happy Janus shouted back. "Ready then?"

He held out his hand, and Quinn watched as a blue energy danced in front of it, eventually swirling into a beautiful mask. The left half was made of a fine, white alabaster. It was shaped like a half skull, coming to a stop just under the nose.

A large portion of the right eye was missing, carved into a shape that looked like it would fit perfectly as it laid upon the new wound Quinn had just received. It was an eerie feeling that made him shiver. The rest of the right half melted into black obsidian, flaring out as though a shadow were engulfing it.

"This mask is *Persona Umbram,* meaning...."

"Person of Shadow," Quinn interrupted.

"Oh good," the intense Janus said sarcastically. "He's a scholar too."

Happy Janus continued on before Quinn could interrupt him again. "He who wears it is one with the darkness. It is truly a unique gift."

"Yes," said the intense Janus, "But what is more of a gift? A glorified piece of jewelry, or the chance to save a life?"

Quinn turned to face him. "What do you mean, 'save a life'?"

He gave Quinn a predatory smile. Again, blue energy swirled before him before settling into the shape of a small girl. She looked at Quinn pleadingly with large, scared eyes.

"Where did my mommy go?" she asked, tears beginning to spill down her cheeks. "I want my mommy. Please!"

Janus rolled his eyes and covered her mouth with his hand. "The choice is simple. Attain a powerful item or save the life of an innocent child."

"You're right," Quinn agreed. "The choice is simple. Clearly saving a life comes before power. Why would I need that mask? I've been trained to fight since I was young."

"Well then," intense Janus shrugged, "If it's that easy we might as well get this over with."

He was just about to push the girl when the other Janus spoke.

"Hold it." There was no joy left in his voice. Instead he fixed

Quinn with an intense stare. "What if I told you that without this mask, you'll lose that girl you're so fond of?"

Quinn began to feel uneasy. How could he have known about Ashe?

"What girl?" Quinn asked, feigning ignorance. "There is no girl I am fond of."

Janus grinned. "So, the name "Ashe" means nothing to you? How do you think she would feel about your response?"

Quinn paled. "How do you…."

Janus waved him off. "That's not important. What is important is that without this mask, she will die. But with it, you will have the power to save her life. Let me show you," he said, staring directly into Quinn's eyes.

*Ashe knelt at the entrance to a massive stone doorway. She stared at the silhouette in front of her with hatred in her eyes. A single tear traced its way down her face. Quinn felt a pang of sadness shoot through his body.*

*He hated seeing her cry. Quinn couldn't see whatever it was she was staring at, but he could tell it hurt her. The room was lit up by the bright orange lava below them, painting it a deep vermilion. Shadows danced along the stone walls in the uneven lighting, adding an even more sinister tone to the events unfolding.*

*Just then, Ashe let out a sharp gasp. Quinn looked back to see a sword sticking through her chest.*

Quinn snapped back to reality, absently wiping a tear from his face.

"What I have just shown you is the future should you not choose to catch this mask. I swear it on my essence to be true." And just like that the intensity was gone and Janus was smiling again. "Now then," he chirped. "Time to choose!"

He dropped the mask.

"Gods damn you! You were supposed to do it at the same time as…ah to Hades with it," yelled intense Janus and he too pushed the child from the ledge.

Quinn didn't have a lot of time to think. His instincts screamed to save the child. He didn't want to believe the vision Janus had shown him. If it was true, he *would* find a way to save Ashe, but that girl could only be saved by him.

Yet his heart screamed for Ashe. He loved her more than life itself, and he just watched her die. It may not have happened yet, but just knowing it might, scared him to death.

The girl let out a high-pitched scream as she fell. She had her eyes closed tight, repeatedly yelling "Please!"

It was time to choose. If he waited any longer it would be too late, and he would fall to the abyss below. The girl. It had to be the girl. Ashe was a fighter. There's no way she would let herself be killed without at least taking her attacker with her.

But the girl falling now was relying on Quinn to save her. It came down to saving a life now and possibly losing one in the future or letting a child die for selfish reasons.

Quinn took a few steps back to give himself some space and then sprinted at the gap. When he reached the pit, he put all of his strength into his legs and jumped.

Reaching out, he thought about the vision Janus had showed him and then about what Ashe would say if he let an innocent child die because of it. Quinn plunged through the icy water and landed hard onto the stone on the other side, rolling through the doorway.

*The choice has been made,* Janus' voice filtered into the cave, distorted by the rushing water.

*Please*. The word seemed to be echoing off the walls of the cave, now nothing more than a whisper.

Quinn looked down at the mask in his hand and cried.

Some time later Quinn felt the goddess' presence in the air again. He hadn't bothered to relight the crystal around his neck; instead choosing to sit in the pitch black of the surrounding cave. He didn't want to see the mask anymore, though he still felt the weight of it in his hand, mocking him.

"I'm really not in the mood for any more games," his voice rasped.

When the goddess spoke, her voice was gentle and soothing. "I know. I only wish to speak with you now. Come talk with me at my hearth and then I will send you back to your world."

Quinn grudgingly pulled himself back to his feet and began trudging down the corridor. A ways down the path, the air began to heat, soothing his frayed nerves. The walls of the cave pulsed all manner of golds and oranges, thrumming with the same essence Quinn felt when he and his friends first entered the cavern.

The path opened up into a vast chamber the likes of which left Quinn breathless. The walls were covered with ancient art depicting all of the legendary heroes Quinn had grown up learning about. Silken drapes hung from the corners, doing an excellent job at disguising the fact that this was a cave.

In the center of the room sat a small ring of stones, with a handful of burning coals inside. The goddess was seated next to the flame, watching embers float up into the air. She was small compared to the average adult. For a moment, Quinn thought she looked like Ashe, until he realized that her hair was brown, not blonde, and that it only looked lighter due to the light of the fire.

In the back of the room was a small walkway, leading up into the air. At the end of it was a curtain of fire, stretching from floor to ceiling. This was no ordinary fire. It burned a bright gold, and the heat felt warm and welcoming. Uncertain whether it was due to the flame, or his trials, Quinn felt a surge of emotion well up within him.

"Welcome to my chamber, young hero. Come sit and talk for a moment if you please. You have my word, on my essence, that no harm shall come to you."

With an effort of will, Quinn looked away from the golden flames, and toward the girl crouching near the fire. She was wearing a simple brown toga, made from a rough fabric.

A red shawl with intricate golden stitching, resembling the curtain of fire on the other side of the room, was draped around her shoulders. He made his way down to the circle of stones and sat on a large stone across from the goddess, staring into the dying embers.

When she spoke, her voice was soft, and far off. Quinn wanted to comfort her but wasn't sure why.

"In the century since the tower has appeared in your world, many heroes have tried to obtain my flame. Only three have made it this far. That was to be expected however, for none were right for the throne. The heroes had not yet grown into their prime."

Quinn looked up at her. She somehow seemed even smaller than before. He realized with a start that, as the fire died down, so did she. Soon, there would be nothing left of either of them.

"There is a prophecy you know," the woman continued. "Quinn, when you leave this place, I will die. I have given all that was left of my essence to you and to your friends." She smiled at the look on his face.

"Do not feel guilty, young one. It was my duty to do so. I swore an oath that this time when the tower appeared, I would give my essence to three heroes with the potential to claim the throne and end the cycle of misery my family has inflicted upon your people. It is no fault of yours that you were chosen. Fate can be cruel, even when necessary."

She poked again at the dying coals, sending a small shower of ashes into the air.

"You're Hestia, goddess of the hearth." He placed a hand over his heart and bowed his head as a sign of respect.

She smiled at him. "Among other things."

"But you're a goddess. Shouldn't you be helping the gods to reclaim the throne?" Quinn asked.

Hestia scrunched up her nose. Shaking her head, she said, "Though it is true I am a goddess, I am against them in this war. I do not care for my brothers and sisters. They had their time on this world, and it was a time filled with greed and lust."

The fire in the pit had fallen to a fading glow and Hestia began to shake, drawing her shawl around her shoulders.

"Our time has come to an end. I must grant you my essence and send you on your way. Remember what I said about your path, Quinn. The decisions you make, like the one you made today, will affect you in the end. Stay true to yourself."

Quinn was tired. He couldn't help the bitterness in his voice when he asked, "What must I do?"

Hestia smiled. "Walk through the golden flames. They will grant you what is left of my essence and send you back to your world. Go now and claim your throne."

Quinn got up and walked the path, stopping in front of the golden flames. They were not hot as he imagined they would be, but rather warm, like a gentle breeze on a summer day.

Despite all that had happened, he couldn't stop the small smile from presenting itself upon his lips. It was calming. He took one last look back at Hestia and walked forward. As he stepped through the fire, he heard Hestia begin to sing, almost too quiet to be heard:

*Three heroes shall rise to lay claim to the throne*
*To see the evils of the world undone.*
*But with the light comes shadows abound*
*Where corruption, betrayal and sadness are found.*
*Oh heroes, my heroes stay true to yourselves,*
*Lest you see your world come crumbling down.*

# CHAPTER 3:
# Ashe

Getting drenched in the Minotaur's rancid saliva was the last straw. Ashe had been wandering this accursed labyrinth for what felt like hours. The cobbled stone floors matched the high walls perfectly, making everything blend into one.

When she looked up, she saw nothing but black nothingness staring back at her. Bones littered the floor, each step precarious and uncertain. The foul smell of human remains was thick in the air, choking her. She had *finally* blocked out the constant stinging of the many cuts she had received from the numerous traps throughout the maze.

She could even live with the fact that when she turned the corner towards what she thought was the exit, a crude, bronze axe embedded itself in the wall behind her, only inches from her scalp. But when the Minotaur let out a battle cry directly into her face, frothing at the mouth and spewing its spittle over every bit of her, she finally snapped.

"*Split up* they said," Ashe yelled as she dove behind the

Minotaur, landing in a crouch and loosening her twin knives from her sleeves. "*Great* plan guys!"

Ashe parried another chop from the axe and jumped back, putting more space between herself and the beast. "If you need me, I'll just be wandering through this *bloody* maze and killing the *freaking* Minotaur."

At the mention of its name, the Minotaur lowered its head, bellowed, and charged directly at her.

"This had better be worth it!"

Just as the beast reached her, she jumped high in the air, flipping forward, and landing on the Minotaur's beefy shoulders. She wrapped her toned legs around its neck, holding on tight as it tried to shake her off. With a battle cry of her own, she slammed her blades into each side of its head, sending the beast face first into the rocky terrain.

She got back to her feet, wiping off her knives on the one spot of clean clothing she could find, before carefully slipping them back into the sheathes inside her sleeves. They weren't just any knives, after all. They had been a special gift from Quinn, celebrating their first anniversary together.

Up ahead she could see a faint light shining from around the corner of the maze wall. With one last attempt at getting some of the, whatever was even on her at this point, out of her hair, she took a steadying breath and made her way toward it. As she turned the corner, she found a sickly green portal suspended in the air, swirling and giving off a low hum.

"Hey magic voice," her voice echoed off the walls of the labyrinth, "There is no chance in Hades I am blindly walking through that. Is there any chance I could ask for some information first?"

The room began to warm up, slowly causing the spit and ichor covering Ashe to crust.

"I swear, you heroes and your questions. Back in my day heroes were always eager to leap into battle."

Ashe suppressed a smile. "And how far into life did your heroes tend to make it?" she asked.

"Yes, yes," the voice responded. "Point taken. Ahead of you lies a portal to your next trial, where you will be subject to a test of character. There is no physical danger to you, just something for me to observe. Now that is all I have time to tell you as your friend is nearing my chamber and I must speak with him."

"Of course," Ashe nodded, grateful for the tidbit of information the voice shared. "Thank you."

"Be truthful with your choices." The voice advised as the warmth receded from the room, leaving Ashe staring into the portal. After taking a second to gather her courage she stepped into the swirling energy.

Though it did not take long to go from one side to the other, stepping through the portal left her feeling very disoriented. For a brief moment it was as if gravity had increased tenfold.

Pressure crashed down onto her, forcing her shoulders to slump against the weight of it. Just as she thought it was going to push her to the ground, she popped out onto the other side.

However, more disorienting than the portal was where she had appeared. She was in a small room surrounded on all sides by cave walls. In front of her was a stone table, with a single, crudely carved wooden chair pulled up to it.

Across the far end of the room she could see another portal swirling, presumably the exit. The portal was the only source of light within the room, giving it a sickly green hue. Though she wanted nothing more than to walk over to it and leave, she knew that was unlikely to be allowed, so she sat at the table and patiently waited.

It hadn't been more than five minutes before a hearty chuckle came from in front of the portal.

"Ye see, I told ya she wouldn't make a break for it. This here little lady has class. I could smell it the second she walked in!"

Ashe sniffed at her sleeve; nose wrinkled in disgust. She smelled like a lot of things, but she doubted class was one of them.

"Yes, I see I was mistaken. I thought she would have been smart enough to see a way out and take it."

Ashe felt a rare twinge of annoyance at that verbal jab.

"Oh," she smiled with mock sweetness. "But why would I want to leave when I am being treated with such politeness by my invisible hosts? Insults, making me wait, not showing yourself and introducing yourself to me? Truly manners are an area in which you excel."

For a brief second, the pressure rose within the room. Ashe cursed herself for losing her temper. Then, as quick as it had appeared the pressure faded followed by another hearty laugh.

"Well she got ya there Janus. Hurry up and make us seen. This one is feisty, and I like it."

The air in front of the portal began to shimmer and distort until a handsome man stood in front of it. His hair was the color of caramel and his eyes were cold and piercing. Ashe shuddered.

"I'm sorry," she began. "I…."

"Nonsense," a voice from behind the man boomed. "Don't let skinny britches here intimidate you. Bring back that fire you had before!"

Ashe had heard the voice, but the man's lips hadn't moved at all since being visible.

"Um, are you telepathic? Or.."

"Turn around you stiff oaf let me have a look at her," the voice boomed again.

The man did as he was bid, revealing a second face on the back of his head.

"Well now, aren't you a looker," he said. "Hair so blonde it's nearly platinum, eyes that sparkle blue and green in a way that would rival the Aegean Sea, and a wit so fiery it will scorch those that are unworthy. Do you have a husband?"

"Erm," Ashe stuttered, thrown completely off balance by the turn of topic, "Actually, I'm spoken for."

"Ah yeah, the skinny kid with the facial wound." he grumbled.

"Facial wound?" Ashe asked, worry creeping into her voice.

"Never mind him," the voice grumbled. "Are you sure you don't want to come with me? I can show you a whole new world your mortal eyes have never-"

The room of the cave flared with heat so severe, that for a second Ashe thought she would spontaneously combust; before fading away.

"ALRIGHT YE FIREY WENCH I GET IT, HANDS OFF," he roared. From behind him Ashe could hear a faint chuckle. When he had smoothed his already perfectly unrumpled clothing to his content he stepped forward and split in half in front of her.

"Well never mind all that," the clean-shaven Janus said. "I suppose we had better just get on with the test then. As I'm sure you were told, this is a test of character. There will be no bodily harm done to you in this room whatsoever. We are just going to play a little *would you rather*. But be warned, as what you choose here will have dire ramifications for your future."

At this point, Ashe couldn't have said whether she was in danger, or if she was just witnessing a really horrible comedy routine, but she was sore, tired and covered in so much sweat, drool and ichor, that she just wanted it to be over.

"Alright," she took a deep breath, keeping her knives ready in case this was all just some big show to get her to drop her guard. "Let's do this."

"Are you sure?" the clean-shaven Janus asked with genuine surprise. "No questions or comments or anything? Isn't that like, your shtick as a hero?"

"You heard the lass," the bearded Janus growled. "Just give her the questions and be done with it." His arm was crossed, and he was refusing to make eye contact with her.

"Very well, we'll start out easy then. Which would you rather eat rabbit or pheasant?"

Ashe quirked an eyebrow. "I'm sorry, but didn't you just ominously tell me that my choices are going to have *dire ramifications?*" she mimed.

"How is this going to affect my future? If I choose rabbit, am I going to get mauled to death by a herd of ravenous bunnies?"

"They're called a colony," Bearded Janus grumbled, still refusing to make eye contact.

"That's...adorable," Ashe said. "But still, how does this affect my future in the slightest?"

"Normally we start with meaningless questions as a way to calibrate the magic for the real heavy hitters. However," he said with a sly grin, "If you would like to skip these and take the risks associated with improper calibration, we can do that."

Ashe's trainers at the Citadel would have paled at her making light of testing fate, but in all honesty, she missed her friends and just wanted to see them again. Feeling uneasy, she agreed that calibration was unnecessary and skipping to the tough questions was best for all involved.

"Very well then," clean-shaven Janus said, almost gleefully. "In that case, I have three scenarios for you."

From the corner, the bearded Janus finally made eye contact again and sighed, slowly shaking his head. That sent shivers up Ashe's spine.

"Scenario One: You are a doctor, and a little boy comes up to you complaining of a severe headache. You discover that the boy is gravely ill due to a parasite in the brain. The only way to save him is to do a surgery that only has a 5% success rate.

"Without the surgery, the boy will die a horrific and painful death. However, if you attempt the surgery and fail, you will be branded a murderer by the kingdom, lose your title as doctor and be locked up in the dungeons for the rest of your life.

"Do you go through with the surgery and try to save the boy? Or do you save yourself in the hopes that you can use your talents to save more lives down the road?"

Ashe knew that this was supposed to be a difficult and thought-provoking question, but she knew her answer right away.

Without hesitation she said, "I would choose to operate on the boy and try for the 5% chance at success. If I chose not to save him, and he lived a tortured existence because I wasn't willing to do what needed to be done, then I wouldn't be doing my job as a doctor."

"Even though by failing at the surgery you would be potentially sacrificing many more lives in the future from those who would have come to you?" Janus asked.

"The thing is," Ashe replied. "In this make-believe universe, you never said that I was the only doctor. If I failed the surgery and was thrown in the dungeons, there are plenty of other doctors available for people to see. But I would not be able to live with myself knowing I sentenced a young boy to die for my own safety."

"Very well," clean Janus conceded. "Your answer has been recorded. We will now move on to scenario two. In this scenario, you will not be making a moral choice. Instead you will be blindly choosing one thing or another.

"When I say blindly, I do not mean that you cannot see them, rather that you will not know the purpose for which you are choosing them. It could be for something good, or for something terrible. Are you ready?"

"Sure thing," she replied.

"Scenario Two: You have the choice between a widowed mother with three children who rely on her to survive, or a little girl who is on her way to finally adopt the puppy she has been wanting for her entire childhood."

"That's it?" Ashe asked. "I know you said this was blind but, can I ask any questions about them?"

"Alas, I have given you all of the information I have been allowed to give. Please make a choice."

Ashe didn't like this scenario at all. It seemed too random. The details that were thrown in seemed as though she was meant to pick one of the choices over the other.

She doubted that anything good would happen to whichever person she chose, and the creepy grin on Janus' face was starting to make her think this wasn't just hypothetical. The fact that she had been told the mother was single and that her children still relied on her made Ashe think she wasn't meant to choose her.

After all, if something bad were to happen, what is a new pet compared to the lives of children relying on their mother? But the fact that it seemed to be heavily influencing her to choose the little girl didn't sit right with her either.

"Something the matter?" Janus asked gleefully. "Come now, don't make me put you on a time limit."

Ashe was stumped. This was too random and too weighted. But if something bad was going to happen to one of them, she figured the lives of three children were more important than the life of one and a puppy. The decision didn't sit right with her, but it had to be made.

"Very well," she said with a sigh. "I choose the little girl."

"Excellent," Janus sounded genuinely pleased. "That will surely come in handy at a later time!"

Ashe paled but kept her mouth shut. She was getting the sinking suspicion she was affecting other people's lives and that sickened her. But she didn't want to show Janus he was getting to her.

"Let's finish," she said, shaken. "I'd like out of here."

“Awwww,” Janus purred, “And here I thought we were becoming friends. Very well last scenario and you are free to meet the goddess.”

“Scenario Three: You stand at the base of a waterfall. At the top of it, two people are on either side of the river, holding an object. The man on the right is holding a beautiful mask said to grant immense power to the wearer. Powers that could potentially change the future.

The other man is holding a child over the fall. At the same time, both men drop what they are holding, plummeting down into an abyss below. You see a cave on the other side of the falls and know you can leap to safety, saving one of the falling items in the process. Which do you save?”

Janus asked this with a glint in his eye. Ashe looked over to see the bearded Janus, staring at her intently. This question definitely seemed to have implications which she did not understand. It was very clearly weighted one way.

“Like before, am I allowed to ask any questions? Or….”

“Just answer and be gone,” bearded Janus snapped.

That took Ashe by surprise. He had gone from, jokingly? proposing to her, to moodily ignoring her and now was snapping at her. She felt anger creep up her neck.

“Apologies,” she replied, doing her best to keep her temper under control. “I would save the child. Life is more important than power.” She stood up quickly from her seat. “All of your questions have been answered. If you’ll excuse me….”

Clean Janus chuckled and beckoned to the portal. “Of course, Ms. Grey. You have performed admirably. I wish you luck in your future endeavors.”

As she was about to step through, she felt a cold hand gently rest on her shoulder.

“Ah,” Clean-shaven Janus said, “If I may ask you just one more question? Nothing to do with the game we just played of course, just for my personal amusement. What would you call someone who chose the mask over the child? Someone who, say, chose power over innocence?”

Ashe narrowed her eyes at the smiling god, pulling her shoulder from his grasp.

The last thing she heard as she stepped through the portal was Janus' gleeful cackle.

She had been much more prepared for the pressure of the portal this time around and came out onto the other side gracefully. Or at least, as gracefully as she could considering her clothing was so crusted over by this point, she could barely bend her arms. That could prove unfortunate if she had more fighting to do up ahead.

As if reading her mind, the sing-song-y rasp of the voice called out to her. It felt as if the voice had gotten weaker from the last time she had heard it.

"Peace, child, the danger is at an end. Come sit by my fire so that we may chat. I swear on my essence that I am no foe."

Ashe followed the narrow path toward a flickering light in the distance. The cave walls here were red in the light, soothing and warm to the touch. If she didn't know she was in the lair of a goddess and in potential danger, she could have easily curled up and napped.

The end of the path opened into a wide room. Further down the path, in the center of the room, was a medium sized fire, being tended to by what look like a young lady. Across the room, up a path made of stone, a brilliant golden curtain of fire fell from the ceiling. Ashe stood, watching the way the fire fell and folded in on itself, mesmerized.

"Beautiful isn't it?" the young lady tending the flame asked in a familiar voice. "Come," she patted the ground next to her. "Sit in front of the flames and chat with me. You have had a tiring day."

Ashe, feeling fully at ease for the first time since entering the cave, walked to the fire and sat, soaking in the calming heat.

"Allow me to apologize for all that you have been through by my hand today." The lady began. "Though please understand, it was necessary. Many have come seeking the power I offer, but only three may walk away with it. For it is my life force, and only the worthy may take it from me."

"I don't understand. It's said that a powerful artifact lay dormant in this cave; one that can help the wielder reach the throne at the top of the tower. Are you saying the artifact is not an artifact at all?"

The lady nodded, staring into Ashe's eyes for the first time.

"Only those worthy of wielding my power may be granted it. There is a prophecy you see. One that states that three heroes are all that stand in the way of the destruction of this world. Should the gods once again claim the throne, this world will see ruin like it has never seen before."

"But aren't you a goddess?" Ashe asked. "Why wouldn't you seek the throne for yourself and for your family?"

The goddess laughed. "Funny," she smiled. "He will ask me that exact thing."

"Who is he?" Ashe asked.

"Never mind that now. The time of the gods is at its end. We will not claim the throne. We MUST not claim it, or humanity will face extinction. Look into my eyes and grab my hand, child."

She thrust her hand out for Ashe to take. With only slight hesitation, Ashe did what was asked of her and stared deeply into the girl's amber eyes.

"Ashelia Grey," her voice rasped. "I grant you a portion of my power. May it help your soul continue to burn bright, and may it scorch the evil that stands before you. May you be a guiding light for all humanity to follow, and a beacon in the darkness to help bring those that are lost, home. Go forth now, as a phoenix, reborn into your world."

As she was speaking, a soft warm light entwined their hands together. For a brief second Ashe felt a searing pain, but it was gone as soon as it began, leaving the glowing imprint of a phoenix on the top of her hand. As the glow faded, she felt a warmth pass through her body.

On a whim, she snapped her fingers. A small ball of golden fire coalesced into existence at the tip of her finger. With shock, she looked over at the girl, only to find her no longer there. Where there had been fire before, now sat embers.

A soft voice spoke from the air. No longer did the room heat as it spoke, but it was unmistakable all the same.

"Go," the voice said softly, guiding her in the direction of the fiery curtain.

Ashe slowly made her way up the winding path, playing with the fire she was able to summon along the way. She could feel the heat radiating off it, though it never got too intense for her to handle. As she reached the golden curtain in front of her, she stopped in her tracks.

"Are my friends ok?" She asked, hoping the voice was still in the room.

After a small delay, the voice responded, "Time within the many realms that make up my domain is fickle. The muscular one has already passed through my room. You will see him again on the other side. As for the other one, he is...struggling."

An image appeared up in the smoke being given off by the embers. In it she could see Quinn. He looked as if he were in a daze, staring down into an enormous cavern. Behind him, a hulking warrior slowly approached. His sword was drawn, and an ugly sneer was plastered across his face.

Panic surged within Ashe. "QUINN ALESIA, DON'T YOU DARE DIE."

As if he had heard her voice, a little life snapped back into Quinn's eyes.

"I have shown you more than fate would allow." The voice spoke again, causing the image to fade.

"But I must know," Ashe pleaded. "What's the outcome of his fight?"

"I cannot allow you to stay here any longer child. For both his sake and your own, I ask that you step through the curtain and return to your realm."

She knew the goddess was right. Ashe didn't know if it was the essence flowing through her that alerted her to it, but there was a presence in the room that was none too happy about what had just occurred. With a sigh of understanding, Ashe stepped back up to the curtain.

"Thank you, Hestia." she said, quietly. And with a silent plea for Quinn to be safe, she walked through the curtain of fire, feeling its warmth wash over her. For the first time in a while, she was at peace.

# CHAPTER 4:
# Levy

Levy was having a great time. Ever since he had walked through the gate with the bear carved over it, he had been attacked relentlessly by all manner of chitinous, snaggle-toothed monsters. His path appeared to be nothing more than a long, single stone walkway.

It was narrow; allowing him only enough room to swing his sword in suppressed arcs. Craggy, rock walls hugged him on either side. Every so often he would glimpse pale eyes glaring out at him from the crevices and he knew an attack was imminent.

By this point he was soaked with sweat and covered in all kinds of little scratches and bites, but he hardly felt the wounds thanks to the adrenaline coursing through him. It was giving him a high he hadn't ever experienced before.

Usually the only time he got a workout like this was when he and Quinn sparred at the Citadel. This easily topped that. The trainers would always stop them before they could reach a satisfying conclusion. Here though, he could fight to his heart's content.

A group of harpies came screaming at him out of the little crevices along the cave walls. Slowly but surely, he was cutting a path through them all towards a softly lit gateway in the distance. He could have reached it already had he tried to, but he was having too much fun carving his way there.

The slaughter continued until about 10 paces from the gateway when a large shadow dropped down from the ceiling, blocking his path. The monster was easily seven feet tall, though he could not be described as fit.

From the waist down it was wrapped in soiled linen. Around its waist was a belt made of weathered rope. Sporadically around the belt, bits of rope dangled with a severed head knotted to the end. Each head was in a different state of decay. From the waist up the creature was hideous.

A protruding belly folded over the front of his waist. But it was the head that caught Levy's attention. The creatures head could only be described as bald, bulbous and incredibly shiny given the small amount of light that was currently present in the cavern. And sitting smack dab in the center of its forehead was a large, bloodshot eye.

"Cyclops," Levy muttered, plugging his nose from the raw stench wafting his way. "Great".

Hearing Levy mutter to himself, the cyclops opened his maw, emitting a fresh wave of stink and yelled, "HUMAN, WELCOME TO MY LAIR. PRAY TO WHICHEVER GOD OR GODDESS YOU CHOOSE, FOR TONIGHT THE MIGHTY STEROPES SHALL DEVOUR YOU WHOLE."

Levy opened his mouth, attempting to throw a rebuttal back at the foul-smelling oaf, but was immediately cut off by another boisterous proclamation.

"I SMELL YOUR FEAR, PUNY ONE. IT IS NORMAL FOR MY PREY TO QUAKE BEFORE ME. FOR I AM THE GREAT SON OF GAIA. NONE HAVE EVER BESTED ME. NOW COME DIE SO I MAY FILL MY BEL…."

Before the cyclops could finish what Levy was sure was going to be a rousing speech on why it was good for him to become dinner, a spear struck the back of the monster's head, leaving a silver tip protruding through his eye. Not even three drops of ichor had splashed to the floor before the light faded from its eye, and the beast crashed to the ground, dead.

"For many, many years I have had to listen to that dead weight boast to his prey," a smooth voice spoke from beyond the doorway. "I just couldn't take it anymore. Come, hero, and let us chat."

Despite being at the gateway now, Levy could see nothing but the smothering blackness that made up the substance of the door. He couldn't help but feel annoyed at whomever had thrown the spear.

He had been enjoying himself, and with a swift strike, his biggest prize had been taken from him. With a hesitant poke, he stuck his finger into the darkness. A cold sensation washed over his skin, sending an unpleasant tingle down his spine.

"Honestly," the voice taunted. "You take your sweet time slaughtering many monsters that would normally make the average human cry to their mothers, but a little gateway has you spooked? Please. If I wanted you dead, that spear would have entered your skull instead of our smelly friend over there."

Levy couldn't really argue with that logic. It's not like he could turn around now. He couldn't wait to meet with his friends again. The thought of comparing their experiences in this cave with Quinn while they sparred made him nearly giddy with excitement. With a deep breath, he stepped through the gateway, making sure he kept his eyes open the entire time.

The room Levy stepped into was very out of place considering where he had just come from. For starters, it was blindingly bright. The floor and ceiling were covered in tile so silver it sparkled. The walls were painted with an impressive mosaic that looked like it had been taken from the pages of history. It depicted a volcano spewing lava onto a muscular man.

Debris blew onto the other walls, choking a civilization in ashes. Then, just as he had taken in every detail of the painting, the tiles shifted, rearranging themselves as if it was one of the sliding puzzles he had played with as a child. It now depicted a waterfall. On one side of it a man stood, dropping an item Levy could not make out.

On the other side, a young girl was falling. Jumping towards the waterfall was the back profile of a man. The scene changed again. This time it depicted Levy holding a magnificent broadsword above his head. In the background was the entrance to a throne room.

*Is that what the tower looks like?*

All that stood between him and the room was a shadowed figure. Their hand was in the air, as if warding off the blow that was about to fall. Levy was mesmerized.

"Do you like it?" the smooth voice asked with mirth. "I call it the wall of choices. Each painting depicts a choice that has been made, or will be made, that changes the course of history. Some of the choices on this wall have caused kingdoms to rise, while others have fallen into ruin."

"I saw myself," Levy murmured, still staring at the changing wall.

"Yes, I would imagine you did." the man replied. "You will make a choice in the future that will end this war. And I would say that is worthy of this wall."

Levy finally broke eye contact with the mosaic and looked over at the speaker for the first time. He was a slim man in a grey pinstripe suit. Each side of his head had a face on it, though so far only one of them had spoken. The other appeared to be sleeping.

"Allow me to introduce myself," the man spoke. Each word from him was calm and soothing, almost lulling Levy into a sense of peace. "My name is Janus. I am the God of choices, and I am a big admirer of yours Levy Sylva." A crooked grin sat upon his face.

"How do you know me?" Levy asked.

He knew that a god knowing his name was likely not a good thing, but he felt that this one meant him no harm. Perhaps it was the smooth way the voice talked, but Levy felt a connection to this god.

"I have followed you from the moment you were born Mr. Sylva," Janus said. "You see, there's a prophecy that exists about three heroes. One of the three is supposed to claim the throne, ushering in a new age for the world.

"Now fate would surely smite me down for telling you this, but honestly with how faded the powers of the gods are these days, who cares? You are one of the heroes of prophecy Levy. Can you guess who the other two might be?"

Levy's eyes widened.

"That's right Levy. The three of you did not happen upon this cave by chance. The information was fed to your little Citadel specifically. The powers of this world all have a horse in this race so to speak.

"The humans believe the hero who claims the throne will usher in a new world for mankind to prosper in. And with the gods' power fading, they believe now is the time to steal that which does not belong to them."

At this Janus's voice took a venomous turn. His lips were peeled back, baring his teeth. Catching the look in Levy's eyes, he composed himself, falling back into his smooth demeanor.

"Why is the power of the gods so weak in this world? And for that matter, why would you tell me this?" Levy asked. "In case you've forgotten, I'm human. I am clearly fighting on the human side and would like to see a new world for us to thrive in. No more monsters devouring us everywhere we go."

"Are you sure?" Janus asked with a grin. "As I said, I have watched you all your life Levy Sylva. I know your hatred for monsters is real, but I also know your ambitions. I know you value strength and power. What if I told you I could help you achieve that and more?"

Levy quirked an eyebrow. "I'm listening."

Janus smiled an eager grin. "As I said before, the power of the gods is fading. Why that is doesn't matter. What does matter is that we cannot claim the throne for ourselves. We are stuck in our own dimensions, too weak to walk what was once our kingdom. So instead, we need a champion who can walk it for us.

"The traitorous goddess would see you be another pawn for the good of humanity. I have pulled you from her dimension to make you this deal. Be our champion Mr. Sylva. Claim the throne in the name of the gods and we will make you one of us.

"You can kill all the monsters you wish. You can have the power to do what you wish, when you wish it. Claim the throne for us, and join us, so that the world may once again be ours."

Levy narrowed his eyes at the offer. "You say you've been watching me since I was a child Janus, yet you seem to know so little about me. It is true that I crave power. And I would be lying if I said your offer was not tempting.

"However, to join you would be to betray my friends. If you

truly knew me as well as you think you do, you would know that I am not willing to cross that line. I appreciate the offer, and the information, but I will have to respectfully decline."

Levy tightened his grip on the handle of his blade. It was not wise to turn down a god. The truth was it bothered him how tempted he had been to take the offer. He looked back at Janus, prepared to fight his way out of his domain, or die trying. Instead he saw a smile.

"Though I admit I am disappointed, I am not surprised. I sense the temptation within you, but I also know that you are hesitant to betray the friends you grew up with. So, I offer you this gift instead, as a token of MY friendship."

Janus raised his hands in the air, and a bright silver orb began to swirl above them. The swirling picked up speed, and the orb began to elongate until hovering just above his palms was a silver broadsword.

The blade was three feet of bright, folded metal. The hilt matched the blade in color. A black leather grip crisscrossed down the handle leading to a snarling wolf head pommel with onyx eyes. As the sword finished forming, it began to levitate over towards Levy.

Without thinking, he reached out to it, grasping it in both hands. The light faded as it made contact with him. He swung his new weapon a few times, amazed at how light it was. Looking up, he saw Janus grinning down at him.

"This changes nothing," he said, though he could hear the lust for the blade in his own voice.

"Of course not." Janus cooed back. "As I said, it is a gift. When you leave here and visit with the goddess, she will give you a gift as well. This will act as a conduit for it. You'll see what I mean later. Just know that, even with the power you get from her, you could be even greater.

"Should there ever come a day where you wish for that power, you need only pray to me. I will appear and open up an entirely new existence to you. Now our time together has reached its end. If I keep you here any longer, she will notice. For now, tell Hestia not where you received this sword. It would raise questions I am not yet prepared to answer. We will speak again."

With a wave of his hands, the ground opened beneath Levy's feet, sending him falling into darkness.

When his vision cleared, Levy found himself in a warm cavern. The walls around him glowed vibrantly, switching between red and gold. Further within he could hear a woman humming. He assumed he was about to meet "the traitorous goddess" as Janus had called her. Without thinking, he reached down to the hilt of his blade. A tingle ran through his arm, calming him.

With a deep breath, he began walking towards the voice. After passing under an archway, Levy found himself staring down at a circular chamber. In the center, a roaring fire was being tended to by a woman with light brown hair. At the far end of the chamber hung a curtain of golden flame.

"Come hero," the voice called out, not coldly but none too warmly either. "You are the first to reach my chamber and there are matters we must discuss."

Levy walked down to where the woman sat tending to the flame, though he felt a rebellious urge to stay standing. The woman looked up at him, a knowing twinkle in her eye.

"That is a nice sword. Though, not the one you entered with it seems. May I ask, perchance, where you got it?"

Levy smiled down at her, tension in every word. "It must have been dropped by another in this cave. I saw it when your cyclops attacked me and decided it was nicer than what I entered with."

"Despite the fact that the one you entered with was engraved with the essence of the gods?" she asked with a raised eyebrow.

"This seemed to get the job done just fine." he said, staring her dead in the eye. He'd be damned if he was going to show weakness to her.

The goddess narrowed her eyes before looking away, staring at the flame in front of her. "Very well, I will not pry. You…oh for goodness sake, one moment please."

Though he didn't see her move, Levy saw the woman's eyes lose focus and flash with power before refocusing back on him. "My apologies. I had a situation to deal with. As I was saying, you have made it to my chamber, and are thus, a hero of the prophecy. As it stands, I have nothing more to say to you.

"Please make your way to the golden flame and step through it. A third of my essence will transfer to you, so that you may better fight for the throne, and for a new age of *peace*." She put particular emphasis on the last word, shooting him another knowing look.

Levy took a step towards the flames before turning back. "What of my friends?" he asked.

Without even gazing in his direction she said, "Your friends will be along shortly."

Sensing that was all she would say on the matter, Levy shrugged and made his way over to the curtain of flames. Just before he stepped through them, he heard the goddess call out to him.

"Levy Sylva beware the gifts immortals give. They always come with unforeseen consequences."

Levy gripped the hilt of the blade again as he stepped through the fire, feeling a rush of energy fill his body, causing his unease to melt away.

# CHAPTER 5: Quinn

Quinn was pissed. He had camped outside of Hestia's cavern for two days after exiting her domain, hoping his friends would come back for him. The goddess had warned him he was the last to see her in her chamber, but he figured he couldn't have been that far behind the others.

Besides, what kind of friends wouldn't want to make sure he made it out ok? After the two days had gone by with nothing to do but hunt and practice his swordsmanship, he worried that maybe he had been in Hestia's dimension for longer than he realized. That fear was quickly put to rest after a quick trip back to Gall; the town they had left from in search of the cave.

The villagers, all surprised to see him still alive after his trip into the mountains, informed him it had only been five days since they had left. With that information, he could only assume his friends had gotten tired of waiting for him and headed back without him. He expected that from Levy, but it stung a bit coming from Ashe.

He and his friends went back all the way to his earliest memories. They had all grown up and trained together from the moment they met. Levy, having been orphaned a few years before and being slightly older, had gotten a head start on them. Quinn had looked up to him for the longest time.

He followed him everywhere around the Citadel, challenging him to races, fights and anything else he could to prove he could stand up with "the big kid". Eventually, after a heated sparring session, Levy acknowledged Quinn for the first time, and they had been inseparable since.

And of course, wherever Quinn went Ashe followed. They had both been abandoned as children. Quinn knew little of his parents, other than that they had been killed on a trip into the city; hoping to procure goods their people no longer had access to in the barren landscape of the Wastes. The Citadel had intervened in time to save him but had been too late for his parents.

Ashe on the other hand, was infamous in their town. She had an affinity for fire from an early age and ended up accidentally burning down a healthy portion of the slums. Facing the wrath of the town, her parents had given her to the Citadel to better focus her attention. She and Quinn had taken to each other immediately, bonding over being in an unknown environment and feeling abandoned by the world around them.

Together, the trio's strengths complemented one another, making them a ferocious weapon to be wielded against the hordes of monsters; completing missions with ease and even taking down the Citadel soldiers they trained against with little difficulty.

Which is why it left him feeling irritated that they had left him behind. He knew it had been Levy's idea. It had to have been. There was no way Ashe had suggested they leave him behind to make his own way back. Quinn kicked a rock as he walked, sulking.

At least it was a warm, sunny day out. Storms were never fun to travel in. Most of the roads between villages were made of dirt which rapidly turned to mud at even the slightest bit of rain.

Quinn reached into the pocket of his cloak and ran his hand along the cool alabaster of the mask. He had caught himself subconsciously doing it after leaving the village, and since then hadn't been able to stop.

Sleep had been difficult for him to come by ever since the events at the waterfall. He wasn't sure the girl had even been a real person, but he couldn't shake the feeling that she was. Even if she hadn't been though, he still felt immense guilt over his decision. Hestia had kept calling him "hero", but right now he wasn't really feeling like one.

The vision Janus had shown him had shaken him to his core. He loved Ashe more than anything else in life, and seeing her lifeless body had driven him to such emotional depths that as he jumped, fully intending to save the child, his body had reacted on its own, reaching out and grabbing the mask instead.

In the end, the truth was simple, he would do anything to save Ashe. And while it sickened him to let the girl fall, it would be worth it in the end. It had to be. A happy memory floated to the front of his mind of the first time he'd finally worked up the nerve to kiss her.

*It had been a hot Summer's night and they were both drenched in sweat after a particularly long sparring session under Master Darrik. Afterward, Ashe mentioned needing to cool off, and Quinn had gotten an idea.*

*Taking her by the hand he led her out into the city, leaping across the rooftops as they liked to do, toward the tallest tower in the distance. It was a long climb to the top, but he assured her it would be worth it.*

*He guided her to the edge, and they sat, dangling their legs over the boundary and staring out over the city far beneath them. A cool breeze sang to them as they sat in each other's arms; her head resting lightly on his shoulder.*

*He could feel her eyes on him, and as he looked down his gaze met her own. Feeling a surge of courage, he leaned down and met her lips with his. Time stood still as they bathed in one another's presence.*

He found that he often went back to that memory in trying times.

As he ran his finger along the mask, he felt a strange power flow into him. The goddess had said she would transfer her essence into him, and he certainly felt stronger.

Colors were more vibrant, things seemed to move a little slower around him and his body felt much lighter. But he wondered if the mask had taken some of the essence as well. And if so, he wondered if she had intended it to be that way. Janus seemed like a bit of a wild card to him. His eyes were just too sharp; too cunning.

He still hadn't put the mask on his face. The first night he camped outside of the cave he attempted to, but as it was about to touch his skin, the image of the girl flashed in his mind and he spent the night retching in the bushes.

Since then he had only touched it, feeling the warm energy spread up his arm and into his body. It felt like a presence was within it. The longer he touched it, the more he thought he could hear a slight whisper. But he always broke contact before it became coherent. It was both intoxicating and terrifying.

A blood curdling scream snapped him out of his daze. The sun had disappeared and the air around him was hazy and stifling. In the distance he could see black smoke rising up from beyond the tree line. He was close to a town he and his friends passed through on the edge of a forest. It was where they'd restocked supplies on their way to the cavern.

The townsfolk had been very carefree and welcoming to them then, refilling their travel sacks for incredibly low prices. Happiness was not something many villages had in this day and age, and Quinn remembered how refreshing it had been to witness. Now, however, the town was ablaze; shrieks echoing amongst the surrounding trees.

A figure bolted from the edge of the forest, sprinting up the path in the direction of Quinn. She appeared to be young, only about eight or nine years old. Her face was the same color as her fiery red hair, probably due to the exertion of sprinting through the forest away from the blaze. The fire must have been bad based on how singed her clothing appeared to be.

"Help us," the girl screamed, still a decent distance from Quinn. "Help us please! Our town is burning and it's killing everybody!"

Quinn knelt down and steadied the girl as she ran into his reach. Her face was covered in soot, the only clean lines coming from the trails the tears had left.

"Calm down." He said in the voice he used to use when Ashe

would cry as a child. “I need you to tell me exactly what’s happening so I can help.”

The girl took a few deep breaths, trying her best to stop the wracking sobs from breaking up her words.

“There’s a...m-monster attacking,” she cried, wiping her eyes. “She came from the forest a-asking f-for a sacrifice. The adults tried to s-scare it off, but it got angry and started spitting fire at people.”

“Can you describe this monster to me?” Quinn asked.

“It h-has a mane and a s-snake tail.” she said, hiccupping as she spoke.

“Thank you,” Quinn grimaced within. “I’ll do what I can. Stay here and keep hidden. If I don’t come back soon, keep going up the path. You’ll reach another village in a day.”

The girl nodded to him and ran into the bushes just off the main path. Quinn got up and stretched, unsheathing his sword and steeling himself. If the girl’s description was accurate, he had no doubt what he would be facing was a chimera.

Chimeras were vicious monsters. They often hunkered down near villages, asking the humans for one sacrifice every so often in return for peace. But more often than not, as they ate humans, their appetite grew. Eventually they would start demanding two sacrifices. Then three, five, ten and so on until either the villagers refused, or the chimera became too hungry. Neither option ever ended well for a village.

The strategy for facing a chimera was simple. Avoid the head, cut off the tail and attack its blind spot. However, that was much easier said than done. For starters, they spit deadly fire from the lion’s mouth, and even if one could out maneuver that, they’d have the snake with which to contend.

If the strike didn’t kill you, the venom would, and swiftly at that. If Quinn’s friends had waited for him, they could have taken it out easily. Ashe would distract the head, keeping the fire close to her.

Levy would jump on the back of it, keeping the snake distracted while Quinn went in for the kill. But of course, they weren’t with him. He took one last deep breath, and with sword in hand, walked into the forest, ready to face the chimera on his own. Man, he was pissed.

# CHAPTER 6: Ashe

Ashe felt terrible about leaving Quinn behind. After she exited Hestia's domain, she and Levy had waited for a day outside. The goddess practically promised Quinn would safely meet them again, but she didn't say when. Time tended to move differently inside the realms of the gods after all.

They spent some time comparing their "prizes" with one another when they had first emerged. Apparently, Levy had only been waiting for an hour or so before Ashe came out. After greeting her, he unsheathed a beautiful silver broadsword.

He said it was light as a feather and filled him with energy, allowing him strength he had never dreamed of. He demonstrated it by kicking a medium sized bolder, scooting it a few inches.

"I feel like if I practice with it, I'll eventually be able to pick something that size up." he said with a self-satisfied grin.

In response, Ashe formed an orb of golden fire in her hand. She tossed it back and forth a couple times before hurling it at the boulder he'd kicked. With a loud crack, chunks of rock sprayed off in all directions, leaving a smoking crater in its place. Levy's grin fell away, leaving his lower lip slightly protruding in a pout.

"That is so not fair," he said, shooting her a weak grin. "I get a shiny sword and a teeny bit of strength and you become little miss Queen of Fire."

Ashe just smiled. Levy had always been ambitious. It's what drove his rivalry with Quinn. The two were always competing, constantly trying to one up each other until someone ended up hurt. That was likely what drove him to leave Quinn behind. So, after a day of waiting, Levy grew impatient and suggested they head back.

"We can't just leave him to find his own way home, Levy." Ashe argued, trying to change her friend's mind.

"He'll be fine, Ashe," Levy replied. "He studied the same maps we did. And if what Hestia said is true, he'll have some kind of new power as well. That will be plenty to keep him safe on the roads.

Besides, it will give you and I some time together. It's been a while since we've really hung out with one another without Quinn tagging along, and I think the quality time will do our friendship some good."

Ashe couldn't argue with that. In the past, they had been much closer with each other. However, once she and Quinn had begun to date, they slowly drifted apart. She knew Levy had feelings for her at one point, and though she didn't reciprocate them, she still loved him as a friend and missed the bond they had once shared.

"Alright," she agreed, hoping it would begin to bridge the gap that had formed between them. "But only if we stop somewhere along the way so I can wash this filth off of me."

"Agreed," he said with his signature, charming smile.

As fate would have it, they didn't have to travel far. Less than ten miles into their trip back from the caves, they came across a natural spring, just off the path they had been walking. It was tucked away in a little grove of trees, nestled among the thriving plant life.

Though levy thought it might be nice to bathe together, Ashe insisted they take turns so that one could keep watch. The pretty landscape didn't diminish the threat of the monsters that roamed the land.

As Levy was taking his turn in the water, Ashe noticed a small caravan of traders making their way toward her. They were all older women, each dressed in a similar fashion to those they had seen in the town of Gall where they'd stayed before making their way to Hestia's domain. Praising her luck, she waved them down, hoping to catch their attention. Their supplies had been running precariously low, and while she thought they would just be able to scrape by until they made it home to the Citadel, she was thrilled to know that now they didn't have to.

Having made her purchases and thanking the nice women before seeing them off, she made her way back toward the spring. She couldn't wait to show Levy the delicious, fresh caught rabbit they'd be feasting on that night.

She had only used her own money, hoping to surprise him with something nice. As she entered the grove, she found him with his new sword out, practicing his stances. Though she did her best not to, she couldn't help but notice he was only clothed from the waist down.

His broad chest moved gracefully with the momentum of his swings, causing the muscles on his back to ripple as he moved from stance to stance. She traced the scars down his back with her eyes before realizing what she was doing and snapping herself out of the trance she was in.

"Levy, what was the point of bathing if you're just going to get sweaty immediately after?" She tried to sound light-hearted in the hopes he hadn't noticed her checking him out.

He looked over his shoulder and smiled. "Gotta keep the skills sharp, and the muscles sharper. Otherwise pretty girls won't drool over me." He looked down to the parcels in her hands. "Whatcha got there?"

She smiled back and raised the parcels in the air. "Dinner is served."

They spent the remainder of the night laughing around a campfire and planning their route home. With their new powers, they didn't feel a need to keep to the relative safety of the roads. They both agreed that the sooner they got back to the Citadel, the better.

~~~
~~~

"Didn't you say you knew where you were going?" Ashe questioned as they made their way down a precarious mountainside path.

"I said I knew the general direction to go," Levy fired back. "We studied maps back at the Citadel, remember? From these mountains, it's a straight shot northeast until we hit the river. From there it's a day's walk east and we hit Stormhaven."

"Did it ever occur to you that roads exist for a reason?" Ashe asked. "Like, maybe as ways for humans to travel easily and avoid uneven terrain like a mountainside cliff or dense forest?"

Though the bath had been nice, the sweat that now cascaded from her brow had practically negated the cleanliness she had felt just a day before. Lucky for both of them, there was a healthy breeze that day or else their combined stench would have made travel even worse.

"Look, you agreed to this plan alright? I said 'Hey, want to cut our travel time in half and go straight to the Citadel?' and you were all 'oh my gods yes that would be lovely will you lead me there, sir?' and off we went!" He narrowly avoided sliding off the ledge for the twentieth time.

"I do NOT sound like that," she responded, holding on to the rock wall for dear life. "And I DEFINITELY did not call you sir."

He shot her a white-toothed grin over his shoulder, cool as a cucumber even in the situation in which they found themselves.

Levy was an attractive man. He normally wore his cropped brown hair slightly spiked up, though the sweat had matted it down currently. He was broad-chested and wrought with muscle due to the vigorous training the Citadel had put them through.

And while he was as cocky as they come, he was always able to back that confidence up. All of that was nice, but he didn't have the heart, or the compassion Quinn had.

Levy scowled when their eyes met. "You're thinking about him again, aren't you?"

"Of course, I am," she responded. "I miss him, and we left him behind. What if he gets into trouble?"

They were nearly at the bottom of the cliff they'd been scaling for the last few hours. Once they reached the ground, forest greeted them as far as the eye could see. From the top of the cliff they had seen a break in the tangle of trees, indicating a river. From there it would only be one more day until they made it home.

"He's going to be fine." Levy reassured her. "Quinn is the strongest person I know, second to me of course," he winked. "And besides, look at the strength we got from Hestia. Surely, he received a gift from her as well. Nothing is going to happen to him."

As they reached the forest floor, the air became smokey and harder to see through.

"There's a big fire East of us," Ashe said feeling the heat interact with her newfound ability. "We should check it out. If it spreads it could burn down this whole forest. I think I can stop it."

"You just want something to take your mind off Quinn," Levy accused.

Ashe smiled. "Yeah, kind of. Is that too much to ask? Besides, I don't know about you but I'm dying to play around with these new abilities."

"Alright." Levy walked off in the direction she pointed. "But I'm telling you, everything is going to be absolutely fine."

# CHAPTER 7: Quinn

Everything was absolutely not fine.

The first thing Quinn saw as he stepped from the tree line into the village was the monstrous form of a chimera, gnawing on the lower half of a young woman. Her glassy eyes stared back at him, betraying the scream of terror and pain frozen on her face.

The chimera was five feet of bulky muscle and sharp teeth. Its mane was thick and curly, matted down with fresh blood. Quinn heard the lion snuffle loudly at the air, before picking up his scent and whipping its head around.

*"OOOOOOOOH,"* it screeched. *"NEW FOOD HAS COME WILLINGLY TO ME."*

Quinn took a step back, taking in his surroundings. The village had been torched beyond repair. Most of the buildings had already collapsed, and any still standing were soon to join them. All around him the stench of burnt flesh clung to the air. With the exception of crackling flames and splintering wood, nothing could be heard. That didn't bode well for the townsfolk.

"Be cautiousssss," the snake whipped around, hissing into the lion's ear. "Thissss one hass the sssmell of human and god on him."

Quinn raised an eyebrow. *Who knew that chimeras had two separate minds in one body?* That had never been brought up in any of his studies, so he had always just assumed a chimera had one consciousness.

*"I DON'T CAAAAAAARE,"* The lion head roared. *"ALL WHO COME INTO MY TERRITORY SHALL BE MY PREY."*

It opened its mouth, and an orange glow lit the back of its throat.

Quinn realized he was about to be scorched and decided not to stick around long enough to see that happen. Instead he sprung toward his right, hoping that with the cover of the forest, he might be able use stealth to his advantage, or at the very least use the trees as barriers between himself and the monster.

But about five steps into his run, the snake's face shot into his vision, striking at his throat. He raised his blade up just in time to deflect the blow, but the momentum of the strike knocked him off balance and he stumbled back toward the village.

The chimera, seeing him stumble, jumped into the air, spinning around in an attempt to land on top of him. Quinn rolled forward, not wanting to be pinned and cooked. He had to try and stay out of the lion's sight, lest he contend with fire he had no protection from.

As he rolled behind the chimera and shot back to his feet, he saw another flash of green, barely bringing his blade up in time to halt the snake's blow. He felt something warm hit his cheek, burning the flesh it touched. He ducked under another jet of acid, narrowly avoiding the caustic liquid.

Quinn knew he needed to strike a decisive blow quickly. If this kept up, he would get tired, and realistically, the chimera only needed one hit to kill him. In one more attempt to put a little distance between himself and the chimera, he sprinted toward one of the only buildings left standing, putting it between himself and the chimera and allowing him to catch his breath a little.

He reached into the pocket of his cloak, hoping to find some knives or anything else he could throw that might make finishing the monster slightly easier. His fingers once again brushed the mask and he felt that familiar tingle of power run up his arm.

*Put…on…..*

The faint whisper came to him again, lulling him away from the threat at hand.

*Let...help…Power.*

The chimera smashed through the other side of the building, causing him to jerk his hand away from the mask, and the tingle faded from his arm. Although this was a dire situation, he still wasn't sure he could stomach using the mask. He listened to the crashing coming from within the structure and jumped just as the monster clawed its way through the other side.

Channeling his inner Levy, he landed on the beasts back, wrapping his hand around the snake's neck and letting the momentum roll him off the other side, pulling the snake's body tight. With a roar, he struck down with his blade, slicing the tail from the chimera and killing the snake in the process.

A thrill ran through Quinn as he spiked the lifeless body of the snake into the ground, watching it bounce a few feet from him. But as he turned toward the lion, a colossal paw swung past his vision, smacking him in the chest, throwing him into the side of a smoldering building.

To his surprise, though the fire around him was very warm, it did not burn him. He wondered if that was thanks to Hestia's essence within him.

He looked down in a daze at the three gouges in his chest. He could feel the warmth of his blood soaking his shirt. The chimera, sensing its victory, slowly stalked toward him with an orange glow lighting the back of its throat. It reminded him of Hestia's fire.

*The mask, Quinn.*

Her voice flitted around in his mind. It was strange that he couldn't remember her saying anything to him about the mask when they had spoken.

*Use the mask. It will help you. Use its power, but do not lose yourself to it.*

With her words floating around in his head, he could almost feel the power humming in his pocket. Reaching with his hand, he wrapped his fingers around the mask. Time seemed to slow around him. Trance-like, he pulled the mask from his pocket and with no hesitance, pressed it to his face.

Time snapped back to normal around him. The chimera roared and leapt at him, claws extended, ready to finish the job. Just as they were about to make contact, Quinn felt the ground beneath him give way and he fell into blackness.

When he pulled his arms away from his face, he found himself standing in a nightmare. The sky and the ground around him were the same shade of black, causing him to feel disoriented. He could not tell what was up or down.

He felt as though he were hovering in place, despite his feet being on solid ground. Around him, the skeletal remains of structures shone a ghostly white. He realized with a start that it was the village. The fire that licked at the structures was a dark grey, giving off no light and frozen in place. Inversely, the shadows shone white.

The chimera, though not frozen, was slowly inching forward, claws extended in the direction Quinn had just been sitting.

*"Welcome,"* a voice rasped. A silhouette outlined in white rose from the ground in front of Quinn. *"I have waited a long time for a hero to claim the power of my mask. I am happy you decided to harness it, rather than meet a grisly end by our whiskered foe."*

He pointed to the chimera, still slowly crawling its way toward the side of the building.

"What is this?" Quinn asked the silhouette.

*"You are in the Realm of Night."* The silhouette responded, gesturing around itself. *"It is a realm that exists alongside the mortal realm within the shadows of your world. He who wears the mask has mastery over the Realm of Night, and as such has mastery over gateways in the shadows that lead between the realms."*

Looking at the white shadows the frozen fire was giving off, Quinn began to put together exactly what that meant.

"So, you're saying I can use the shadows as doorways when I wear the mask? I can see time in this realm moves slowly. Does that mean it's possible for me to rapidly move back and forth in the real world, so long as where I am going has shadow for me to use?"

*"Precisely."*

"What is the energy I feel when I touch the mask?" Quinn asked the outline. He was wary of all of this but trusted that Hestia did not intend to harm him. She had seemed to treat him as though he were her last hope and wanted to honor that. If it meant accessing this power, he trusted she would not lead him astray.

*"The Realm of Night is a realm created by Nyx, the goddess of night. By wearing the mask, you are channeling godly essence into your body. As such, you are bound to feel increased power. However, a word of caution, as I am bound to serve the master of this realm.*

"The essence of the goddess you have within you is the only thing keeping you from being lost to this power. Normally, this realm would be too powerful for a mortal. The more you rely on the power within this mask, the more likely it is to consume you."

Quinn felt a chill run through his body. He was suddenly thankful he hadn't tried putting it on before. Thanks to the vision Janus had shown him, he knew he would need it in the future to keep Ashe safe, and swore right then he would never use the mask unless it was absolutely necessary.

"Thank you for your guidance," he said to the shadow before him. "What can I call you?"

*"You may call me Chaos."* And with that, the silhouette sunk back into the ground.

With a newfound confidence, Quinn walked to one of the shadows directly behind the chimera and jumped through it with newfound determination.

# CHAPTER 8: Ashe

The smoke had become chokingly dense around them. Relying on her sense of the flame roaring in the distance, Ashe lead them through the maze of thick trees. Behind her, Ashe could hear Levy coughing and hacking, doing his best to keep clean air in his lungs.

The forest was dark as night, due to the thick canopies and the black smoke smothering any light that tried to filter through. Any animals that lived in the forest had long since fled the scene, creating a foreboding silence.

As she crept closer to the heart of the blaze, Ashe began to feel another presence within it. It was dark, and incredibly cold and lifeless, seemingly the exact opposite of the fire inside her. She shivered, imagining what kind of evil could possibly give off such a feeling.

"We're close," she murmured to Levy, trying to keep her voice low. "There is something in the heart of it though. Something I don't like the feel of. Be ready for a fight."

Without a word, Levy slid his new sword out of its scabbard, eyes fixed ahead. Ashe appreciated that he trusted her enough to listen and take the warning seriously, and that despite him usually taking the lead, he was willing to step back and allow her to test and get a grasp of her new abilities.

Feeling her powers at work was exhilarating. She felt the warmth of the fire within her at all times, moving through her body as though it were her blood. When she felt fire nearby, that warm feeling would extend out of her as though it were reaching for the other flame. It was how she had initially felt the blaze they were heading toward now.

The stronger the fire around them, the stronger the reaction would be. The campfires they had made had been just a small pull, yearning to connect with it. However, as they moved further toward the direction of the blaze, the pull was becoming more and more urgent. It was almost as if it were dragging her along.

She still had control of her body, but it felt as though that control was slipping away with each step she took. She realized she should have been freaked out by that, but instead she felt excitement. This power was now a part of her, and she couldn't wait to flex it.

A little further in they encountered the first patch of flame. The trees of the forest here had just begun to smolder as bits of leaves and debris littering the forest floor smoked and lit ablaze. Ashe reached her arm out, stopping Levy.

She gestured to the ground, indicating he should get low and out of the smoke while she went to work. With an uneasy nod, he crouched down and watched. Ashe closed her eyes, feeling the warmth within her. She imagined grabbing the power from within and pulling it to the surface.

It took a small amount of coaxing but eventually it came willingly. It crawled over every inch of her skin, sending pleasing tingles all over her body. With a confidence she had never felt before, she walked up to the largest flame and stuck her hand into the hottest part of it. She heard a small gasp from Levy, but he didn't try to stop her, for which she was grateful.

Everything she had done with her power up to this point had been purely instinctual. She assumed sticking her hand in the fire would not hurt her though this was the first time she had actually tried it. Bringing her power to the surface had been something she figured would work since she had spent the last couple days poking and prodding at the sensation within her.

It was only now that she realized that she had no idea what to do next. She began to feel a slight sense of panic, having dragged Levy out here only to find out she did not know how to stop the fire from burning. In her panic, she began to feel her connection to the power waver.

If she lost it, she had a feeling her protection from the flame would be gone and it would be incredibly painful. Just as she was about to lose the connection all together, she felt a warm pressure on her hand.

*"Peace, child,"* the whisper of Hestia came to her. *"Trust in yourself. You already seem to have a good grasp on the power I have given you. Silence your mind and allow it to lead you. My essence is one with you, and with that comes the instinct of how to use my gift."*

The panic Ashe had been feeling receded and with it came the warmth of the power again washing over her skin. Using the same technique as when she had coaxed the power from inside her to the surface, she opened herself to the fire around her.

She could feel the wild energy the flame was giving off. All it needed was to be tamed. She enveloped the fire with her energy, pulling it to her. She could feel the flame become part of her power. Opening her eyes, she saw all of the fire around her reaching out toward her, swirling around her hand.

As it touched her skin, she felt it join the energy inside of her. Before long, a large area around them was free of the blaze. Ashe felt an incredible sense of jubilation at the feat she had just performed.

She heard the crunch of leaves behind her and turned to see Levy step beside her.

"Woah," he muttered looking deep into her eyes. "That was…."

"Incredible?" she asked with a smile.

"Um." Levy backed away one step. "Your eyes are…yellow."

He peered at her with…was that fear on his face?

"…and glowing. It's…pretty creepy."

Ashe closed her eyes, releasing the mental grip she had on the energy. It immediately sunk back within her, continuing its course through her body.

"Better?" she asked, opening her eyes.

"Much. Now come on and lead us into the heart of the flame. I want to fight whatever caused this fire and get back home. I think I speak for both of us when I say we sorely need a bath."

Ashe was about to compare his stench to a particularly smelly cyclops, when a guttural roar filled the air. All humor left their eyes and both she and Levy turned toward the sound. "I don't know what that was, but it doesn't sound friendly."

Levy had a huge smile on his face as he swung his sword in a small arc. "About time I get to test this bad boy out. Come on, Fire Queen, lead me to the bad guy."

It was another twenty-minute jog through thick smoke and smoldering vegetation before they reached their destination. Along the way Ashe had put out a few more fires that had been threatening to spread to more of the forest. With each patch of flame, she felt more and more secure with her power.

By the time they reached the remains of a village, she felt as though she was firmly in control. Her power still desperately wanted to reach the heart of the blaze, but it was no longer pulling her in the direction of it. It was much more like the needle of a compass now, pointing her in the right direction.

Levy whistled, looking at the destruction around them. If Ashe's mental map was correct, this was the village they had stopped at to resupply on their way to the cave where they had met Hestia. The people had been so happy and carefree.

It saddened her to see what remained of it. All around her, charred bodies littered the dirt streets. The foundations of buildings splintered and crumbled in the wicked heat of the fire lapping at them.

"What do you think caused this?" she asked Levy, unable to tear her eyes from the wreckage. A loud crash sounded in the distance, followed by a roar.

"I think we're about to find out," he replied, holding his blade out in front of him. "Whatever it is, let me handle it. You've gotten to have your fun. Now it's my turn."

Ashe was about to lecture him that just because they had been given powers didn't make them gods when the enormous form of a lion came tearing around the corner of one of the lone standing buildings a few lengths away. Its eyes were wide, and it frothed at the mouth.

"That's a…."

"Chimera," Levy finished, setting his feet and readying his blade. "And it's running right to its death," He shouted with a smile. "Be ready to do that flame thing you do if it spits at me. Otherwise stay out of my way."

"It looks scared," she reached once again for her power.

"Of course, it's scared!" Levy grinned. "It knows its end is near."

"I don't think…." Ashe was unable to finish her sentence as twenty meters before it would have reached them, a figure encompassed in billowing black energy appeared between them and the chimera. The creature let out a screech as it desperately tried to halt its progress, skittering on its haunches as it attempted to change direction.

With a flick of the wrist, the shadowy man sliced out with a familiar looking blade, opening a gash across the monster's nose. It reared up on its hind legs, bellowing a roar of pain. Just as Ashe was about to call out, the shadow disappeared in front of her eyes, before reappearing on the scaffolding of a burnt building. Levy swiveled his head around, tracking to where the shadow reappeared. "What the fu…."

With another flourish of his blade, the shadow leapt into the air, flipping forward once and stabbing his blade down, plunging it to the hilt into the forehead of the chimera. With one last roar, it fell to the ground before going limp.

The shadow hit the ground next to it and rolled, before coming to a stop next to the beast's head. Placing his foot upon the chimera, he grabbed the handle of his blade and pulled, yanking it free. The ichor flew off of it with a flick, and the man re-sheathed it, before turning to face Ashe and Levy.

Levy looked at Ashe with a question in his eyes. With a start, Ashe realized the cold presence she felt was radiating from the shadowy energy enveloping this man. She began to ask who the man was but before she could get the words out, Levy charged.

He got within range and let loose with a vicious horizontal strike, intending to take the shadow's head clean off. However, just as the sword would have made contact, the man slipped into the ground, disappearing. He reappeared a moment later, directly behind him.

With a quick, fluid motion, the man reached out and smacked Levy in the rear, slipping back into the ground as Levy swung around. He appeared right behind him not even a second later and delivered another quick smack to the back of his head before playfully jumping backwards out of the reach of Levy's blade.

Levy, now fuming, charged after him. He had always had a ridiculous amount of strength, but it was easy to rile him up. Though he had made great strides in eliminating that weakness, every now and then he still slipped up, allowing his opponents to take advantage.

Every time he swung, the man would disappear, only to reappear behind him and deliver some kind of physical taunt. Ashe started to realize now why the chimera had shown up the way it did. It hadn't been charging after them. It had been running away from this shadowy being.

"Levy just come back and let's try to talk with him. This is clearly getting us nowhere and he is obviously not trying to hurt you."

Levy looked like he was about to burst. A vein bulged precariously far out of his forehead, and his face was a shade of red she had never seen before. It was obvious he wanted nothing more than to stick his sword through the shadowy man.

He must have realized he was outmatched because with a rare show of deference he switched into a defensive stance and slowly backed away until he was even again with Ashe, never taking his eyes from the man wrapped in darkness.

The shadowy man reappeared a few meters in front of them. When it was clear they no longer intended to attack, he began to let out the eeriest laugh Ashe had ever heard. It sounded as though two voices were overlapped, with the deeper one happening just a millisecond after the higher one.

However, the higher voice was a laugh she recognized, as it was a laugh she had heard a thousand times. "Oh, you have got to be kidding me," Ashe said, staring at the man. Levy looked over at her confused. Finally, getting over the laughing fit, the shadow slowly reached up, grasping something white that could be vaguely seen through the flickering energy, and pulled it off. The shadows immediately receded back into the item, until standing before them was a man with long black hair that fell just past his chin.

"Quinn, you little prick," Levy said, sheathing his sword.

Ashe ran forward, throwing her arms around him. "Oh, thank the gods you're alright!"

Wrapped in his arms, she looked at the item in his hand that the shadows had receded back into. It was a beautiful white mask in the shape of a half skull. Onyx jutted out from the opposite side, representing the shadow that had retreated back into it. With a chill, Janus' taunting about power came back into her mind.

Quinn must have sensed her change in demeanor because he pulled her out at arm's length.

"What's wrong?" he asked.

Ashe had known Quinn for so long. There was no way he would ever have sacrificed an innocent life for power. She doubted even Levy, the most ambitious of the three of them, would do something so cold. She refused to let that creepy god mess with her life.

"It's nothing," she smiled, taking her eyes off the mask. "Just feeling guilty about leaving you behind."

"Yes well, as you can see." He gestured to the burnt down village around him, "I am clearly doing just fine on my own."

Despite the grim scene they were standing in, Ashe couldn't help but giggle at his sarcasm. They had been through so much in the last few days, and now all of that tension was bleeding out. She wrapped him in another hug, letting all of the fear and exhaustion leave in his arms.

Levy walked up beside them as she was letting him go and clasped Quinn on the forearm. "It's good to see you. There's no way we'll make it back to the capital tonight so we may as well camp until tomorrow. We have a lot to discuss, I think."

Quinn grinned and wrapped the big man in a hug. "We'd have less to discuss if you hadn't left me back at that cave. Meeting back up here is surely the fates giving me a chance to kick your ass for leaving me behind."

Ashe chortled. Despite all their trials, all of their fights and weariness, and being covered head to toe in copious amounts of sweat, blood and gods only knew what else, her friends still wanted to fight.

"Yes, well, I'm going to go put this fire out while you two boys finish your measuring contest," she walked toward the heart of the flame.

She was going to try and reach her powers out as far as she currently could and get all the remaining blaze in one go. "When you're done, I would very much like to get home."

~~~

It had taken the better part of an hour before she was able to get the rest of the fire put out. The boys had beaten each other bloody; laying on the ground in a worn-out heap of heaving limbs. Quinn surged to his feet, remembering a girl he had to make sure was okay. It was well after dark by the time he returned to their makeshift camp, having had no luck in finding her.

He said he'd told her to go up the road toward the next village if he didn't come back, but the guilt of not finding her didn't leave his face. Ashe scooted in closer, snuggling up to him as they sat around the fire. Her presence tended to ease his mind, and she saw him relax as he wrapped her in a hug.

Levy returned a little later with a couple of rabbits he had hunted. They spent the next hour in silence, waiting for the meat to cook. When they had filled their bellies, they each shared their stories of the trials and guardians they had to face in Hestia's domain.

Levy told them about how Janus had tried to turn him to the side of the gods, confirming Ashe's fear that he was attempting to mess with their minds. She told them as much, concerned that Levy
~~~

may give in to the siren call of power that came with Janus' offer. He offered her an easy smile, patting his blade and saying he had all he needed.

When it was Quinn's turn, he told them about how he battled Perseus. Ashe gripped his hand when he told them about how he had felt hopeless staring into the abyss until he heard Ashe's voice. They shared a quick kiss as Levy mimed throwing up in the background.

However, when he got to his encounter with Janus, he got quiet. It was clear he was uncomfortable with whatever had happened, and Ashe didn't want to push him into talking about it unless he wanted to. He gave a very vague description of having to pass some kind of test before being allowed to move on but didn't elaborate any further.

While he spoke, Ashe noticed him briefly reach into his cloak. He seemed to realize what he was doing and briskly pulled his hand back out; not making eye contact with either of them. She felt a wave of anxiety wash over her as Janus' parting question came unbidden to her mind.

It was clear he felt guilt about it. She could feel it radiating from him. She figured she'd get him to talk to her in due time, when they were alone. For now, she just wanted to make him feel better. They settled down after Quinn finished his story.

Tomorrow they would finish this leg of their journey, returning to Stormhaven and to the Citadel by evening. They would be busy the next few weeks. After all, they were fighting a losing war. But with this new found power, and her friends by her side, Ashe was hoping they would finally be able to turn the tide.

As she drifted off to sleep, the soft murmur of Janus' words played on repeat in her mind.

*"What would you call someone who chose power over life?"* It mocked.

# CHAPTER 9:
# Levy

*Levy found himself back in a familiar silver room, watching historical events unfold before him. This had been one of his favorite parts of his trial. He was mesmerized by the images he was seeing; Images no mortal alive today had borne witness to. His trainers at the Citadel would be beside themselves if they saw what he was getting to see.*

*Two images in particular continued to show themselves with increasing frequency. The first was himself, holding his sword high in the air as the entrance to the throne room sat behind him. He liked that one.*

*It filled him with a sense of pride and victory. The second was the picture he had seen during his trial of the man leaping at a waterfall. This time however, he was able to make out the object the man reached toward. It was a mask. The very same mask he had seen his friend take off his face and hurriedly shove back into his cloak.*

*"That's right Mr. Sylva," a smooth voice spoke around the room.*

*"That is the very same mask your friend had upon his face. That must upset you."*

*Levy looked around the room for the speaker. "Stop playing games with me Janus. Why would that upset me?"*

*"Why would it not?" Janus made no attempt to hide the pity in his voice. "All three of you entered the cave together. Yet, the girl who chose your friend over you, left with the power to control fire, and now your best friend can access the power of shadow. And what did you get from the goddess?"*

*Levy felt guilt rise up within him. He was truly happy that his friends had gained so much from their journey, but he had asked himself that same question over and over.*

*"What if you had gone down one of their paths instead?" the voice mocked, as if reading his mind. "Why did they get such powerful gifts, and all you got was a little extra strength? The sword I gave you channels it, but it seems to me as though the goddess barely gave you anything at all."*

*"Stop," Levy choked. "I see myself in these images. You said they show important events. Clearly, I was given enough to claim the throne. Your words will not sway me from my path. They are only serving to push me from yours."*

*"Are you so sure? I hear the waver in your voice. This is my domain after all. What makes you think that what you see is the truth of the future. You see what I want you to see Mr. Sylva. And what I want you to see is your success. However, if you choose to continue with the meager power you were given, well...."*

*A snap filled the air and Levy once again saw the image of himself in front of the throne room. Only this time, he watched as the doors to the room slammed shut, leaving him firmly on the other side.*

*"I can help you achieve what you desire Mr. Sylva. You need only ask. All I will require of you is to claim the throne for the gods. We will turn your world into a utopia. Allow me to help you, and the doors will open to you once again. Think on what I've said."*

*"Leave," Levy said hoarsely, "And do not call me to your realm again. I will not give you what you seek."*

*A mirthless chuckle filled the air. "Young man, I do not call you into my realm. Your yearning for power brings you here of your own accord. We will meet again soon, I think."*

*As the voice left, a pressure lifted from the room. The floor beneath Levy fell from beneath his feet, dropping him into the waiting darkness.*

~~~

Levy woke with a start, jumping from his bed, sword in hand. His shirt was drenched in sweat and clung to his body. Soft rays of light filtered in through his window, indicating the start of his day had arrived. That was fine by him. Since returning to the citadel, his dreams had been haunted by that insufferable god.

He would rather be awake, training and planning, than face that snake again. It was clear to him that Janus intended to turn him against his friends. He didn't even try to hide the fact. He may have promised no harm to them if he gave the throne to the gods, but he couldn't stomach the thought of betraying his friends, let alone all of humanity. The gods could not be trusted.

At first the trainers had been disappointed when they hadn't returned with a trove of weapons to help the war effort. However, it had turned into a hero's welcome after they had told them about their trials and shown what they could do.

It had been a long time since the world had seen actual demigods, though they weren't demigods in the traditional sense. That would imply they had been born of mortal and god. But the trainers assured them that having been infused with the essence of a goddess was the same thing.

Though they were happy to see Levy's feats of strength, and Quinn's improved speed, sensing, and endurance, they all fawned over Ashe. To them, she may as well have been crowned the new goddess of fire. She was immediately taken into special training.

It appeared as though she had become the main strategy for taking the throne. Levy figured they would have included Quinn in that as well, but for some reason he hadn't shown them the mask or its capabilities.

He seemed very skittish when the topic of the mask came up and begged his friends not to share that detail with the Masters. With
~~~

Levy's newfound knowledge of how he got the mask, he was beginning to understand why.

They promised to keep his secrets, leaving Ashe as the sole star of the Citadel. Because of that, it gave Levy and Quinn a lot of time to talk. And since today was going to be another day of the Masters and Ashe locked behind the council doors, Levy figured it was time to do just that.

~~~

Levy found Quinn eating alone in the mess hall. The Citadel was a colossal structure at the heart of Stormhaven. Despite being the main quarters for the war effort, it housed more than just soldiers. However, that didn't change the fact that no matter how packed the mess hall was, Quinn always occupied a table by himself.

Despite the many victories and achievements Quinn accomplished for these people, it didn't change the fact that he was Abyssillian, and those prejudices were always present in human society. It made Levy sick that his friend was treated so poorly by the very people he was constantly putting his life on the line to protect.

It was one of the reasons he started allowing Quinn to follow him around everywhere when he had first arrived. Eventually that bloomed into a wonderful friendship. They constantly bickered and competed, but when it came to a fight, there was nobody else in the world Levy would rather have at his back. He was also the only other person at the Citadel that could keep up with Levy on a battlefield.

At least, that used to be the case. Now Levy wasn't so sure. If he wore his mask, Levy didn't think he would stand a chance against him. And Ashe was the same way with her fire. A pang of jealousy jolted through his system, immediately followed by a wave of guilt.

"I know I'm a handsome man, but I'm spoken for, sorry. So, unless there is something else I can do for you, I'm going to have to ask you to allow me to eat my meal in peace," Quinn looked up at Levy with a grin on his face.

Levy had a moment of embarrassment as he realized he had been standing over him staring for an uncomfortably long time. With
~~~

a slight shake of his head, he snapped out of it and smiled back at him.

"Don't flatter yourself Alesia, you're lucky Ashe is willing to come within a mile of you. I hope she has control of those powers of hers. Wouldn't want any accidents during any nocturnal activities." he winked.

"Oh?" Quinn sharpened his grin. "I'm surprised you know about these 'nocturnal activities'. I didn't think you were experienced in such things. Where'd you learn about that, your hand?"

Levy looked around, seeing disapproving stares thrown their way from the other patrons in the room. With a placating smile he said "Come on, let's go spar a little. I want to talk, and it doesn't seem like the Masters have anything planned for us today."

Quinn drained his bowl and got up from the bench, following him out of the room. If he saw the fearful looks he got, he didn't show it. He was probably used to it by now. Levy wasn't sure how he could tolerate it.

If he got dirty looks everywhere he went, he would lose his temper. They exited the Citadel through a rear entrance and walked across the courtyard toward the training grounds. As it became clearer where they were headed, the soldiers on their breaks or days off began to follow in their wake.

Abyssillian nature aside, Quinn was still one of the best fighters here. So, when he and Levy, also considered one of the best, sparred, their matches became quite the spectacle. Money tended to be bet and exchanged based on the outcome. At first, when they were young and showing promise, Levy would wipe the floor with Quinn.

As time went on, and Quinn got more training, beginning to learn what his Abyssillian blood could do, he became much more of a threat. As of now, their record against each other was only a couple of matches in Levy's favor.

They entered through the doors on the other side of the courtyard into a spacious room. In the center of the room was a pit of sand in the shape of a large oval. That was the arena floor. Sand had many uses when it came to sparring. It forced fighters to exert more energy, strengthening more of the muscles in the body than a typical solid floor would. It also gave fighters experience in fighting on uncertain footing.

War was an ugly thing, and you didn't always get to choose the battleground. Monsters were killers no matter where they fought. It also helped to mitigate damage if the combatant fell too hard. Because of that, it opened up the ability to continue a fight if one of the combatants lost a weapon, allowing for hand combat and throws.

Wooden bleachers surrounded the arena pit. This room was commonly used for tournaments and other events between the soldiers when morale needed to be kept high, so seating was a necessity. The roof was made of a large glass dome. Good for keeping natural lighting during the day and keeping out rain during a storm.

As Levy and Quinn entered the pit, about fifteen soldiers clambered in, taking seats spread out around the bleachers. Quinn quirked an eyebrow at Levy, who shrugged back in response.

"They know a good fight when they see one."

Quinn shrugged back and asked, "How do you want to do this? Hand to hand, wood or steel?"

"Let's do wooden staves today," Levy looked over at the weapons rack. "We'll give the audience some fun."

Staves were neither of their preferred weapons which made them the perfect things to train with. Levy had a lot of strength, especially since coming home from the mission, so if he used the big wooden sword he liked to use against the skinny one of Quinn's choice, it was likely to splinter it, bringing an end to the match quickly.

With staves, both fighters would be forced into unfamiliar territory and would have to be careful about how they fought. Granted, they had trained with all of these weapons since early childhood so "unfamiliar" simply meant not preferable. But the staves were sturdy and would hold up against Levy's onslaught.

Quinn grunted his agreement and stepped up to the rack, twirling a white oak staff around a few times. Levy grabbed a similar staff and took his place in the center of the ring. As Quinn walked up to match him, Levy lowered his voice, "Do you have it with you?"

"No," came Quinn's clipped reply.

"You should use it," Levy responded, watching for any sign of emotion that might play across his friend's face.

"Not here Levy. Not in front of everyone. Nobody but you two can know about it. Not until I have no other choice."

"Why?" he asked, raising his voice a little. He just didn't understand how Quinn could have such a powerful item fall into his lap and refuse to use it. "You're unstoppable with that thing!"

"Shhh," Quinn hissed, looking around at the soldiers to see if anybody heard. "Enough. If this is what this is about, I'm not sparring."

Levy raised his hands in resignation. "Okay, okay, I'm sorry. I do want to know about it and why you're so afraid, but I won't push you here in front of all of these people. Let's spar and get some good training in. We can talk later."

Quinn nodded and raised his staff, holding it out in front of him and bowing like they were taught to do before a match. "I'll give you the same answer then as now. I don't want to talk about it."

Levy matched his bow, "How about a bet then? If you win, I will never bring it up again. If I win, we find somewhere to talk privately, and you tell me everything about it. I'm your friend man, and I want to be there for you. This is clearly bugging you. It will help to talk about it."

Quinn just sighed. He knew Levy very well, which meant he knew he wouldn't give up. This was going to be his one chance to make him stop. Plus, he was competitive and liked a good wager.

"Fine," he relented. "But if I win, you not only have to stop asking me about it, but you also have to cover all of mine and Ashe's chores for the entire day the next time we have a day off so she and I can go into town. It's been forever since I've gotten to take her out."

"Deal," he smiled. "Now en garde!" He lashed out a quick strike, attempting to catch Quinn unready and off balance.

Alas, Quinn was never in such a way. He walked around ready for a fight at any moment. Levy supposed if he had to walk around, hated by almost everyone for what he was, he would always be ready for a fight as well.

Quinn caught the end of Levy's staff with the tip of his own, pushing it to the left and bringing the butt of his own up in an uppercut. Levy jumped back, feeling the air as the wood narrowly avoided contact with his chin.

"God's sake man, are you trying to take my head off?"

The ever-increasing size of the crowd cheered at the near miss. Quinn let lose an impish smile of his own. "Just trying to do what the Masters never could and knock some sense into you."

Levy let out a booming laugh and swept his staff down at his friend's legs. Just short of making contact however, he stabbed it down into the sand, using it to vault himself in the air and launch a kick aimed at Quinn's chest.

Quinn, having had his staff down to block the leg sweep, found himself in no position to defend, and did the only thing he could. He jumped backwards, taking less impact when the kick landed. The momentum of the jump combined with the push of the kick launched him backwards, landing hard on his back.

Levy heard the pleasing "oof" of air shooting out of his friend's lungs. The crowd roared in either agony or support as gold changed hands quickly.

"So, about that mask," Levy said with a cocky grin. Quinn's legs shot into the air and he kicked out, bringing himself back to his feet. The crowd let loose another roar as they realized the fight wasn't over yet.

"You're going to regret asking that," Quinn said. His eyes blazed red as he crouched into an offensive stance. Quinn's eyes had always been striking, being as different as they were, but Levy had never seen them do that before.

Before he could think about anything else, Quinn vanished into a blur as he darted into motion. Movement in the corner of Levy's eye alerted him to Quinn's presence, allowing him to bring up his arm just in time to block his kick. The impact stung more than any kick he'd taken before, and he had taken many.

As Quinn hit the ground, he disappeared again, streaking around to the other side and sweeping out with his staff. Again, Levy saw just a flicker of movement, and stuck enough of his staff out to turn what would have been a finishing strike into a glancing blow. Still, it was a glancing blow that sent pain coursing through him.

He sent a haphazard strike out to where the blow had just come from, but his staff met only air. It was then that he felt his legs sweep out from under him, planting him hard on his back.

Moments later the end of Quinn's staff rested against his throat with only the slightest bit of pressure. His friend stood over him, staring down at him with shining red eyes. Levy realized with both jealousy and anger that it must be the goddess' essence fueling this increased speed. Quinn had been holding out on him.

With a burst of anger, Levy swept the staff from his throat and surged to his feet. He grabbed Quinn by the collar and yelled, "If you're too much of a coward to use the power of that mask, then give it to me. You're clearly fine without it!"

Quinn's eyes widened and Levy realized he had just shouted that to a room that at this point was filled with not only quite a few soldiers, but some of the Masters as well.

"Quinn, I'm so sorry, I…."

His friend grabbed the hand that was holding his collar and forced it away from him. With a look of fear and betrayal, he stormed out of the training grounds.

# CHAPTER 10: Quinn

Quinn was devastated. It had been weeks since he'd grabbed the mask, and still, that girl haunted his dreams. Sometimes he would dream of her falling into the abyss; the maniacal laughter of Janus mocking him as he watched helplessly.

Other times, the girl would appear before him with the mask on her face. She would look at him, tilt her head to the side in an unsettling way and ask, "Why?" to which he had no answer.

Over and over, he told himself it had been to save Ashe. The vision had shaken him. But even he knew how flimsy that excuse was. Everyone knew the gods couldn't be trusted. They used humans for their own pleasure and abandoned them when they were finished.

Quinn had fallen right into that trap. Janus had sworn on his essence that the vision he showed Quinn had been true, and that, to a god, is binding. But gods are infamous for their half-truths. There was no guarantee that anything he saw in that vision would come to pass in such a way.

The fact was, Quinn had let an innocent child die for the sake of power, and no excuse as to why he needed that power could ever wash away that sin. He felt every bit the monster the humans in the capital saw him as. His one hope had been that he could keep it hidden: Never use it again, never let the Masters know of its existence and never face that demon again. But even he knew that was never to be.

Eventually he would have had to face the music. And thanks to Levy, now everyone knew. It was only a matter of time before he was dragged to the front lines with Ashe.

*Ashe.* The name brought even more dread. Even more so than the Masters not knowing the truth of the mask, he did not want to tell Ashe. She was the absolute protector of the innocent. He cherished their relationship more than anything else in his life, and he worried that as soon as she found out what he'd done, she would never see him the same.

That would break his heart. It would shatter the very core of his being, and it was only a matter of time now. He had a note he'd written when they first got back to the Citadel. It explained everything on it; what happened, why he made the choice he made, and the guilt he felt over it.

He hadn't had the guts to tell her so he had written it down in the hopes it would ease some of the anxiety he felt. Once the truth came out, he figured he'd better have that ready in case she never wanted to speak to him again. That was the worst part. He knew it was selfish to keep it from her. And it was selfish to the little girl he let die.

What worried him more than anything else about the whole situation was breaking Ashe's heart. She was the kindest person he had ever met, and the thought of him being responsible for inflicting any kind of pain on her tortured him. She had been the only one outside of Levy to ever look at him as a person and not a monster.

Even the Masters had a disapproving look in their eyes when he first came to the Citadel. But Ashe had taken his hand and immediately welcomed him into her life, red eyes be damned. He felt as though his heart was being ripped in two.

*Maybe I am the monster they all think I am.*

"Bull," A familiar voice said. Levy sat down next to him,

leaning against one of the large stone gargoyles that decorated the rooftops of the Citadel, dangling his legs off the edge.

From this height, the entirety of Stormhaven was laid out in front of them. Just past the gates of the Citadel, the busy streets wound their way to the marketplace where even from this height the murmur of the crowds could be heard.

It was surrounded on all sides by the city's housing. Unlike in most other settlements, Stormhaven was rather rich; thanks in part to the wide variety of business the Citadel brought in. As a result, even the poorest citizens were able to find shelter. A little further out were the slums.

Though not as nice as the stone and brick housing closest to the market, even these buildings were made from sturdy wood. Around the perimeter of the city the towering walls stood vast and strong. It was thanks to these walls that Stormhaven was able to prosper where so many other settlements could not.

"I didn't say anything." Quinn said, not making eye contact.

"You didn't have to," Levy replied. "I know what you're thinking when you have that solemn, 'woe is me' look in your eye."

"How did you know I was up here?" Quinn asked, not bothering to get mad. The truth was out and there was no point in being upset.

"You always hide up here when you're upset." His friend answered, staring out at the city beyond.

"Ever since you were little, when I would beat in a match, you would come hide up here. We all knew you did it. You were kind of a sore loser."

His grin was distant. "Look, I wanted to apologize. Losing my temper is no excuse for being a bad friend. The Masters asked me about it, but I didn't tell them anything. I'm sorry for making them aware of it though."

Quinn shrugged. "Don't be. Keeping it a secret was a fever dream at best. It was bound to come out eventually. It's not like I'd just ignore it in a fight for the tower if it meant surviving. I just... I'm scared, Levy. I messed up bad."

Levy glanced over and saw the pale face of his friend. He'd assumed Quinn was keeping the mask a secret for selfish reasons; wanting to keep it as a surprise and end up a hero. It was now obvious just how terrified he was.

Quinn was fighting an internal battle and he was at the point of breaking. With a sigh Levy said, “Look, I don’t know what’s going on with you and that mask, and since I lost our match, I won’t ask. But if it helps, I have been fighting my own internal battle ever since getting back from our mission.”

Quinn looked over, hopeful. Sharing wasn’t something he liked to do outside of anybody but Ashe, but if he was going to confide in anyone else, Levy was the most appropriate. “What do you mean?”

“I just….” Levy shook his head. “Look, Ashe came out of that cave with the ability to control fire, and she’s getting stronger every day. She went from struggling to put out one small fire to being able to completely extinguish an entire village in an hour. That’s some serious fire power.”

He must have seen Quinn’s narrowed eyes because he smiled and added “Pun intended.”

Quinn snorted as Levy continued, “And then there’s you. You come back with this ridiculous enhanced speed and endurance, not to mention you have this mask that when you wear it, makes you a teleporting shadow, and even though you are too scared to use it, it’s there for you.

“But me? I left that cave with the ability to nudge a boulder and a shiny new sword. I know it’s petty, but I have all of this jealousy coursing through me. I’ve trained to take that tower every single day since the moment I could hold a sword.

“And this was supposed to be a chance for me to lead that fight. But instead I watch my friends become more powerful than any human alive, while I get sent to the sidelines as a support. It’s just burning me up inside.”

Quinn looked at his friend in shock. In all of the years he had known him, Levy had never talked so in depth about his feelings and his emotions. It left him speechless.

After composing himself he said, “If I could trade you I would. I know it seems like this mask is something great, but I promise you it isn’t.”

“I’ll be honest with you,” Levy said, staring off into the distance, “I‘ve had dreams since returning. In them I see you leaping at a waterfall. On one side the mask is falling and the other, a human. I think I've worked out what's eating at you so much.

"If you want to talk about it, you can. You won't get any judgment from me. The fact of the matter is, what we went through in that cave, our trials, they scarred us. We'll carry the trauma with us for the rest of our lives, no matter how long they are. They're experiences few humans have gone through before. So, while some may think one thing of you, I won't."

Quinn was silent for a long time, watching the sun sink lower in the sky and listening to the sounds of life around him. Finally, he sucked in a fresh breath of air and said, "After I defeated Perseus, I was given the choice of two paths. Hestia asked me what I was afraid of and I answered 'choices.'

"So, she destroyed one of the paths leaving me only one to go down. When I met Janus, I recognized him pretty quickly. I thought it had all been one sick joke, since he's the god of choices and all."

Levy was watching his friend speak, a mix of interest and concern on his face.

"After introducing himself to me, he led me to a waterfall where he split into two and offered me a choice. He would drop two things. One of them a child, the other my mask. I could choose only one to save."

"I know you," Levy interjected in honest confusion. "There must have been some extenuating circumstance. Otherwise there's no way you wouldn't have saved the child."

Quinn looked over; pain etched across his face.

"Ashe," Levy whispered.

Quinn took a shaky breath before continuing. "He showed me a vision, Levy. A vision of Ashe being stabbed through the back. I couldn't see who did it or for what reason, but she was killed. He swore to me, swore on his *essence*, that this would come to pass if I did not choose the mask.

"With it, I would be able to save her from that fate. Even still I swore to save the child. Yet, when I jumped I…."

He looked back over at Levy, tears taking residence in the corners of his eyes. "My body just reacted, Levy. It just reached out and took it."

Levy wrapped Quinn in a hug. He had no idea the severity of

the guilt that had plagued Quinn. “Easy, man, easy,” he murmured.

“You aren’t a monster. You’re mortal. We have to make tough decisions. Sometimes they are right for the wrong reasons. This may be the fates at work, but I assure you one thing, you are not a monster. Ashe wouldn’t think so either.

“And just because they know about the mask now doesn’t mean you have to share how you got it. Let them see it and see what it can do but keep the story to yourself until you’re ready to share it. I will not tell a soul.”

With that Levy stood up. “The Masters want to see you in the training grounds when you’re ready. You’re a good person, Quinn. This doesn’t define you.”

Quinn listened to Levy’s footsteps fade as he composed himself. It had felt good to get that off his chest. Levy was helping him support the burden of it and it meant a lot to him. But he knew his friend was wrong.

Maybe he wasn’t a monster, but there was no way if Ashe found out what happened she would be okay with it. That just wasn’t her. With a final sigh, he stood up and started making his way back to the training grounds. It was best not to keep the Masters waiting.

# CHAPTER 11: Ashe

Ashe was ready for a break. She knew her power was invaluable to the Citadel and all of mankind, and she was pleased and even eager to help however she could. In this moment, she was spent. Council after council the Masters caught her up with the ancient secrets of their order.

Nobody knew why the tower existed, but it was a magic of a fickle creation. In the past millennia, the gods had easily claimed the tower when it would appear thanks to their potent essences. The humans never stood a chance with their mortal lives and their squishy bodies.

The magic of the tower would attract droves of monsters to it, making it only possible for one with the power of a god to make it to the throne room without dying. Even then some gods were known to perish along the way.

However, thanks to years of the Masters storing away godly artifacts of power in secret, sealed vaults, effectively draining the world of their power and locking the gods from the mortal realm, the humans stood an actual chance. This time when the tower appeared, humanity was ready.

They had melted down many essence-infused weapons and forged a mighty chain. With this chain, when the tower appeared, a large group of humans fought their way to it and bound the tower to the earth, stopping it from fading from their realm.

Although they couldn't figure out how to open the doors leading into the throne room, their sacrifice allowed for time. Now that Ashe and her friends had the power of a goddess within them, the Citadel decided the moment to strike had come at last.

While all of this information thrilled her, filling Ashe with purpose and a sense of duty, the councils tended to drag on and on. It was with a sigh of relief that when Master Enkar came busting into the council chambers tittering on about some newfound power, she packed up her belongings and followed them out to the training grounds.

When she arrived, she found it empty with the exception of Levy. He leaned back against the wall surrounding the pit and followed their entrance with his eyes. As she made her way over to him, she realized that despite his relaxed demeanor, he held tension in his neck and eyes.

"What's this about?" she asked, leaning against the wall beside him. He just shook his head and stared at the Masters filing in.

There were twenty Masters that made up the elite of the Citadel. Each of them specialized in a different area ranging from politics to fighting and everything in between. A master of each aspect of war is what they always told her growing up.

They all sat together now in a huddled mass, whispering excitedly amongst themselves. Down in the center of the arena, with his arms crossed and staring at the door, stood the grizzled, Master Darrik.

He was Master at Arms and was responsible for the training of she and her friends growing up. He turned them into the fighters they were today with a harsh, unforgiving training regimen. He was not a kind man.

Just then the door to the training grounds swung open and Quinn walked into the arena with a slight look of fear on his face. Ashe's stomach dropped when she realized that in his hand, he carried his mask.

"Did you know about this?" she asked Levy, concerned.

"This is my fault." His mouth twisted into a frown. "We were sparring in front of a crowd earlier. I got angry when he beat me and yelled about it. There were some Masters watching us and they heard me."

Ashe looked to him; concern etched onto her face. "Are you ok?"

"I'm fine," he said. "I'm more worried about him. That mask is eating at him. He needs to get comfortable using it if we want to reach the tower."

Ashe shook her head. "If he's that scared of it then he shouldn't keep using it."

"He isn't scared of it." Levy kept his eyes locked on Quinn.

Following Levy's gaze, Ashe began to feel dread rise within her as she finally sensed what she had been blind to. "He feels guilty about something."

Levy just shrugged, watching as Quinn and Darrik met in the center of the arena. "Ask him about it. It's not for me to say. But one way or another, we need the power that mask provides. You need to convince him it's ok."

Ashe was stuck between a range of emotions. She was sad that Quinn was feeling so helpless and lost. She was scared of what could have happened to have caused him to become so distant and unlike himself. But more than anything, she felt dread.

Dread at knowing, in the back of her mind, that Janus was still meddling in their lives. For it was Janus that brought that mask to Quinn, and it was Janus who was likely pulling the strings of his guilt.

Through it all, the words that haunted her since first seeing that cursed mask kept playing through her head. "*What would you call someone who chose power over life?*"

But she didn't think Quinn would do that. He was constantly putting his life on the line for a people who hated his guts because of the blood that ran through his veins. He would sacrifice himself in a heartbeat to save the innocent.

Whatever had caused this mask to fall into his hands, she knew the real monster was Janus. Still, the fact that those words so closely connected her fears to that mask terrified her.

Because if Quinn had come into that mask in a way that made him feel so guilty he couldn't talk to her about it, she who he told *everything*, then he might have done something he considered to be unforgivable. And, even though she knew she would always love him no matter what, that scared her more than anything else.

# CHAPTER 12: Quinn

"What took you so long?" Master Darrik's voice boomed when Quinn entered the training hall. "And why does it look like you've been crying? You think the monsters are going to just run away when you start crying? They are going to *eat you alive* if you show them that kind of weakness."

Master Darrik really had a way with people.

"And what are you dawdling for, soldier? I taught you better than that. Come here and show me this damn mask!"

Quinn heaved out a sigh, stressed and on edge, and walked forward. Master Darrik had always hated him growing up. He was of the strong belief that Abyssillians were monsters.

Though not all of the Masters hated him, some even went out of their way to try and make him feel like he belonged, a lot of them seemed to. It got tiring.

As he walked up to Master Darrik, he looked over and saw Ashe and Levy leaning up against the wall. Levy was looking at the mask with a hunger in his eyes. Knowing what he knew now, he didn't blame the man.

Levy wanted power. He wanted to be the hero of humanity and he felt as though he didn't get his fair shot at it after leaving the cave. Ashe on the other hand was staring directly at him, concern prevalent in her eyes.

Quinn worried that Levy may have told her what happened anyways, but he didn't see any anger in her. Only worry and sadness. The sadness scared him more than anger would have.

As he reached the stern master, Quinn held the mask up so he could see. Darrik looked it over, asking Quinn to rotate it; being very careful not to touch it himself. Humans feared what they didn't know, and as far as the mask was concerned, it certainly gave off a sinister aura.

Another master walked over from the side and placed his hands over the mask, closing his eyes and concentrating. Quinn could sense him reach out at it with his mind, feeling it for any kind of indication it was essence engraved. With a brief nod to Darrik, he pulled his hands back and returned to his seat.

"Does it have a name?" Darrik took a step back.

"Persona Umbram," Quinn replied, transfixed by the power he felt tingling up his arm.

"Person of Shadow." One of the Masters from the side translated. "Intriguing."

"And what does it do?" The master stared with a lustful look in his eye.

"It would be easier if I showed you master," Quinn responded, looking Darrik in the eye. "Why don't you grab a weapon and try to hit me before I disarm you?"

With a little smirk Darrik replied, "Very well. But don't think I'll go easy. I don't like that look in your eye and I plan to smack it out of you."

Quinn bowed his head in response. Slowly, he raised the mask to his face, slipping it on and allowing the power to wash over him. He heard a few gasps from the Masters before all went silent.

When he opened his eyes, he found himself standing in the Realm of Night. Chaos stood in front of him, still a silhouette but now with a more pronounced outline.

"You are clearer to me this time," He observed, looking the

outline up and down.

*As I said before. The more you use the mask, the more you assimilate with it. As that happens, more power will be opened to you, though it will also be more probable that you will lose yourself to this place.*

"Don't worry, I'll be quick." He pointed at the outline of Darrik.

*Do as you will,* Chaos responded. *Just beware the attraction power leaves.*

And with that he faded back into the blackness, leaving Quinn to himself.

# CHAPTER 13: Levy

Levy smiled when the shadow energy enveloped Quinn. He had only seen the power of the mask briefly before, but seeing it again firsthand, from start to end was going to be magical. All around him the Masters gasped. And then, as quick as a blink, Quinn was gone.

Quinn hadn't told him about how the mask worked when they had talked earlier, but based on his prior experience, and what he saw now in front of him, he assumed it had to do with travel through another realm.

He always exited and reentered through the darkness of a shadow. Likely he was traveling in a realm that ran alongside their own, invisible to the human eye. This was exhilarating.

Quinn always reappeared before he struck, so he wondered if he was unable to inflict any kind of physical damage from the other realm. So many questions he wanted answers to. He wondered if Quinn would let him try it out, though he highly doubted it. Beside him, Ashe looked like a nervous wreck.

She was pale as a ghost and biting at her nails like she always did when she was anxious.

"Relax," he said to her, trying to be reassuring. "The mask won't harm him, and Darrik won't get the chance to. I can beat Darrik in my sleep and Quinn literally kicked my ass when I fought him before."

"I'm not worried about the mask or Darrik," she wiped at the tears in her eyes. "I'm worried about Quinn. Janus messed with his head somehow. Whatever he had to do in order to get that mask has scarred him and he doesn't know how to talk about it."

Levy twisted his mouth in thought. She needed to know the truth about the mask if Quinn was ever going to move forward with harnessing its power. Even if the truth of it ended their relationship, Quinn wasn't going to be able to help if he was spending all his time moping.

Personal relationships meant nothing to the survival of humanity. Why is it he was the only one of them who seemed able to see that? And yet, he was the one who had been left with hardly any power.

"Just talk to him after this. Listen to him. Humanity living through this war is what matters. For that we need him to be able to use that mask and the power it provides him."

Ashe bit her lip and nodded. He knew she cared more for him than anyone. If anybody would be able to make him see sense, it would be her.

Out in the center of the sand, Darrik paced relentlessly, attempting to locate where Quinn had disappeared to. His sword was at the ready, not that it really mattered. Quinn was going to wipe the floor with the old man. Levy couldn't help but grin.

Quinn may have lucked into the most powerful thing out of all of them. He surveyed the battle field, locating all of the shadows and trying to decide where his friend might pop out. As if reading his mind, a shadowy figure slowly emerged out of Darrik's own shadow, directly behind the man.

It was ominous the way he moved, so slowly and so silently, with power surging around him. The Masters all gasped, alerting Darrik that Quinn had re-emerged. With a quick swing he turned, bringing the wooden sword around in a wicked strike. Quinn, however, had been ready for it.

Before the sword got even halfway around, Quinn had the master by the back of the neck, left arm outstretched keeping his sword arm locked straight and away from his body. With a quick twist, he jarred Darrik's wrist, causing the blade to tumble from the man's grasp.

For good measure, he then lifted the master over his head and dropped him down hard so that the master landed on his upper back with his legs up in the air. The Masters in the area were all silent as Master Darrik recovered his breath and slowly pushed himself back to his feet. Levy let out a booming laugh at what he had just witnessed.

"What do you say Master? Ready to admit defeat?"

Darrik's eyes narrowed before slowly raising his hands in the air. "Come to the council room tomorrow, Quinn. You're a part of the plans now."

Levy's nostrils flared in annoyance at being once again left out. He couldn't be the hero humanity needed if he wasn't involved. With that having been decided, the Masters all shuffled out of the room, a mixture of excitement and fear in the glances they threw Quinn's way.

It was only after the last master had left the room that Quinn removed the mask, allowing the shadow to retreat back into the alabaster. Levy walked up to him, his back stiff, and clapped him on the back.

"See, that wasn't so bad right? And now you get to be part of the big boy plans."

Quinn just shook his head back.

"Are you okay Quinn?" Ashe asked with a soft voice from behind him. "Come with me back to my room and we can talk. I know something is eating at you. You know I'm here. Let me help."

She walked up to him and grabbed his hand, leading him out of the arena, giving Levy a reassuring pat on the way out.

When he was sure they were gone, Levy let out a groan of frustration. How could they be so blind? They were sitting on the power of the gods, and all they could do was mope around. It was so unfair!

He had the willingness and the fortitude to see this through to the end; to see humanity sitting on the throne and dictating a better world. And all he got was a little sword and a small boost of strength?

The Masters had been clearly disappointed with him ever since they had gotten back. Before he was a leader. Now he was on the sidelines; relegated to training the basic soldiers and fetching materials for Ashe, the prodigy. He was sick of it. He needed to find a way to bring humanity into their golden age.

If his friends were unwilling to do it, then it was up to him. He saw the picture of him in front of the throne room in his mind. He just had to make it there. Levy would do whatever it took to be the hero his people needed. They would thank him in the end.

# CHAPTER 14: Ashe

They walked across the grounds of the Citadel, hand in hand, under a beautiful night sky. Ashe led them down a path they had walked many times in the past, hoping it would jog some pleasant memories and make Quinn more open to talk.

The walkway was made from carved marble blocks; the white stone providing a stark contrast against the blazing reds of the roses surrounding it. The weather was just beginning to cool down as the season shifted from summer to autumn, and a pleasant breeze blew leaves dancing across their path.

The moon above was nearly full, casting a silver glow down upon the two. Normally this was the kind of night that Quinn would love, taking Ashe across the city on the rooftops. Stormhaven was a sprawling city, surrounded on all sides by towering stone walls.

It was the safest place to be for humanity, so long as you had the right kind of coin or trade to make it. On their first date, Quinn had taken her up to the highest rooftop in the city, where they had been able to look out across its entirety.

The sights had been beautiful, and the air fresh and clean. Since that night, whenever they wanted to get away, they would jump from roof to roof, making their way back to that spot. It was one of Ashe's fondest memories.

Tonight however, despite the beautiful weather, Ashe was practically dragging Quinn along behind her. Anytime she would look to him behind her, he would look down, avoiding eye contact entirely. Ever since they had gotten back from their mission, he'd been elusive and withdrawn.

Both qualities that were incredibly unlike him; at least with her. He had always been the type of person to face a storm head on. Any problem had a solution so long as he cared enough to find it. And she was always beside him to share in the burden. It was one of the things that had bonded them. But now, he avoided her at all costs. It crushed her.

"Quinn," she prodded gently. "Please, talk to me. Whatever is bugging you, you know I'll listen." She could tell, even in the silver moonlight, that his face paled even further. "Let me help you." She said, trying to coax it out of him.

"I don't want to talk about it Ashe, please."

He looked up into her eyes for the first time. There was genuine fear there and it broke her heart. He was one of the bravest people she knew, yet whatever bothered him had shaken him to his very core.

"You're going to have to eventually. You can't keep whatever this is bottled up inside. It's toxic. Look at you, you're deteriorating."

It was true. Ever since they'd returned, he had hardly eaten. The shadows under his eyes were deep and dark, indicating his lack of sleep. Whatever was bothering him, it was killing him.

He bit his lip. She didn't want to pressure him too much. She knew that it would only lead to him sealing it further away. She was treating it like she had when she had first been practicing with her power. Slowly coaxing it to the surface.

For his own well-being, the truth had to come out. Both because it was hurting him, but also because she feared she knew what the truth was, and she refused to believe it unless it came from his own lips. It was selfish and that gutted her, but she had to know.

Curse Janus for putting such nasty taunts in her head. Finally, he seemed to reach a decision and looked back into her eyes.

"The mask is dangerous." He began slowly, as if trying to decide how much to divulge. "When I wear it, it takes me to this place called the *Realm of Night*. A being exists there who calls himself Chaos. He has warned me that the more I use the mask, the more likely I'll be to lose myself to that power.

"Hestia's essence protects me from the pull of it, but lately the urge to wear it has been growing within me. It's like the realm is addictive to me, and the more I come in contact with it, the stronger an affect it has on me. I fear what losing myself to its power entails."

Ashe wasn't expecting that answer. She assumed he would discuss the details of how he got the mask in his trial, not what the mask was doing to him. Why would he be so scared to talk to her if this was what was bothering him?

Of course, she would be on his side. The only thing she could think was that he was worried that he wouldn't be willing to sacrifice himself to this power, even if it meant taking the throne and saving humanity, and that he didn't think she would agree with him on that. But he knew her better than that. That was something Levy, and the Masters would resent, not her. There was definitely a deeper pain.

"Quinn," she began carefully. "If you are afraid of losing yourself to that mask, then don't wear it. You're still a strong warrior, even without it. You still have Hestia's essence within you, making you a stronger soldier than any of the others.

"Let me be the head of the spear, and you can be my wielder. You don't need to fear that I'll turn on you for being afraid to use this dangerous power."

They had reached her room now and stood outside her door. He shot her a smile that did not reach his eyes.

"Thank you, Ashe. You have no idea how much that's been eating at me." He pulled her into his arms placing a soft kiss on her lips.

Having known Quinn for almost all of their lives, she knew he wasn't telling her the full truth. He may have been able to fool most other people, but the truth was written all over his face. There was still more he was hiding from her. As he began to turn away, she grabbed his hand again, pulling him closer.

She kissed him then, parting his lips with her tongue. She felt his reluctance fade away as he melted into her, all of his fear bleeding out of him until all that was left was passion. Their passion for one another blended together, until neither knew where they ended and the other began. As they separated from each other, both catching their breath, she nodded toward the door.

"Come in with me. I know something is still bothering you. But you know that no matter what it is, I want to be with you and help you through it. I'm here for you."

She felt his arm stiffen before quickly relaxing again. He shot her a look, hoping she didn't notice. He leaned in one more time, cupping her face in his hand.

"We have to be up early for council tomorrow. We should both get some sleep. We'll talk soon, I promise."

With her eyes still closed, she felt him slip his hand from hers, and listened as his footsteps slowly faded away. When she opened her eyes, he was gone. With a shuttering sigh, she unlocked the door and went inside.

"Little bit of a lover's quarrel, eh?" A voice greeted her from the darkness of her quarters. Ashe immediately dropped into a crouched stance, bringing fire to her hands. It lit the room in a golden glow, showing the sneering face of the bearded Janus.

"Relax, love," he cooed, raising his hands in a placating gesture. "I didn't come here for a fight."

"How are you even here?" Ashe asked, not bringing her hands down. "I thought the gods were all trapped in their realms."

"Aye, that's true. But there are still places of power in this world that we can project ourselves to. As you can see," he passed his hand though the cup sitting on her table, "I am not here in the flesh, just in essence. This Citadel of yours holds immense power." A twinkle lit his eye. "Want to know why?"

"With all due respect, not particularly. Why are you in my quarters, and where is your other face?"

Janus scrunched his nose in distaste. "He's off speaking with another at the moment. Thought I'd take the opportunity to sneak away and give you some advice."

This time it was Ashe's turn to scrunch her nose. "Why would

I want any advice from you? You've done nothing but cause problems since the moment I met you."

Janus smirked, resting his ghostly hand on his forehead. "Everything we do is for a reason. For the good of your world and ours. The humans would see us locked away in our realms for the rest of eternity. We only want our freedom back. We have no quarrel with you lot."

"Except for the fact that you want to rule us like in the old days. So long as we accept your abuse without rising up, we don't get squashed under your giant, godly feet."

Janus raised an eyebrow, staring at the sole of his shoe. "My feet are smaller than your friend Levy's, love. Nothing to worry about there."

Ashe flared the fire in her hands brighter, hoping it would convince him to leave. Seeing it, Janus got serious again.

"The bottom line is this. The gods are going to claim the throne, as we have since the dawn of time. You can either be on the winning side, or you can die. There is no middle ground.

"And let me tell you, if you think I'm being dramatic, ask your boy toy about it. Based on information I've been given by someone in the know, so to speak, it's still haunting him.

"But surely you know all about that, right? You guys talk about everything. I'm sure you don't see him as a monster for the choice he made. That poor girl…."

Ashe's stomach plummeted. She had her suspicions that Quinn had done something he regretted during his trials that led him to the mask. Janus had taunted her with it when she was leaving his room during her own. But she wanted the exact details.

"Anyways, my offer still stands, love. Let me make you my wife. Become immortal and live the glory days alongside us. Or don't and die. That would be such a waste though. So much potential within you."

With a sad shake of his head he began to fade from her room.

"Janus," she commanded with false bravery. His fading paused as he looked at her, hopeful. "Never visit me again."

He gave a snort of derision before shaking his head and disappearing.

With a last, mocking word he said, "What will you do, little phoenix, when you are abandoned by all you love, and have pushed away your last ally? Who will save you then?"

# CHAPTER 15: Quinn

Quinn walked down the cobbled *roads* of Stormhaven, making his way toward the marketplace. After his conversation with Ashe the night before, he wanted to go and get her something nice.

He'd been eyeing a silver heart locket for quite a while now and was just waiting until he had saved enough to get it. Things would be tight for a little while after this but putting her at ease would be worth it.

All around him the city was alive with the sounds of its citizens. From children running between the legs of the people crowding the stalls, to the voices of the merchants hawking their wares, the ignorant bliss of those who lived their lives protected behind the walls of the city were loud and vibrant.

Contrary to most human cities scattered around the land, the people of Stormhaven lived privileged lives. The walls, made of towering stone, were built high and sturdy. Quinn could feel them humming with an ancient power, though where that power came from, he was never able to track.

As such, the people had nothing to fear from outside threats. Thanks to the Masters, and the Citadel, the city was far advanced in other ways as well. There was a large sewer system that ran beneath the city, connected to each home. Buildings all had their own hatch which the people could use to dump their wastes.

Thanks to this, the streets smelled constantly of baking bread and the rich spices that were traded on a daily basis, instead of the slop thrown on the streets like in other cities.

As he continued along the street, listening to the bustling people around him, he ran his hand along the surface of the mask inside his cloak, feeling each detail and groove individually. He felt a small high as the power of the Realm of Night trickled into him, slightly slowing down the world around him, allowing him to take everything in with greater detail.

The urge to use the mask increased every day as the energy he received just from touching it weakened. Though he knew he shouldn't, he was growing increasingly addicted to the power he felt when he wore it. The worst part was, despite Chaos' numerous warnings, as well as common sense dictating his thoughts, his temptation was beginning to win out.

Each day he had to convince himself not to put the mask on. It would be one thing if a situation presented itself in which he had no choice but to rely on its power, but to just nonchalantly wear it just to feel that energy course through him? That was something he couldn't allow himself to do.

Movement in the corner of his eye brought his head around just in time to see two men in all black drag an elderly man with them into the darkness of a nearby alleyway. It was as if they had read his thoughts and offered to comply.

Without thinking, Quinn removed the mask and went to slap it on his face before realizing what he was doing. Though this was a situation in which he felt the need to step in, surely, he didn't need the masks power. He was a trained warrior infused with the essence of a goddess. Combined with the power of the mask, that was sure to be overkill.

Without giving himself the chance to hesitate further, he set the mask on his face, stepping into the Realm of Night, feeling a sense of ecstasy as its power washed over him.

"You're beginning to enjoy this place too much," Chaos said, standing just to his right.

"I just need to stop them from hurting that man," Quinn replied, defensively. "And then the mask will be right back in my pocket."

*"Are you telling me you need this mask to stop two mortal men from committing a robbery?"*

Quinn felt a sense of shame run through him. Chaos was right. He'd beaten Perseus, an ancient hero of legend, without the mask. Yet now he was frivolously relying on it just because he wanted to feel its power again.

*"You don't need to convince me. I am only trying to warn you. Now go. Even with time moving slowly here, if you stand still any longer you will likely be too late."*

Chaos was right again. He would have to chastise himself later. For now, there was someone in need of his assistance. He made his way toward the entrance of the alley.

Thanks to the buildings surrounding it on each side, it was enveloped in shadow, making it as bright as a well-lit room in the Realm of Night. It also meant Quinn could appear practically anywhere. *This would be fun.*

At the far end of the alley, with his back pressed as close to the brick wall as he could get, the elderly man cowered; his hands held above his head.

"Please, I don't have anything on me. I was just out for a walk," He pleaded.

"Shut it, old man." The mugger on the left growled. He wore a black, leather tunic, cinched at the waste with rope. The sleeves had been ripped off, revealing tanned, weathered skin, kissed too long by the summer sun. Scars of all shapes and sizes wound their way down his arms, ending precisely at his wrists as though they were cut intentionally.

"Yeah," his compatriot snickered. "Better listen to the boss and keep your lips zipped if you don't wanna die. Besides, we saw you make a visit to the marketplace. We know you have coin."

This man was dressed the same, though he was considerably shorter and more rotund than his fellow mugger. When he spoke, his voice came out high and shrill, wavering in such a way that Quinn wondered if his sanity was entirely present. Both men wore black hoods, pulled tight around their heads keeping Quinn from seeing their faces.

"Please, I'm begging you," the man wailed. "My daughter is visiting in a few days and I just wanted to get her something nice. I spent what I had."

"Hear that boss?" The short one laughed. "Says he ain't got no coin left on him. That's a real shame, ain't it?"

The taller man walked up and kicked the cowering elder in his face, knocking him onto the dirty cobblestone.

"We don't have time for those who don't have coin," The tall man said in his baritone voice. "If you can't give us what we ask, then you'll pay with your life."

Quinn had seen enough. When the tall mugger's boot had struck the old man, a white-hot rage filled him. Pulling on the power of the Realm around him, he stepped into the shadow portal, sliding up ominously out of the cobble ground between the old man and his attackers.

"Sorry, boys." He spoke in his double voice. "But I'm afraid your fun ends here."

From this angle he could see the smaller man's beady little eyes widen from beneath his hood.

"What the Hades is this thing," he squealed at his boss.

"I don't know, but whatever it is we'll kill it too," He pulled a jagged, steel knife from the belt of his tunic.

The tall man struck out, attempting to slice open Quinn's throat. Thanks to the power of the mask, combined with his natural instincts, the move was far too telegraphed to be even remotely affective.

Without hesitation, Quinn reached out and grabbed the man by the wrist, giving it a sharp twist and wrenching the dagger from his hand; catching it as it fell. With his other hand, he grabbed a handful of hair on the side of the mugger's head.

"Don't fret, this will be over before you know it."

With a swift push, he slammed the man's head into the side of the building, splattering blood across alley. The smaller mugger let out a strangled squeak before turning and running back toward the entrance.

*Not a chance*, Quinn thought.

He slipped back into the Realm of Night, gliding past the hobbling mugger, before stepping back again into the mortal realm; directly in front of his prey.

Falling to his knees, the man begged, "Please don't kill me. I don't want to die."

"That's funny," Quinn responded. "That's similar to what the gentleman you were just robbing was saying. And yet you were going to kill him anyway."

Faster than the man could respond, Quinn slashed out with dagger he had taken from the first mugger, opening the man's throat. Beside him, the old man hobbled toward the exit of the alleyway, moving as fast away from the carnage as his brittle legs would take him.

*"That was brutal."* The voice of Chaos said, with no hint of emotion.

Quinn looked around at the fallen forms of the muggers as the blood began to slowly cover the surface of the alley. The realization of what he had just done hit him like a punch to the gut. With a surge of panic, he ripped the mask from his face, falling to his knees and retching into the pooling blood.

He looked down at the mask in his hand with vitriol and disgust.

*Never again. I will never again wear this mask.*

With a determination he didn't feel he rose to his feet and wound his arm back, readying himself to smash the mask against the stone floor. Yet, just as his arm came down, the image of a blade sticking through Ashe jumped to the forefront of his thoughts.

*You have my word, on my essence, that this will come to pass.*

The words of Janus came unbidden back to his mind.

At the last second, he stopped the momentum of his strike, keeping the mask firmly in hand. He spent the next few minutes staring at it, before pounding feet sounded in the distance. With one last look at the mask, he tucked it back inside his pocket and slipped out from the alleyway, blending in with the crowd as he made his way back toward the safety of the Citadel.

# CHAPTER 16: Levy

*'Jealousy is one of the most common fatal flaws we see in the ancient heroes we study, second only to hubris.' The instructor lectured to Levy.*

*You need to let go of yours or it will eat at you until you are just a shell of what you were.*

Levy rolled his shoulders, working at the knots that had built in them as he slept.

*'You say that as if I can just turn it on and off like a switch, Master. It isn't something I can so easily control. I don't want to feel the way I do. I want to be happy for Quinn. Ashe is...beautiful. And he deserves somebody who doesn't think of him as subhuman as most of the people here do.'*

*Master Brendan was one of the oldest Masters at the Citadel. He had served it for many decades as Master of Whispers. With years under his belt of subterfuge and information gathering, it was no surprise to Levy that he had sought him out.*

*Anytime the possibility of discord rose up among he and his friends, Brendan was there to calm it. The Masters didn't want their future heroes to be at odds.*

*Young Quinn is certainly in need of a steadying hand.' The old master replied,*

*'Ashelia will be good for him. As for your feelings toward it, while it is admirable that you believe such a thing, your actions betray those thoughts.*

*'I was young once myself, Levy. I remember what it was like to love and not be loved in return. But how you act is the measure of a man. You must rise above your feelings and steady yourself if you are to take the throne someday. And make no mistake, you will take the throne. We Masters will help see to that.'*

*'If I am to take the throne, why train Quinn and Ashe alongside me?' he asked. While he enjoyed having his friends around, he always worried that someday they may outshine him.*

*He had known from a very young age that he was destined to sit on the throne and usher in a new age of prosperity for humanity. The Masters raised him on such promises every day.*

*Then one day they brought Quinn into the fold, followed by Ashe. Soon the Masters talked about the three of them reaching the throne together. Though they still assured Levy it would be he who took it, he couldn't help but worry they might be telling his friends the same thing.*

*'Fear not, Levy. In order to rip through the hordes of monsters the tower calls to it, you will need weapons. That is why we brought them here as well. I assure you that is still the plan. Let this be another moment for you to meditate on when it comes to controlling your jealousy. Every man has within him a fatal flaw. Do not fall victim to yours.'*

~~~

Levy grunted with exertion as he beheaded one of the training dummies in the yard. The air outside was particularly muggy today, though a nice breeze had picked up as the sun began to sink in the sky. He often thought back to his conversations with Brendan in times of turmoil, or when he started to feel the jealousy rise within
~~~

him.

Though he loved his friends, he constantly felt like an outsider to them. Quinn had followed Levy around, constantly pestering him when he first came to the citadel before Levy relented and they had finally become friends. And then Ashe came along, and Quinn was immediately enamored with the pretty blonde girl. If that hadn't been bad enough, Levy developed feelings for her as well, only to have her shut him down and choose Quinn.

Though they still spent time together often, Levy couldn't help but feel as though a rift had slowly developed between them, with him alone on one side, slowly drifting apart from them.

When they came back from the Arholm Peaks as demigods, he was sure his time to shine had finally come. Yet the Masters, who had whispered promises in his ear from an early age, had all but abandoned him; instead fawning over Ashe and Quinn.

And so, the rift got wider. Then there was what happened just the day before. After their heart to heart, something that still made Levy slightly uncomfortable, he thought he had begun to shrink that rift a bit with Quinn.

Yet when Quinn had come back from the markets, Levy tried to call him over so he could see the gift he got Ashe. Quinn made quick eye contact before immediately lowering his head and rushing away, acting as though he had never even seen Levy waving. He spent the rest of the night ignoring Levy's requests to hang out.

Now Ashe and Quinn were locked behind the doors of the council room, being let in on all of the secrets of the Citadel and planning for a war that it seemed Levy would no longer be a part of.

*No, that's nonsense.* He thought to himself. *Just because I don't have some mystical power doesn't mean I am not useful. I still have Hestia's essence. I'm still the best fighter they have. They promised to help me claim the throne. I'm sure they're just prepping them to help me.*

He was doing his best to clear his mind of the jealousy that threatened to poison him. His friends didn't deserve his ire, and there was no proof the Masters plotted against him either.

Levy looked up at the deep purples and oranges of the sunset, wiping the sweat from his forehead. As if on cue, the bells of the

Citadel tolled; a deep, somber sound. He waited, listening closely for the sixth ring; indicating the council would be just about over.

Normally he liked to train in the pit, using the sand as extra conditioning. Today however, he thought he would use the outdoor training ground, as it was conveniently placed next to the council chambers. Now that Quinn had been invited to sit in on the council, Levy decided it was time he got some information as well. At the sound of the sixth bell, he ran lightly to a small crenulation in the stone wall, tucked away just next the entrance to the council chambers.

He pressed himself flat against the stone, using the shadows of the structure to hide from sight. It wasn't as affective as whatever Quinn could do with his mask, but he doubted he would be found unless somebody was looking for him. His heart quickened as the sound of footsteps came closer.

"Meet back here again tomorrow. There is much more to discuss," Master Enkar said in his mousey voice. He was a very short man with curly grey hair that covered his ears.

Small, round spectacles sat perfectly atop his short, bulbous nose; though they were so small, Levy was convinced they were nothing more than a fashion choice. Enkar carried with him an air of self-importance.

Honestly, a lot of the Masters did, though at least most of them could back it up. In Enkar's case, Levy believed the man was far above his station.

"Master Enkar," a sweet voice, that could only have come from Ashe, asked. "When will we be taking our powers to the front lines? These councils are all very informative and I am grateful for the guidance, but if what you say is true and soldiers are dying on a daily basis so that we have a foot in the ground when it comes time to take the tower, I would love to head there and help."

"Miss Grey, while that is all well and good, there is so much for you to learn before you take the throne. If you are to lead our people into the next age, you must know all there is to know about our land and our history."

Levy's head whipped up when he heard the Master say those words. What did he mean "Before you take the throne."

Surely, they hadn't forgotten about him already.

"I understand Master, thank you for your wisdom."

"Very well, Miss Grey. Now run along. I must have a word with Quinn here."

With a bow to the master and a gentle squeeze of Quinn's arm, she walked off toward her quarters.

*Curious.* Levy thought to himself. *What could the master want to talk to Quinn about. As far as I know, Enkar is not very fond of him.*

As soon as Ashe was out of earshot, the small master rounded on Quinn, grabbing hold of his arm.

"Now you listen here, boy," He said in a snarling whisper. "I don't know what you were up to in that marketplace yesterday, but I have heard the reports.

Ashelia is the best shot we have at taking that throne, but for her to get there she needs every able body we can get. You're our best hope at keeping her alive long enough to reach the tower. So, do whatever you need to do to smother your monstrous urges, but do not screw this up. Do you understand?"

"Yes, sir," Quinn responded. Levy hadn't heard such a quiet response toward one of the Masters since they were very little.

"Good." Enkar replied, seemingly satisfied. "Now go whack at one of those training dummies and keep your skills sharp."

As the master scurried off, Levy ducked out of his hiding spot.

"What did he mean about the marketplace?" Levy asked, feeling slight amusement at seeing his friend startle.

"Never mind it," Quinn replied. "There was a mugging and some things got out of hand is all."

As Quinn made to step past him, Levy stuck out a hand, blocking his path.

"What was all that about Ashe taking the throne?"

Quinn's eyes widened a fraction before he regained his composure. After a brief moment of indecision, he came to a conclusion and said, "I'm sorry I have to be the one to tell you this Levy. The Masters really should have told you already.

"They want Ashe to take the throne and you and I to help her to it. I know you've been dreaming of that since you were young, but the Masters seem to think Ashe is the closest thing to a god humanity has. They believe she gives us the best chance of survival."

Levy could feel his eye twitch. Though he had always feared this would happen, until this very moment he never fully believed it would. The words of Master Brendan came back to him, but he threw them from his head. He had no interest in what that old man had to say anymore. His future had just been stolen from him by the very Masters who had promised it to him.

"Levy…." Quinn began, but Levy just waved him off.

"It's fine." He said, moving around his friend, back toward his quarters.

Quinn reached out to stop him, but Levy smacked his hand away.

"I said it's fine. Leave me alone Quinn."

"Let's talk about it. You helped me when I needed to talk, now let me help you."

Levy looked over his shoulder. "It's all good, seriously. All that matters is that we reach the tower, right?"

"Right," Quinn sounded unconvinced.

Levy nodded, turning his back toward his rooms.

"Where are you going?" Quinn asked, "Do you want to go spar?"

"I'll catch up with you later," Levy replied, not turning around. "First, I have someone I need to speak with."

As he continued down the path, he reached down and grabbed the pommel of his broadsword, feeling that familiar energy trickle through him.

# CHAPTER 17: Quinn

For the second time that day Quinn found himself back in the training hall. His body was drenched in sweat, and his knuckles were raw and bloody from continuously beating on the dummies. Three of them had already fallen in the brief time he had been there.

The Masters would no doubt be upset with him in the morning. Those dummies were made from Mageia wood, a type of tree only found in the snowy northlands and were not cheap. But he didn't care.

After the incident in the marketplace, he had so much pent up fear, this was the only thing he could do to keep himself occupied. Ever since he had grabbed that stupid mask he felt like a changed person. Not only because of the circumstances of why he had it in the first place, but because of the power it held.

Every word of what he had told Ashe had been true, if not the truth she had wanted from him. The power of the mask was alluring. Ever since the first time he put it on it called to him. When he wore it in his fight, if you could even call it that, with Master Darrik, he had to really push hard to take it back off. And the fact that he jumped straight to using it at the first sign of trouble only made it more dangerous.

The power that enveloped him felt so good. When he wore the mask, he didn't feel the guilt or the anger. He felt like a god. When he took the mask off, it did nothing but make him feel even worse. He didn't want to be a god. All of this was only feeding into what he knew the humans already thought he was.

It was clear that Levy wanted him to embrace the mask. If he couldn't have the power for himself, he wanted it to be used to win the war. He didn't understand the dangers it posed. Janus had made it pretty clear by this point, based on what Levy had told them, that he wanted a champion for the gods so they might claim the throne again.

If Quinn lost himself to the powers of this mask, would he even realize it if he became said champion. The mask brought out all of the worst sides of him. A violent glee, a bloodlust and thirst for battle. When he had fought Darrik, he wanted nothing more than to snap the Master's wrist when he held it in his hand.

The thought repulsed him. Darrik had been a bastard to him all his life, but Quinn prided himself on being better to people than what Darrik had thought him to be. When he used it against those muggers, he had actually thought of one of them as his prey. That thought alone made him shiver.

Then there was Ashe. She scared him more than anything. He didn't care as much if the world thought of him as a monster. He never wanted to lose her trust, but he feared that if he told her about how he let the little girl die in order to grab the mask, she would be upset.

It wasn't like he had consciously decided to sacrifice her for the mask, and that defense might save their relationship, though with how strongly she valued saving innocent lives over hoarding power, he wasn't so sure. But if she knew he had done it, and she was involved in his reasoning why, she would be heartbroken.

It echoed everything she hated about the gods. Power over all, innocents be damned. And that terrified him. In the barren landscape of hatred and darkness of his young life, Ashe had been one of his brightest lights. He wasn't sure he could recover from losing that.

After destroying a fourth training dummy, Quinn decided he should stop there. That was going to cost a good chunk of money to replace, and he didn't want to go any further into the red with the Citadel. Not bothering to put his shirt back on, he walked out into the pleasant night breeze.

Despite being both physically and mentally exhausted, his mind was still racing. He couldn't remember the last time he'd had a good night's sleep. Knowing how unlikely it would be that he would get any this way, he decided to sit in the center of the courtyard, under the watchful gaze of the moon.

One of the first lessons the Masters had taught him growing up was to quiet the mind through meditation. It opened up his senses to the world around him, easing his burdens in the process. Since nothing else had helped him up until this point, he decided he would give it a go. He closed his eyes, clearing his mind as best he could, focusing on the nature he was surrounded by.

It was always easiest for him to achieve meditation when he started by grounding himself. The soft breeze blew by, making the leaves in the trees sway to its rhythm. He felt the cooling sensation as it dried the sweat on his skin. The fresh scent of the nearby roses lining the courtyard drifted across his nose, calming him even further. And then, all was quiet.

*He was back in a familiar room. He sat in a circle of stones, watching a small fire burn. A little way up a stone path, a light, golden curtain of fire fell from the ceiling to the floor. Despite everything that had happened the last time he'd been here, he felt strangely at peace. Beside him sat a small woman, gently prodding at the fire with a stick. 'Hello Hestia,'*

*Hestia looked up at him, sadness reflecting back from her eyes. 'Hello, Quinn,' she said somberly. 'Sorry to have brought your mind to a place I'm sure you wish you'd have never seen again, but it has been my home for many years.'*

*Quinn shook his head. 'I don't mind this place.' He said looking around. 'Of all of the rooms I saw in my trials, this was the one in which I felt most at peace.'*

*He had never once felt threatened by Hestia. Even when she launched him back from the gate he and Levy had tried to go through together, he hadn't sensed any kind of malice. Besides, she reminded him a lot of Ashe. The way she spoke and acted, the fire in her eyes, it was all very warming to him.*

*As if reading his emotions, she asked, 'How is she?'*

*'Ashe?' he asked. "She is doing wonderfully. She seems to have almost complete mastery over the gift you gave her. The Masters think she will be the one to win the war for humanity.'*

*A small smile spread on her face at that news. 'That is wonderful to hear. She has such a warm heart. She will be the guiding light for mankind that the gods were never able to be.'*

*At this she turned sad again, looking deep into Quinn's eyes. 'I am sorry for the pain I have caused you.'*

*Quinn tilted his head. 'What pain have you caused me? You have given me the gift of your essence, enhancing every part of me. Any pain I have from this place is due to Janus.'*

*She shook her head, looking down at the fire.*

*'I knew Janus planned to betray me. For a long time, he had watched hero after hero enter this place, failing every test we gave them. At first, he believed, like I did, that the time of the gods was truly over, and humanity deserved to have their place in the world.*

*'But as more and more came through here, failing the tests due to their greed and fear, he began to have a change of heart. Eventually he decided mortals were nothing more than primitive beings, living based on their most primal instincts, and that they did not deserve the throne.*

*'So, when you and your friends finally reached my domain, he had hatched his own plan. But I have a plan of my own, and for it to succeed, two of you have to reach the throne room together. I never wanted that mask to fall into your hands. But when I saw his vision, the one of Ashelia dying in front of it, I knew I had no choice.'*

*A tear rolled down the goddess cheek at this. Instinctively, Quinn reached out and wiped it away. Hestia only smiled and shook her head.*

*'I need you to understand, Quinn, that Ashe is the future of your kind. She is filled with a kindness and warmth that no other mortal possesses. If you want to see true peace in your world, it must be her that sits upon the throne. You must be her guardian. There are those*

*vying for this throne that you don't even know about yet; many who would see her dead.*

*'She will not succeed without you. And yet by allowing you to have that mask, I have set you on a path of separation. It is a problem that I was not able to work out before you reached my chambers. So now, I must ask your forgiveness as I have no choice but to leave it to you. No matter what happens, no matter how much she tries to push you away, you MUST keep her safe. Do you understand?'*

*Quinn only nodded. He knew, deep down, ever since he had recovered the mask, that their time was coming to an end. Ashe was light, and warmth and love. She was everything the mask was not.*

*But if what Janus showed him was the truth, he needed its power to see her reach the throne. He would do whatever it took, even if it meant losing himself in the process. With new resolve, he felt a lot of his anxieties fade away.*

*'I swear to you, I will do everything in my power to see her succeed. Whether that's with me or not, will be entirely up to her. But I will tell her the truth of things. Thank you for your guidance, Lady Hestia.'*

*'One last thing before you go.' She spoke into the fire, already beginning to fade. 'This will be the last time I am able to speak with you. My essence has almost fully assimilated with you now.*

*'When it does, the last traces of me in this world will be gone. Before that happens, allow me to leave you with one warning. Be cautious of the creature within the mask.'*

*She faded completely after that, taking the warmth and light of the fire with her. Quinn gave the chambers one last look, burning it into his mind. He knew it was plausible that this would be the last time he ever saw this place, and he wanted to remember the warmth and the hope it had given him.*

*Because when he got back, he knew he had a difficult conversation ahead of him. And he wasn't sure he would ever feel this at peace again.*

~~~

Quinn opened his eyes to a hand clamped on his shoulder,
~~~

vigorously shaking him back and forth.

"Quiiiiiinn. Hellooooooo, anybody home?" Levy stood in front of him, his typical grin on his face, and the silver light of the moon gleaming in his eyes. His face looked almost sinister, and if he hadn't known his friend for so long, he would think he was up to no good. But after the last conversation they'd had earlier that day, Quinn was happy to see any smile at all.

"Well it's about time!" He said, taking a step back. "I've been trying to get you to wake up for the last ten minutes. I thought maybe you were dead, but you kept muttering something about Hestia and warmth or something. I was starting to get worried that witch had possessed you," he laughed.

Quinn let out an uneasy grin. "Ah, yeah sorry I was meditating. I must have had her on the mind because I was remembering my time in her chamber."

Levy's eyebrows shot up his head. "Well I definitely wouldn't tell Ashe about that," he laughed.

Quinn felt heat rise to his face. "Not like that! I meant before I walked through that golden curtain."

"Look man, I didn't need to know the color of her curtain," Levy joked. He loved getting a rise out of Quinn and did it any chance he got. It was embarrassing how often he succeeded.

"Anyways," he continued, the gleam returning to his eyes, "Come with me. I have something to show you that I think you're going to be interested in. Bring your sword. Oh, and the mask as well!"

"Where are we going that I'm going to need my sword?" Quinn asked, skeptical.

Anytime Levy had some big thing planned that involved Quinn needing a weapon, he tended to end up cleaning out the bathrooms for months. He was not excited about the prospect of that.

"Look, I'm sorry but is there any chance this can this wait? I need to go talk to Ashe. It's important."

"Oh, for gods' sake," Levy rolled his eyes. "Don't tell me THAT drama is still going on. I thought you guys were getting that all squared away when you left the training hall to go *talk*."

"I didn't...we didn't...look just, I need to talk to her," he stammered, feeling the heat in his face again.

Levy just smiled at him and winked. “No worries, I already sent word to her. She’ll meet us there. I wanted her to see it too. Now get off the ground and let’s go! This is going to be exciting!”

Quinn shook his head and got to his feet. There was no saying no to Levy when he got this way. It would be less of a pain to just go and see what had him all riled up, and then talk to Ashe afterwards. Besides, at least this way he’d have something to take his mind off things.

~~~

“Alright,” he said after grabbing his sword and a change of clothes from his quarters. He wasn’t thrilled about bringing the mask with him, but he figured having it in case he needed it wouldn’t hurt. “Lead on then.”
~~~

# CHAPTER 18:
# Levy

*'As I said before.' The man smiled at him. 'Those who yearn for power will always come back.'*

*Janus sat at a table in his silver room, watching the young man before him. His other half had gone off to speak with someone else, but Levy didn't particularly care about to whom or for what reason. Janus was watching him with a gleeful look in his eyes.*

*'You don't have to act so smug about it,' Levy said feeling every bit the petulant child he sounded like.*

*He had spent hours thinking about what he wanted to say to the god before him and he knew he had to play it carefully. He had no interest in being the pawn of the gods. He would be the hero of mankind.*

*If it meant using those more powerful than him to reach that goal then so be it. But that wouldn't be good enough for Janus and he knew it. Janus wanted a puppet that he could control. But just because Levy wouldn't agree to that didn't mean Janus had to know that.*

*He would be playing a dangerous game, but it was one he felt he could come out on top of. 'I've decided to take you up on your offer,' he started, thinking carefully about his next words. 'But I would like to be clear about a few things before we reach any kind of deal.'*

*'Of course, of course,' Janus smiled. 'Let me just get into my negotiation outfit.'*

*He winked before waving his hand in front of his body. As his hand passed over himself, his clothing rippled and changed into a black, silk tunic with sparkling silver seams. On the table sat a black leather satchel with a silver J stitched into it. Opening the satchel, Janus reached in and removed a stack of paper.*

*'Now then, shall we draw up the contract?'*

*Levy had trouble controlling the ire in his voice. 'Will you be serious? I know you live forever, and life is just a big game to you, but for me this is life or death.'*

*Janus got a dangerous glint in his eye then. Taking his feet from off the table, he leaned forward and softly said, 'Young man, I am very serious. This contract is the same as an oath on my essence. I am just trying to put it in terms you can understand.*

*'Don't ever presume to tell me how to act. Keep in mind that, while I am willing to enter a partnership with you, you are still nothing but a mortal playing with a god. Understood?'*

*Levy swallowed the lump of fear that had formed in his throat and said, hoarsely, 'Understood.'*

*With that out of the way Janus immediately lightened up again, a smile back on his face. 'Wonderful! Now then, let's get signing, shall we?'*

~~~

Levy woke from his dream visit with Janus wearing a large smile on his face. Tonight, everything was going to change. Janus had given him one task to complete. It had the added bonus of being an intriguing secret the Citadel was trying to keep. If he succeeded, he would be granted a lot of power; enough to change the world.
~~~

The only promise he had to make to Janus was that when he claimed the throne, he would allow the gods to reclaim their fading power so that they may once more walk the earth. Levy figured that with himself on the throne, he would have enough power to keep them in check, and humanity would not suffer beneath them any longer.

Honestly, he was shocked Janus had given in to that so easily. He figured they must really be desperate to have a horse in this race if they would allow him to make such a bold claim. It wouldn't be long now though. One simple task, and he would have all the power he needed in order to win the throne. His legacy began tonight.

~~~

It had taken him longer than we would have liked to find Quinn in the courtyard. It took even longer than he had patience for to rouse him from his meditation. But he needed to have Quinn with him when he did this. Sides had to be taken tonight and having the power of the mask would help his cause.

He needed Ashe as well. She wouldn't understand what was going to happen, but he needed her power to reach the location so he had begrudgingly left her a note, scrawled hastily and slapped on her door, asking her to meet them at the entrance to the depths of the Citadel.

Ever since they had gotten back from their mission, Levy had been feeling more and more annoyed at the thought of Ashe. It wasn't entirely her fault. He knew that jealousy played a major role in it. That was something he had come to terms with however, and he no longer viewed it as a weakness, but as a way to push himself to improve.

However, after returning from their mission as the leader of their trio, only to see that ripped away from him by the gift that goddess had instilled in her, it made him pretty upset.

Then there was Quinn. He had been Levy's one and only true rival in this place. He easily out sped him, and despite the fact that Levy was much stronger, Quinn was often able to out maneuver him
~~~

in matches.

Levy still won plenty of their fights thanks to his strength, but nobody came close to matching him the way Quinn did. Yet, ever since their return from Hestia's domain, he had been a sniveling baby. He was given a powerful gift and had the love of a beautiful woman capable of controlling fire with a thought, and yet he did nothing but mope. It all left such a bad taste in Levy's mouth. The three of them together held the power to change the world, especially after tonight.

He just had to convince them to see it his way. So long as everything went according to plan, he would become the most powerful mortal alive. The monsters guarding the tower wouldn't stand a chance. And with his friends at his side, they would be unstoppable.

They spent the journey reminiscing of old times; trying to lighten the tension that was thick between them. A couple times along the way they crossed paths with a Master returning to their quarters and had to jump off the path, clinging to the shadows. Though it wasn't out of the ordinary for either of them to be seen out this late at night, the fewer people who saw them the better.

As they approached the large doors that led down into the bowels of the Citadel, a shadow detached itself from the doorway and walked to meet them.

"Hello Fire Queen," Levy bowed, offering one of his friendliest smiles. "Thanks for coming so quickly. I was worried we may have to wait for you. After all, sneaking into a forbidden part of the Citadel seems a little rule-breaky for you."

Ashe smiled, making her way over to Quinn. "I have to admit I'm not overly fond of being here" she said, reaching out and sneaking her hand into Quinn's.

"But you said it was important to the cause, and while I feel like anything you discover here tonight the Masters already know about, I can't help but be a little bit intrigued myself."

Levy winked and said, "Trust me, you aren't going to be disappointed. I'd spoil it for you now but where would the fun in that be? Just wait, once we get these doors unlocked, it will be pretty obvious why we're here."

"And how are we going to unlock them?" Quinn asked, staring at the marks on the door. These were no ordinary locks. They had powerful engravings carved deep into the wood. Whatever they had locked down there, the Masters had gone through a lot to keep it hidden.

"Hmm, yes I see what you mean," Levy made a show of pondering. "If only we had a powerful, essence infused Fire Queen capable of burning away strong engravings like these." He looked at Quinn, purposely avoiding Ashe's ireful look. "You know where we can find one of those? I hear they're your type."

Ashe chortled, shaking her head and making her way up to the door. "I'll do this, but when the Masters find us out, I'm blaming you."

"I assure you; the Masters finding out will not be an issue." he smirked.

"Your funeral," she shrugged back at him. "Stand back." She closed her eyes, reaching her hands out in front of her. Levy noticed Quinn watching her, his eyes moving over her body as if tracking movement that Levy could not see. Golden flames covered Ashe's hands a second later, increasing in heat and intensity every so often.

"Incredible," Quinn said, still staring at her body.

"Quinn, buddy," Levy said with humor, "I know you get excited when you look at her, but now is really not the time."

Quinn looked back and smiled at the taunt. "Not that, I mean her power. I can sense its movement within her. It's almost like meditation. She reaches deep within with her mind, grabbing at Hestia's essence and pulling it to the surface where it ignites with the air. It's fascinating."

"Fancy," Levy said, caring very little about the workings of her powers at all. Though, he did wish he had some of Quinn's Abyssillian blood. He could see how sensing that kind of thing might come in handy in a fight.

"You know," he joked. "With an attitude like that, it astounds me that you have yet to find love."

Levy narrowed his eyes. "I care about winning the war, Quinn. Nothing else matters."

Quinn just shook his head. "That's a lonely way to live, man. Trust me: when crap hits the fan, you're going to wish you had that someone special at your back."

Levy couldn't help but shoot a quick glance toward Ashe.

"GOT IT," they heard Ashe yell. Brilliant golden flames were burning along the patterns of the door, leaving the wood untouched. With a loud sizzle, the essence locking the door disintegrated away. As the final bit of fire burnt out leaving them in darkness, a loud clunk filled the air. The doors swung open of their own accord, as if beckoning them down into the darkness below.

"I have someone at my back," Levy muttered so only he could hear it.

~~~

The darkness underneath the Citadel was total. It didn't even take three steps before they could no longer see their own hand in front of their face. To add to their discomfort, the doors they entered through slammed closed behind them, shutting them in to whatever they were going to find below.

"Illumino."

Levy heard his friend say the familiar phrase, bringing a soft red glow to the walls around them.

"Thanks," Ashe mumbled, clutching his hand for support. "Burning away those engravings took a lot out of me. I'm not sure I'd have been able to light our way."

"Quinn," Levi asked cutting in. "Can you feel anything?"

Quinn closed his eyes, reaching down the corridor with his senses. "There's a strong point of energy deep below us. It feels-" His eyes snapped open, meeting Levy's. "What's down there?"

"An immense power is waiting for us. It's how the Citadel is powering the city and keeping the citizens of Stormhaven safe." Levy explained.

"How did you know this existed?" Ashe asked, a hint of skepticism trickling into her voice. "This seems like the kind of thing the Masters would hold pretty close to their chest. With all due respect, I don't think any of us would be privy to that."

Levy had to be cautious if he was going to get his friends to go
~~~

along with this. "A friend told me," he said hoping that would be the end of it.

"A friend?" Ashe asked, raising an eyebrow.

"Yes, a friend," he repeated. "I have connections you know. I've been at the Citadel longer than either of you. I know a lot about this place's secrets that you two would never dream of. Now come on, we don't have a lot of time. I wouldn't be surprised if the Masters already know their protections are gone and I doubt they would be thrilled to see us down here. I just want to see this power source."

He saw Quinn and Ashe share a look, but thankfully they both followed him as he began to descend toward his prize.

Three-quarters of the way down, the ground turned from wood to rock and from rock to dirt. A bright green radiance lit up the tunnel, making the red light from Quinn's crystal obsolete.

"This is incredible," Quinn whispered, breaths coming rapidly. "Whatever it is they have down here, it's stronger than anything I have ever felt before. And that's including Hestia's domain."

Levy smiled at that. This was getting better and better. He wished he had Quinn's ability to sense energy. People called him a monster for it, but Levy had always thought of it as a gift. Only a little way to go before he found his legacy.

As they reached the chamber, a bright green glow could be seen from up ahead. In the center of the glow was the skeletal frame of a woman. It looked as if she had been trapped for hundreds of years; nothing but skin and bone, held fast in glowing chains. She writhing as if in pain, groaning and seething. Spittle foamed at her mouth, spraying forth with every agonized wail.

"What *is* that," Ashe yelled, running toward the light.

Ashe, Quinn," Levy said gliding past them, his silver broadsword unsheathed and held out in front of him, "Allow me to introduce you to Athena: Goddess of Wisdom. Though I much prefer her title as Goddess of Warfare."

They both sucked in breaths, staring in awe and fear at the trapped Goddess.

"Athena is an Olympian," Ashe said, unable to take her eyes off of the skeletal deity before her. "How is she here? Why is she trapped?"

Quinn's eyes narrowed behind her, slowly reaching back to the hilt of his sword. "What's going on Levy?" he asked. "How did you know this existed?"

"Relax, Quinn," he said with a smile that didn't reach his eyes. "I'm just planning on winning the war." He walked back in front of his friends. It was now or never. Janus had given him all of the information he needed, he just hoped he could sway his friends and save them from what was to come.

"Haven't you ever wondered how a city the size of Stormhaven has stayed alive and untouched for so long in a world where human settlements get wiped out on a daily basis? I mean in all of the time we've been here, have the walls even been attacked once?"

Ashe began to answer but Levy cut her off. "That was rhetorical. Of course, they haven't. Don't you think that's strange? Again, rhetorical. Please, Fire Queen, save all questions and comments until after the presentation.

"The reason behind it is simple. When humanity made the chains, they used to hold the tower in place and anchor it to our world, they began to think about what else chains like that might be able to do.

"So, they made another set, and began thinking of ways to use them that would benefit society. Now obviously the best thing they could do was claim the throne and win the war, right? But they weren't ready for that yet.

"For starters they had just melted down a huge amount of their only effective weapons. But what they could do was make a safe haven. So that's what they did. The Masters built a place where they could spend the next many years planning for how they could take the tower from the monsters surrounding it.

"They erected stone walls around this city, to help keep the monsters out. But no matter how many attacks they survived; the monsters kept coming. What they needed was power. And that's when they got an idea for the chains.

"They reached out to the Olympians, asking them to use what remained of their power to send an envoy here. They claimed that they would be willing to claim the throne for the gods, if in return they granted power to their walls so that they may never be breached.

"And so, thinking they had an easy way to reclaim their power, the gods sent Athena to meet with the mortals. However, when she arrived, she walked right into their trap.

"They used the second set of chains to bind her here. And since that day she has existed in this place, both herself and the knowledge of her locked away in this pit. The chains draw her energy out from her, and the Masters use it to power and protect the city. Look at how she suffers."

Ashe shook her head. Her face had gone pale after hearing what he had said. "That's awful. Nobody should have to suffer like this for so long. Not even a goddess."

Levy smiled. "I agree. Which is why I plan to cut her free. I've made a deal with Janus. If I free her from this prison, he will grant me half of his essence. With his half combined with the third I got from Hestia; I'll have the essence of almost a full god as my own. Together, the three of us can claim the throne and put an end to all of this bloodshed."

"Levy," Ashe said softly, "I agree that this isn't right, but if you release Athena from this prison, she will go berserk, killing every human she can get her hands on."

"Janus has assured me that once she is free from this prison, she will burn out quickly. She has had too much of her power sapped from her. She'll have only enough time left in our realm to destroy the city before fading from existence."

"And you're okay with that?" Ashe asked, aghast. "Levy, this city is filled with thousands and thousands of people. That's thousands of human deaths on our hands, just for the sake of power."

"Thousands are already dying." Levy said, resolute. "That is the reality of war; the reality of the world we live in. It's time for your fairy tale illusion to end Ashe.

"In order to bring peace and safety, sacrifices need to be made. Ask Quinn. I'm sure he sees it the same way I do, considering he has already made sacrifices for his own ideals."

Ashe's head whipped around to Quinn, an unreadable look in her eye.

"Now stand back. If you won't do what needs to be done, I will. Don't get in my way."

# CHAPTER 19: Quinn

"What did he mean by that," Ashe pleaded at him. Quinn was dumbstruck. He knew he was going to have to tell her about the truth of how he got the mask, and he knew it was going to hurt. But he did not expect the bombshell statement to be dropped on both of them from the one person he had confided in who had sworn not to tell anyone.

Quinn grabbed her hands. "Later. I promise I will tell you about it later. But right now, we need to stop him from freeing Athena and killing everybody in the city. And you're too weak to summon your fire. Let me handle this and then we'll talk."

She just nodded at him but left him with a look that this wasn't over.

"Levy, what in Hades," Quinn yelled, running in front of his friend, blocking his path. "Have you gone off the deep end? You're about to kill EVERYBODY in the city. That's a major part of the war effort. You think that just because you get a little godly power out of it, you're going to be able to single-handedly walk through a horde of manticore and into the tower with no resistance? That's madness."

"Get out of my way, Quinn. My path is set. I was hoping you would walk it with me, but if you get in my way, as much as it pains me to do so, I will kill you. I have the backing of the gods. All I need to do is allow them to share the earth with us once again and they will help me reach the throne." Levy rested his hand on the hilt of his blade. "Join me or get out of the way."

"So, you sold your soul to Janus and the gods and in return you get the power you've been craving, is that it? Give me a break, Levy. Has your lust for power gotten so out of control that you're willing to subjugate and kill your own people?

"Because that's what you're signing them up for by allowing the gods back again. Do you not remember the myths we grew up being force fed? Humanity is a toy to them. And when they get bored, they get rid of us."

Quinn couldn't believe what he was hearing. This was not the Levy he had grown up with. "Stop letting Janus twist your mind. There is no way you would have sacrificed so many of our people before you met him."

Levy just shook his head. "Janus has woken me up to the truths of our world, my friend. Sacrifice is needed to reach peace. This is your last chance. Get out of my way, or I will kill you."

With a swish, Quinn released his blade from the scabbard on his back. "I won't just stand back and let you level this city, Levy."

Before Levy had a chance to strike first, Quinn darted forward, stabbing out at his friend.

# CHAPTER 20: Ashe

*'Come on Ashe, I see how your eyes linger after Quinn and I fight.'*

*Levy's hand was pressed against the wall, holding his weight as he leaned his face toward her own. His signature smile blazed white against his tanned skin. His cropped brown hair was swept back today, creating little waves.*

*Ashe smiled back at him. The way his eyes sparkled when he was happy as well as his charismatic leadership drew everyone to him. His muscular build certainly didn't dissuade people either.*

*The problem was, he knew he was attractive. His ego matched his muscles in terms of bulk. "Sorry Levy, while I can't deny your charm, I'm spoken for. Any lingering eyes are just to make sure you aren't hurt."*

*Levy leaned closer, whispering directly next to her ear. 'We did just have a particularly intense sparring match you know. If you want to check me for injuries, I wouldn't be opposed.'*

*Ashe blew air from her nose, sliding out from between his body and the wall. "We have a medical wing for that.*

*Levy groaned, turning back to face her. 'Just give me a chance Ashe. What's Quinn have that I don't? I'm stronger than him. Soon we'll get to finally go to the front lines together. The Masters intend for me to take the throne; you know that. Be by my side when I do. You and I can lead humanity out of this darkness. We can rule them together!'*

*Ashe gave him a small smile. 'I don't want to rule them, Levy. I want to guide them. This isn't about power; it's about growth.'*

*She walked up to him and tapped him on the chest. 'You asked what Quinn has that you don't? The answer is empathy. You have ambitions and passion and strength. You are reliable and strong, and someone is going to love you for it. I love you as a friend because of it.*

*'But Quinn, from the moment he first met me, saw my struggles and led me out of that dark place. Every step of the way, despite his own internal struggles, he guided me out of my pain and gave me happiness where*

*'I thought there was none to have. I don't say any of this to hurt you. You are an incredible person, and I couldn't ask for a better friend. But that is why I love Quinn as I do.'*

*'I can do that too,' Levy said, leaning in to kiss her. Shocked, Ashe pushed him away.*

*'Levy, stop. I'm sorry but I just don't feel for you that way.'*

*Levy looked down at his feet with a mix of anger and sadness. 'Sorry Ashe. I shouldn't have done that. It won't happen again.'*

*Ashe's eyes softened, feeling bad for hurting him. 'Levy, I don't want to hurt our friendship. You'll find someone, just give it time.'*

*'Yeah,' he said with his hands in his pockets, shuffling away from her. 'We'll see.'*

Ashe felt as useless now as she did back then. She had burned away all of her energy on the door's engravings that locked this place away. Now she sat watching her friends fight each other, unsure of what to say that could diffuse the situation. Her body was heavy, and it was all she could do just to keep her head up.

Quinn was a nonstop blur, darting in and out of Levy's reach, needling at him and bouncing away. She could tell he was trying hard to not seriously injure their friend, while also trying to make him unable to continue the fight. As much as it hurt watching Levy succumb to his desires for strength, she could understand why he made the decision.

It was no secret he was feeling left out and neglected since their return from Hestia's realm. She wanted to talk to him about it for a while now, but her days were consumed with war councils and the Masters. Seeing where that isolation had led him, she couldn't help feeling as though she'd failed him as a friend.

While that had likely pushed Levy into action, it didn't surprise her at all that what tipped the scale was Janus. He had been messing with their lives ever since they were first introduced to him, and it was no shock that he was able to prey on the turmoil inside of Levy.

Her heart was as heavy as her head. She hoped that Quinn could stop him while also salvaging their friendship, but as the fight went on it seemed increasingly unlikely. And all the while, Levy's words about Quinn weighed heavily in the back of her mind. What sacrifices had he made for his ideals? She had an idea of course, but until he told her directly, she didn't want to think the worst.

*Please Quinn, save him from this darkness.*

# CHAPTER 21: Levy

Quinn was way too damn fast, and it was pissing Levy off. Every time Levy thought he had an opening on his friend, Quinn would bob back down out of the way and open another shallow cut somewhere on Levy's body.

"Come on Quinn," he taunted, "You're gonna have to take this seriously eventually."

Another shallow cut opened just above his knee and he was forced to jump back, putting a small distance between them.

"I'm taking this very seriously," Quinn responded a few steps away. "I'm not going to kill you. I'm hoping maybe the Masters can talk some sense into you. If not them, then I'll visit you every day until you wake up. Either way, I'm just going to bleed you until you're too weak to stand."

Levy laughed, readying himself for another strike. "You won't be able to beat me with how you are now. Sure, you'll get your little cuts in and it'll hurt, but all it's going to take is one big hit from me and you'll go down. That's how it's always worked. If you really want to stop me, put on the mask."

Levy lurched forward, knowing that mentioning the mask would put Quinn off balance. He swiped his sword out in a vicious arc, hammering a blow down on Quinn, which his friend just barely managed to turn away.

"Is that what this is about?" Quinn asked, now on the defensive. "Your obsession with that mask is unhealthy Levy. You don't even know how it works. That thing is dangerous."

"It's only dangerous in the hands of the weak," Levy shot back, raining blow after blow down upon his friend. "If you are too afraid to use the power that was handed to you, then you are too weak to win this war."

Quinn's arms buckled from the barrage; allowing Levy to slice a shallow cut onto his thigh. He hobbled back, attempting to catch his breath and give his arms some time to recuperate.

"No," Quinn growled. "It's dangerous in the hands of an unhinged psychopath, determined to destroy the largest city humanity has. You're already a puppet for the gods and you don't even realize it. It's not too late to stop this Levy. You haven't crossed that line yet."

Levy released a mighty roar, charging at him with everything he had. He no longer cared if he killed him or not. Quinn was too blind to the truth; too soft to do what needed to be done. A man like that was dangerous to rely on. It was better this way. "Goodbye Quinn."

# CHAPTER 22: Quinn

"Goodbye Quinn." When he heard Levy mutter those words, he knew the fight was over. Levy had now firmly committed to killing him here. Quinn couldn't believe it. He had grown up admiring him. He wanted to be him more than anything else in those days. He'd was so strong and brave.

Confidence oozed out of him everywhere he went and with every decision he made. And now the man he had spent his life looking up to more than anybody else had decided to kill him. He saw Levy running at him as though it were slow motion. The grief and pain were overwhelming. First, he feared he was going to lose Ashe, and now Levy.

*I have sent you on a path of separation.*

Hestia's words rang in his mind. She had foreseen this coming.

As Levy came closer, Quinn felt his hand begin to reach toward where the mask lay in his pocket. If he put it on now, he could save himself and Ashe from the destruction of the angry goddess. But to do so would mean sacrificing the city and all of its people to her wrath.

On the other hand, he could try to fight off Levy and keep him from freeing Athena. He didn't like his odds in that fight though. The cut on his thigh was seriously hindering his mobility, and despite everything he knew, he still wasn't sure he could bring himself to kill his friend.

That kind of indecision would get him killed, which would end up being the same thing as sacrificing the city. Only in this scenario Ashe would likely die as well.

*Keep her safe.*

Yeah, no chance he would die before getting her to safety. He looked over toward her and they briefly made eye contact. When she saw what he was thinking, her eyes widened.

"Quinn you can't," she yelled. But he had already made up his mind.

As Levy descended upon him, Quinn rolled onto his back, kicking up his legs into Levy's chest with all of the power he could muster, and launched him over his head toward Athena's prison. The wound in his thigh screamed with the exertion but he had to push through it, or they would all be dead in seconds. He reached into his pocket and pulled the mask out.

"Ashe," he called to her. "I don't know if this will work but close your eyes. I'm going to drag you out of here through the Realm of Night! No matter what happens, or what you feel, DO NOT LOOK until I tell you it's okay. Do you understand?"

Before she had time to answer an exhilarated cry filled the air. Quinn turned around just in time to see Levy slice the chains from around Athena. As they fell to the floor, he saw Janus appear behind Levy.

"You've done well," Janus said as he reached out. Grabbing hold of Levy's wrist.

A bright silver light shimmered down Levy's arm and into him. When it faded, Levy flexed his hand a few times.

"I feel so alive." he said, victory in his voice.

"That is what it feels like to be a god," Janus replied, staring directly at Quinn.

"I like it," Levy replied, a smile in his voice.

A loud screech interrupted the conversation as Athena glowed bright with surging green power.

"ASHE, WE NEED TO GO," Quinn roared, slamming the mask onto his face. He felt the cold sensation of the shadows wrapping him in its billowing cloak. With all of the energy he had left, he leapt toward Ashe, grabbing her arm and pulling her into the nearest shadow.

"Close your eyes," he reminded her. "I'll tell you when it's safe." With a final look back, Quinn saw his former friend staring at him with his signature grin on his face. Only instead of the brown his eyes had once been, now they glowed silver as the moonlight in the dark night sky.

The Realm of Night was in turmoil. Shadows whipped around in all directions, as if being buffeted by strong gusts of wind. Terrifying wails echoed through the air, adding to the mayhem. Chaos appeared next to him, as was his custom.

Making eye contact, Quinn gave him a quick shake of his head; indicating he did not want him to say anything while Ashe was near.

"Quinn?" Ashe asked, uncertainty laced her voice. Thankfully, her eyes were shut tight.

"Right here," He said, scooping her into his arms. "Relax. I'll get us out of here."

~~~

Hours later Quinn and Ashe sat on a hilltop looking down at the smoldering ruins of their home. Athena had burst out of the ground, laying waste to everything she came in contact with. Screams lit up the night as flashes of wicked green energy sent structures toppling to the ground.

When her energy had finally been expended, she disappeared, fading into the nothingness the gods go to when they no longer have the energy to exist. All that remained of the capital was rubble, and a deafening silence. They hadn't spoken to each other at all since making it out of the tunnel where Athena had been unleashed.

Quinn knew Ashe was upset about his decision, but she also knew that it was either that, or die down there like everyone else.
~~~

And even though the largest part of the war effort had been demolished, this didn't mean it had been wiped out completely. They still had a job to do.

"What did he mean?" a small voice asked, breaking the silence around them.

"What did who mean?" Quinn asked, hating that the silence had come to an end, and that the end had come at last.

"Levy. When he said you had already sacrificed for your ideals."

Quinn sighed. "Ashe, I…."

"No more avoiding it Quinn," she said, turning to him with tears in her eyes. "I have given you opportunity after opportunity to tell me. Do you think I'm dumb?

"I've had my suspicions ever since I first saw the mask. I told you about my trial with Janus. But still I was patient and tried to let you come to me with it. I love you, Quinn, and whatever it was, I was willing to work through it.

"But you never came forward and were honest with me. Instead I had to deal with Janus taunting me over and over, and Levy dropping it on me. Now I want to hear it from you. Tell me how you got that mask."

Tears were falling rapidly from her eyes as she finished.

Quinn felt the lump in his throat as he tried to keep his emotions in check. The moment he had been fearing since they returned had finally come. He took in her image one more time before beginning his story, terrified that it would be the last time he got to spend time with her.

By the time he finished telling her about the vision and how he had grabbed the mask instead of the girl, she was shaking her head, tears falling ever faster from her eyes. "Ashe, I-"

"No. No no no no." She backed away from him. "You're just like him," she said, sticking that verbal knife directly into his heart. "You let an innocent girl die for power."

"I did it for you," Quinn said, feeling tears falling from his eyes freely now as well. "I know I screwed up, Ashe. It has been eating away at me for weeks. But when I saw you die, I just…my body just reacted. You are my entire world and the thought of even potentially losing you hurt more than I can describe."

"We are fighting a war, Quinn!"

Her voice was small, anger now mixed in with the tears. "Dying is a threat we live with every day of our lives. We know it's a risk. But that girl, she didn't sign up for anything. You could have saved her from that fate, but instead you let her die, so that there was a chance I wouldn't because you saw it in a vision of a god who gets his jollies off by playing with our minds and destroying our home!"

Quinn had been shocked entirely into silence. She was right of course. He had known it from the first time his hands had touched that cursed mask. He had all but sold his soul to Janus as well.

"Do you have anything to say?" she asked, a steely finality creeping into her voice.

Quinn just shook his head. "Nothing other than I love you. I messed up, and I know I did. And I'm sorry."

Ashe just shook her head, wiping the tears from her face. "I love you too, I know you did, and don't apologize to me. Apologize to the little girl you let die."

"I do," Quinn rasped. "Every night when she visits me in my dreams."

Ashe's eyes softened a fraction. "I'm sorry Quinn. I know this is hard. I love you. I still do, but I think I might be poisoning you. You just used that mask to save me without thinking; allowing our home and everyone inside it to be destroyed, instead of using it to stop Levy and Janus.

"I think we need a break from each other. If anything, this has shown me that it's time I join the men and women fighting at the front lines. We still have allies there and I think I can do a lot of good.

"And if I see an opening, I'll go for the tower as well. But please, don't follow me. I need time to think, and you need time to experience life without me always on your mind."

Quinn had known it was coming. He had known he couldn't stop it. And yet despite having all of the time in the world to prepare for it, it still shattered him into a million different pieces.

"If that's what you want, I understand." His words were barely audible, but Ashe must have gotten the message.

She stepped forward and placed a small kiss on his cheek. Before she could walk away, he took the red pendant from around his neck and placed it in her hand. She looked at it for a brief second before shoving it in her pocket.

"Goodbye Quinn," She said, one last tear falling from her eye.

"Goodbye."

Quinn lost track of time after Ashe had left him there. He was in a constant war with himself to chase after her, but he knew that would only damage things further. She had said it herself, she needed space to breathe and time to think.

That wouldn't stop him from watching over her of course. He had promised Hestia. But there was nothing he could do as he was, all alone with no supplies and no allies. With the Citadel gone, he doubted he would be welcomed in any other cities or towns.

An aching numbness began to settle over his heart. Getting back to his feet he grabbed his mask again, slipping it gently over his face. He wanted to feel the ecstasy of that otherworldly power wash over him again.

Once in the Realm of Night, he took stock of his surroundings. The more time he spent in here, the more subtleties he was beginning to notice. The ground and sky were not actually one giant black mass, but instead subtle shadows played across its surface.

He had come to realize that those were roads. While it didn't allow him to instantly traverse the land, it certainly allowed him to travel faster than it would in his reality.

Beside him, Chaos rose from the ground. He was beginning to see more detail with him as well. The features of a face were beginning to form, though they were still too undefined to make anything out specifically.

*"Where to now?"* He asked in a slightly more pronounced voice.

"The only place I have left to go," Quinn replied, walking along the shadow road leading a westerly direction. "To the Wastes."

He tried to fight down the butterflies he was feeling inside his stomach. "It's long past time I went home."

# Part Two

# CHAPTER 23:
# Ashe

*'Why are you crying?' A voice cut into the darkness. Ashelia opened her eyes to see a young boy with raven black hair standing in front of her, smiling. 'Are you hurt?'*

*She looked around at her surroundings taking in the unfamiliar interior of the building called the Citadel. She reached up and touched her face, feeling moisture on her cheek.*

*The boy in front of her was looking at her with concern in his beautiful red eyes. She had never seen eyes like that before and was drawn to them instantly.*

*Though he looked happy, she could see the pain behind his smile. 'Helloooooo?' The boy asked reaching out and gently wiping away a tear. 'Do you need help? Want me to get a master? They don't like me very much, but I'll do it if it will help.'*

*Ashelia shook her head, too shy to say anything. 'Oh! Okay then.' He smiled again, rocking back and forth on his feet.*

*'My name's Quinn by the way. What's yours?'*

*'Ashelia,' she mumbled into the floor, clutching at the hem of*

*her skirt.*

*'Ashelia,' the boy repeated it back to her in wonder. 'That's so pretty! What are you doing here at the Citadel, Ashelia?'*

*She couldn't help but smile at the boy's enthusiasm. She had been raised in the slums of Stormhaven where everyone kept to themselves and there were rarely any smiles.*

*This boy was so vibrant and filled with energy. It was refreshing. Feeling a little more confident she answered, 'I accidentally set a fire in the slums and got into a lot of trouble, so my parents gave me to the Masters here for some kind of special behavior training, whatever that means.'*

*Quinn's eyes got wide, showing off even more of the beautiful red. 'Woah that's so cool! I've always been kind of scared of fire. It looks pretty but it hurts when you touch it. I like to stay where it's dark. You learn cool things that way.'*

*"Fire isn't scary," Ashelia responded passionately. "Fire is beautiful and warm. My dad always used to say it gives life to those in need. And the ashes that float up into the sky look like snow as they fall back down."*

*Quinn gasped when she said that. She looked over at him, startled but the fear faded when she saw a big, goofy grin spread over his face. 'Ashes," he proclaimed, as if that was an answer to a question he had been pondering for ages. 'Like Ashelia! Hey, can I call you Ashe?'*

*'Didn't you say you thought my name was pretty?' she asked, pouting.*

*'It is,' he assured her, still grinning like a fool. 'But friends always call each other by nicknames. That's what my friend Levy told me! That's why he calls me Princess! I don't know what it means but it sounds neat.'*

*Ashe tried to hold a snort of laughter back. 'Quinn,' she smiled. 'I don't think you should be happy about being called Princess'*

*'Is it mean?' Quinn asked, his eyebrows scrunched together.*

*'It can be,' she said.*

*Quinn kept his eyebrows scrunched together for a second longer before smiling again and shrugging. 'Oh well, it doesn't feel mean when he says it. I'm ok with it,' he replied, as though that settled everything.*

*'You aren't from around here are you?' she asked the boy.*

*'What gave it away?' he asked attempting to wink, though really it was more of a clumsy blink. 'The red eyes? Pale skin?'*

*'Well the eyes are one thing,' she giggled. 'But you just act differently. Everyone here is so serious all the time. You're too relaxed.'*

*Quinn just shrugged again; a crack appearing in his happy façade before quickly fading. 'What's the point in being sad all the time?' he asked, growing serious.*

*'I grew up here. My parents died before I really knew them. Apparently, they were something called Absilians or something like that. I don't know, the Masters don't talk about it much.*

*'But there's nothing I can do about that so I may as well enjoy my time here. Plus, now I have another friend,' he said, back to his carefree smile.*

*'Hey!' He snapped his head up, excited again. 'Since you live here now, do you want to see my favorite spot?'*

*Ashe smiled. Somehow in the space of a couple minutes, this boy had taken her from heartbroken to smiling and laughing. Things didn't seem so bad when she was talking to him. 'I'd love to, Quinn.'*

*'Great,' he took her hand. 'Follow me!'*

*He pulled her along the grounds of the Citadel. As they walked, he gave her a brief, uninformative tour. 'This is the mess hall, and that is the soldier's quarters. Over there is the council room, but we aren't allowed to go in there.*

*'Levy gets a slap on the wrist when he does. Last time I did it though they locked me in my room for two weeks. Maybe I messed something up, I don't know. OH! And this is the courtyard. Aren't all the flowers pretty? The Masters say it's hard to find flowers like this in the wild anymore.'*

*Ashe followed along, ooh-ing and ahh-ing at the appropriate times. She had already been on a detailed tour with the Masters, but Quinn seemed to be having fun and she didn't want to ruin that.*

*He seemed genuinely excited to be talking with someone. Eventually they came to a small building near the northern most point of the citadel. Quinn had already climbed up the side of the wall and was looking down expectantly at her. 'I don't think I can climb this,' she said, afraid she would disappoint him.*

*'That's okay,' he replied, reaching an arm down. 'I'm stronger than I look. Just grab my hand and I'll pull you up. Promise I won't drop you.'*

*She reached up and grabbed his hand, bracing her feet against the side of the building. As he finished pulling her up onto the roof, he motioned to a small window just barely big enough for each of them to fit through.*

*He put a finger to his lips and whispered, 'Quiet when we go through here. This is the Master's quarters. We aren't allowed in here but it's fun to sneak in. Sometimes you hear fun things that you can surprise them by knowing later. The looks on their faces are priceless. Come on!'*

*They snuck through the opening and climbed their way onto the shadowed scaffolding over what must have been the Master's mess hall. Though it was mostly empty, two Masters sat in the corner embroiled in what appeared to be a heated discussion.*

*Quinn was staring down at them listening with a very serious expression on his face. Ashe crawled over to him and listened as well.*

*'I'll still never understand why in Hades' name Talius took someone like that in,' the man bellowed, slamming his fist on the table. 'That kid is a monster!'*

*Ashe thought for a second they were talking about her and her fire incident, until she looked over and saw tears in the corners of Quinn's eyes.*

*'Calm down Darrik,' the other master said, putting a hand on his arm in a placating gesture. 'He has talents that will come in handy. You don't have to like the boy, just train him as a tool that can be used against the monsters.'*

*'That THING is no boy, Connor. You know how Abyssillians are. Vile blood runs through those veins. If the red eyes aren't proof enough of that then just you wait, he'll turn on us in the end. I'll train it if I have to, but he's going to wish he had died in the attack with his parents.'*

*Quinn shuffled past her, crawling as swiftly as he could out the window they had entered through. When she made it back out, she found him sitting with his back against the wall.*

*'Quinn,' she said softly.*

*'I'm not a monster,' he replied, furiously trying to fight back tears. 'I can't help being born what I am. But I'm human just like everyone else. If I didn't have these dumb red eyes nobody would even know I was Absilian.'*

*Ashe reached out and hugged him. She felt warm water soak into the fabric on her shoulder as the tears could no longer be contained. 'Hush now,' she said to him, stroking his hair. 'I like your red eyes. They're beautiful. And I don't think you are a monster.'*

*The boy in her arms started laughing then. A cold, sinister, double voiced laugh. The air around her grew black and cold. She pushed him out from her arms, looking into his eyes.*

*Instead of red, she saw darkness. A mask was pressed upon his face, enveloping his entire being in dark shadows. As the laughing died down, he quirked his head at her. 'Are you sure?'*

~~~

"ASHE!" A voice rang out, snapping her out of her dreams. A young woman with brown hair and fierce brown eyes stood over her, looking down with concern.

"Sorry, Mallory," Ashe said, rubbing her eyes before getting up from her sleeping pad. She looked around the sparse interior of her tent, trying to find where she had set her clothes.

She wasn't thrilled about wearing the same set she'd worn the day before, but life on the front lines wasn't easy. Other than her sleeping mat and the weathered, wooden trunk that sat at the foot of it, she didn't have much. It was easier to travel that way.

A large table with a map spread out on it stood at the very center of the tent, but that was necessary for her and the captains to plan their trek forward.

"Please don't tell me I missed breakfast again?"

"Of course, you missed breakfast again," Mallory scowled. "You always miss breakfast, sleeping in every day moaning in your sleep for Quinn. Oh Quinn, how I long to see your red eyes again."

Ashe's head whipped around, heat rising up the nape of her neck.
~~~

"Honestly woman," Mallory continued. "What kind of leader sleeps in every day having wet dreams while their men and women are hard at work digging latrines and setting defenses."

Mallory was impossible to stop once she began a tirade like this, so Ashe focused on getting dressed and letting the red creep out of her face. It had been three years since the Citadel had been blown away by Athena. Three years since she had parted ways with Quinn.

And yet, every night his face still haunted her dreams. Though if what Mallory was saying was true, he apparently didn't always haunt them. She hadn't kept in direct contact with him, fearing if she did things would quickly rekindle between them, and she wasn't sure she was ready for that after how everything ended.

However, she had scouts keeping an eye on the lands surrounding the tower, and that included the Wastes. Apparently, he had gone back home after she left him, and became quite the celebrity.

With his powers he was able to bring food to the wastes through means they hadn't had previously. He also used his training to turn a group of rag-tag bandits into his own personal honor guard. With times less tough in the wastes for his people, such extremes were no longer necessary, and as a result the Abyssillians were thriving.

She was happy for him. Though that happiness was brittle, and only masked the hollow pang in her heart.

"And another thing," Mallory continued, either not realizing Ashe had stopped listening or just not caring. "You…."

"Mallory," Ashe cut in. "Your point has come across loud and clear. Thank you."

"That's what you said the last three times I made it," she sulked.

Mallory was her right hand in the war and at camp. She was a fierce fighter, had a great reputation with the soldiers, and was loyal to a tee.

When Ashe had first come up to the front lines, Mallory was the first one to take her seriously. All of the grizzled vets had laughed about the girl who claimed to be a demigod, come from the Citadel to help win the war.

Mallory had convinced them to allow her the chance to prove it. She rode with them into one battle and scorched a large group of half woman, half dragon monsters called dracaenae to burnt husks and ashes. Within a moon's cycle she was a leading voice. She had the power to end this war and rebuild the world in the favor of humanity, and they all knew it.

"Please tell me you at least saved me a little bacon?" Ashe asked, feeling her stomach rumble.

Mallory rolled her eyes and produced three strips of meat. "You're lucky I like you and that 'Fire Queen' thing you do," She teased.

Ashe winced. "Please, never call me Fire Queen. It's what *he* used to call me."

Mallory nodded, looking down at the ground. She was always so curious about Ashe's past. Ashe kept it hidden from most people, not wanting to relive those last memories. Life had been difficult for her ever since Levy had betrayed them to Janus.

"If you won't talk about him," Mallory said, staring at the red crystal Ashe wore around her neck, "Then let's talk about this Quinn you keep moaning about in your dreams."

Ashe froze in her tracks, staring up at the outline of the tower in the distance. They had fought their way through hordes of monsters to get this far, mostly thanks to her and her powers. The tower had been anchored to the mountain over a half century ago with the massive chains shot from ancient cannons the Masters had in their possession.

However, not liking to be held in one spot, as it was against the very nature of the powerful structure, the magic it gave off began poisoning the landscape, melting rock and attracting all sorts of monsters to it. Now it had fully turned that mountain into a volcano, sitting deep in the center of the molten rock.

If Quinn and Levy had just been with her, as they were supposed to have been, they may have a chance of actually reaching it. With just her, the task was a slog through countless enemies. Though she supposed that was partially her fault.

A snap in front of her eyes brought her back to reality.

"Come on Ashe," Mallory pleaded. "Tell me about him. I know he gave you that crystal. He was clearly important. Let me in."

Ashe looked over into her big, puppy dog eyes. "What makes you think he gave this to me?"

Mallory rolled her eyes. "Oh, come on. You never take it off. Not even when you bathe. You absentmindedly play with it when you get that far off look in your eyes. The same look, might I add, you have now when we talk about him. It's pretty obvious."

Ashe's eyes became distant. "Quinn was my first friend. When I was young, I accidentally caused a lot of harm to my neighborhood, and my parents, wanting to be rid of me, sold me to the Citadel.

"I was heartbroken to say the least. But Quinn never let that bother him. He immediately befriended me, showing me all of his favorite places and just being a presence around me when I was feeling sad.

"He helped train me up to where he and Levy were outside of our classes so I wouldn't feel like an outsider when we sparred. He was just really sweet to me, with absolutely no strings attached.

"Honestly, I think he was just lonely and really wanted a friend. Eventually, as we got older, we realized we were way more than just friends. The Masters of the Citadel encouraged me not to pursue anything with him.

"They said he was a monster, and that the fates would not allow us to ever be together. But we couldn't help it. When we were near each other we were like magnets, constantly drawn into one another's presence. And when we were far from each other, it just felt like there was a connection between us.

"It's hard to explain. But he was the first, and the only man I ever loved. And I think vice-versa."

Ashe wondered, with an unwarranted pang of jealousy, if that were still true. Surely there were pretty Abyssillian girls out in the wastes. Did he still feel for her like he used to? She had left him pretty heart broken.

"That's. So. Sweet." Mallory's eyes glistened. "You guys are like, star crossed lovers or something, destined to reunite. Oh my god, I'm so excited for you. Do you think he'll come find you soon?"

Ashe couldn't help but laugh. On the battlefield, Mallory was deadly. There was nobody else she would rather have at her back. But off it, she had to remember she was still fairly young, and acted like it.

"I don't know Mallory. The way things were left, he may not want to see me again. And even if he did, I don't know if I would want things to rekindle. There's a reason things ended the way they did. Now come on, no more talk of past loves. We have work to do."

Their camp was set up efficiently, so that it was quick and easy to take down and move. They always tried to camp in a clearing whenever the forest would allow, so that they could use the sturdy oaks as a natural barrier from any straggling monsters or prying eyes.

They set their fire pits up just inside of that barrier as a way to light up the edges and see into the darkness of the forest beyond. Because Ashe's tent had become the de facto strategizing tent, it was always set directly in the center of the camp; easily guarded and easily accessible by the other captains when necessary.

Ashe spent the next couple of hours wandering around the camp, talking with the men and supervising training sessions. But in the back of her mind, she couldn't help but wonder what Quinn was up to.

# CHAPTER 24: Quinn

The Wastes in the Realm of Night looked eerily similar to the Wastes outside of it. They consisted of hard, cracked dirt as far as the eye could see. The sun never shone there. Instead, charcoal clouds choked the sky, mocking the Abyssillians with the hope of rain.

But that was a lie. It never rained in the Wastes. Quinn looked down at the ghostly outlines of his trio of allies. 'Ally' may have been harsh, considering all they had gone through since his return, but after Levy betrayed him and Ashe had dumped him, he wasn't sure he was ready to throw the word "friend" around yet.

The three he watched now had originated as simple bandits. Before he came back, the wastes were unforgiving. Food didn't exist out here, forcing his people to rely on trade. However, few traders made their way out into the dusty lands they inhabited, fearful of the people with monster ichor running through their veins.

Those that did mocked them, often only allowing them to buy the meat and produce that had spoiled along their journey. That had left them with no option but to poach the borders between the Wastes and lands rich with resources to the east.

On his way out here after the Citadel was lost, the three bandits had mistakenly seen him as a weak target, attempting to take his belongings and send him back across the border. They soon found their judgement to be made in error as Quinn dispatched all three within a few steps.

It was only when they had all been knocked to the dirt that they saw the red eyes staring back at them. They excitedly led him back to Petram, a city hidden in the cliffs of the Waste. When he showed his people the wealth he had brought with him, as well as what he was capable of doing thanks to Hestia's essence within him, they celebrated. They looked at him as a gift from the gods and he found himself rising swiftly in their ranks.

He didn't have the heart to tell these people it was the gods he intended to destroy, instead allowing them their beliefs. While training his trio in secret. To the Abyssillians, it was the humans who were evil. They believed the gods had blessed them with the gifts the ichor had instilled in them, and that humanity hated them for it.

In some ways they were right. In Quinn's experience growing up in Stormhaven, he was treated like dirt for what he was. But it was no secret to him that the gods were the ones who had put that idea in their heads.

All humans, after all, were their playthings. Besides, he knew what it was like to be judged for what you were instead of who you were. While he resented how he was treated by a majority of the citizens of Stormhaven, there were good ones as well. He chose to judge people based on their character instead of their race.

"They have vastly improved in the few years you have trained them" Chaos observed, standing next to him. The more Quinn had used the mask, the better grip he felt he was gaining on its power. Over time, Chaos had also begun to take on a similar appearance to him. He still lacked defined qualities however.

*"They may stand a chance in actual battle. If, of course, that is where you plan to lead them,"* he said knowingly.

"It's not just they who have improved," Quinn responded. "The whole village is coming along nicely. Soon the Abyssillians will be a force to be reckoned with."

"*Yes, but against whom?*" Chaos replied. "*You plan to take the throne and kill the gods, reshaping the world. But they worship those gods still. Not only that, but is a better world for mankind a better world for your people as well? Or will the discrimination against them become even worse? Will they even follow you into battle against their own gods? Will you tell them?*"

"Why so many questions, Chaos?" Quinn took his eyes off the trio for the first time. He enjoyed watching them train with the mask on because he was able to see everything in very slow motion, showing every single mistake they made in their stances.

"I am merely trying to get a read on how you think so I can better serve you, as well as offer council when it is needed. These are all things to consider, as without an army at your back you have no chance of claiming the throne. You are powerful, but the horde that guards it is many. And, considering your friend Levy, there are other forces to consider as well."

"Levy is not my friend," Quinn answered, surprised at the coldness in his voice.

Chaos only smiled. "*As you say. You may want to step in now. If they go much further your trio will be a duo.*"

Looking down he saw what Chaos meant. Sen, a young man only in his late teens, was on the ground. His sword had been knocked away and out of reach. Sen was a small kid with comically large ears and stringy blonde hair. Quinn had done what he could to put some muscle on his body, but he still had a ways to go.

What he lacked in physical stature however, he made up for in speed and cunning. Though his specific bloodline had become weak, he still had a gift residing within him. When he was completely still and focused, he was able to hear things from a very far way off. It had made it simple to find targets when they were living their bandit days.

Above him, chopping down at him with an axe, was his twin brother Nes. If Sen was small and intelligent, the exact opposite could be said of Nes. His talents lie far more in his physical abilities. While his brother was on the shorter side, Nes was built like a mountain.

He wore his thick blonde hair up in a bun to keep it out of his eyes. Each talent an Abyssillian had, left some sort of unique marking on their body. Nes, through large amounts of strain, was able to make a small earthquake happen in his immediate surroundings.

Though incredibly useful in a fight, due to his weak bloodline, it put his body under immense pressure. As a result, his body was covered from head to toe in scars.

The brothers had a fierce rivalry with one another. Nes always touted his physical superiority, constantly getting under his brother's skin. Sen would go out of his way to try and prove him wrong, usually ending up in a physical confrontation he had no chance of winning.

Sen was plenty strong on his own, but when he was in battle, his strongest weapon, his mind, tended to shut off, leaving him acting on an instinct he just didn't have. Quinn threw his hands up in frustration and jumped through the nearest shadow, back to the Mortal Realm.

He appeared with a burst of swirling energy, right between the downed Sen and the attacking Nes. With a flick of his wrist he sent a wave of energy into Nes' chest, shoving him back. Sighing, he reached up and slipped the mask off his face, sending it back into the Realm of Night.

That was one of the neater things he had discovered he could do with it. He and the mask shared a connection allowing him to tap into its power even when he wasn't in physical contact with it. The boost it gave him was only fractional while not on his face, but it allowed him to do fun things like slip it back and forth between realms. Waving his hand over his face and having the mask appear in a burst of shadowy energy was his favorite party trick.

"Nes," he faced the stronger boy. "Were you really about to kill your brother just now?"

Nes looked down in shame. "It's not that I wanted to," he said. "I just lost control. By the time I saw his sword was gone I was already swinging down. I couldn't stop the momentum."

"Oh bull," yelled Sen, struggling to his feet. "You looked right at my empty hand with a smile on your face."

"What did you say, Malaka?" Nes replied, stepping in his

brother's direction.

"Enough!" came a third voice. Andra was the shortest of all of them, standing less than five feet of height.

Sen looked at Andra, his mouth gaping. "Did you just…holy crap Nes, Andra just talked."

Nes joined in with a grin. "She didn't just talk bro, she commanded us! What upside-down world did I wake up in today to be treated in such a way?"

Unlike the other two, her bloodlines were still incredibly strong, giving her the gift to tame and speak with all sorts of different creatures. She was incredibly shy, preferring to speak to the drakons she tamed rather than to other people.

Her hair was long, falling all the way down to her ankles, and shone in all different colors depending on how the light hit it. Because she spoke so rarely, when she did, people tended to listen. As if realizing what she just said, she let out a little squeak and hid her face in her sleeve, reaching up and petting the baby drakon perched on her shoulder.

Drakons were incredibly rare monsters. In the ancient days, they were said to lay waste to armies, paralyzing foes with their eyes and devouring mouthfuls of soldiers at a time. Even now Drakons, though nearly non-existent, were incredibly powerful in the wild.

Andra had initially intended to breed them in a desperate attempt to bring food and wealth to their village. Drakon teeth and scales would fetch a mighty profit with a trader, and the wings made incredible leather. Sadly, after her first was born, the male died of a sickness, leaving her with only the mother and the baby remaining.

"Alright guys, that's enough. Leave Andra alone," Quinn smiled at each. He wasn't sure about the trio when he had first agreed to train them, but they had all come a long way since that first day and honestly, he was starting to like these nitwits.

"Sen, you need to…." he put his face in his palm. "Stop snapping to attention every time I say your name you little smart ass. We aren't an army and I'm not your commander."

"Aye, aye sir!" Sen responded with a snarky grin plastered to his face. Nes and Andra snickered in the background.

"You need to loosen your wrist when you wield your blade. If it's too rigid you will be easily disarmed. You're fast, and you're smart. Most monsters are going to be stupid, relying on base instinct to kill. Use that to your advantage and outsmart them."

He switched his gaze over to Nes. "As for you, quit acting like a big stupid monster relying on base instinct." Sen burst out laughing in the background. "I'll be honest, you don't have a sharp mind like your brother. But you do have what he lacks."

"Personality?" Nes grinned.

"Would you guys please take this seriously?" Quinn stared them down. "You have all the talent in the world and then some if you would just apply it. What I was going to say is you have what he lacks: a warrior's instinct.

"You have the physical build and strength to tank most opponents and overpower them. You just need to be more aware of your surroundings."

Quinn sighed, stretching out his sore arms. He needed to start sparring with them again. It had been a little while and he was worried if he didn't get a decent sparring partner soon, he'd start to get rusty.

"Come on you knuckleheads," he grinned. "Let's go back and get something to eat. My treat." With a "whoop" from all of them, even Andra, they set off back to town.

# CHAPTER 25: Levy

Far to the north, nestled away in a dense, snowy forest of spruce, stood a stone fortress. It was within this fortress that the Masters of the Citadel had stockpiled the ancient items of power once used by the gods. The old fools had been holding out on the front liners. Powerful items such as these would have been an invaluable resource in the war.

Instead they kept them tucked away.

*Out of sight, out of mind. How ridiculous.*

Levy squeezed his eyes shut, refocusing himself. "You know, I really hate it when you do that."

Part of the deal he had made with Janus, in return for loosing Athena from her bonds and unleashing her upon the Masters, was that he would receive half of the god's essence. What he hadn't realized, much to his chagrin, was that it wouldn't be the same as what Hestia had given him.

*Hestia was ignorant.* Janus spoke in his mind. *The dumb goddess split herself too thin, allowing her essence to be fully absorbed by you and the other two. By giving you half of mine, I can stay conscious within you, while my other half goes about his business.*

Levy would have cared a lot less about that if it hadn't been the bearded half that got shoved inside his head.

*Yeah well right back atcha lad. I was away, if you'll recall, when you made that dumb agreement.*

Levy shook his head refocusing on the task at hand. The wind this far north was biting, forcing him to burrow further into his lined cloak. "What specifically are we here for, weapons?" Levy looked down at the silver broadsword he held by his side. The wolf head stared back at him with a predatory smile.

*It's not that kind of weapon we're after lad, it's an orb. Clearly your Masters were holding a lot back from you. This vault is old. It's covered in ancient, powerful engravings that exist for the sole purpose of trapping energy inside. In this case, godly energy.*

Levy could feel his pulse quicken with that information. This entire time, the Masters had been sitting on such a powerful stockpile, and yet they hadn't even tried to use it to claim the throne.

Typical human greed to hold on to their treasures and wait, sacrificing many innocent lives in the process, until someone strong enough would do the job for them. Levy shook his head.

No, he had to remember that it wasn't humans that were the problem. There were a few bad apples, but it was the gods who twisted them that way. Using them for their amusement, offering only scraps of what they could just to see their little pets fight each other for them.

*Focus on the mission, lad. You'll have plenty of time to curse us later.*

"Ok, fine," Levy looked back at the heavily guarded fortress. "So, what's the plan then? Sneak in, grab this orb and get out?"

*You have a large amount of godly essence in you, lad, what do you need to sneak for? Go down there, bust some heads and take what is rightfully ours.*

Levy smiled, feeling the godly energy flowing through his body, invigorating him. He wished he could see his face right now, because he knew his eyes would be shining silver in the night. What a terrifying feeling the traitorous guards would feel, seeing two points of deadly silver slowly approaching out of the darkness.

"Janus, what do you say? Let's go have some fun."

Levy stalked down the main path of the forest, leading to the front gate of the fortress. The landscape around him was serene; betraying the slaughter that was about to occur. The trees were completely iced over thanks the frigid winds, making it look as though they had been sculpted.

All shades of green and purple lights danced in the night sky, dying the snow. Scouts and guards garbed in Citadel attire lined the trees, unaware of the predator that lurked in the shadows. Even with the Citadel destroyed and the Masters dead, it appeared their influence was still alive in the world. Not one of them saw their deaths approach.

One minute they were watching, the next their world went black. As Levy slowly approached the entrance, the two guards on either side called out. "Halt there and turn around. This is restricted ground."

With a smirk, Levy ducked low, shadowing himself at the edge of the darkness, just out of the flickering light of the torches. He waited there, tensing his muscles and allocating his energy into his calves. Just as the guards took their first step toward him, he heard Janus yell *NOW,* and he sprung forward.

He had reached the first guard within three steps. Not bad, considering the distance he had covered, but he felt he could do better. With a vicious chop he swung in a low arc, slicing the first guard in half before he had even seen the blade. Wasting no time, he planted his left foot and swiveled, spinning around and taking the other guard's head clean off at the neck.

*Well done. Now head inside.*

Inside the fortress was a large stone staircase leading down. Though the staircase was wide, the steps were very short and compressed, practically stacked on top of one another. Levy wrinkled his nose at the petrichor coming from the damp stone. He was not fond of the musty smell.

After nearly being skewered by iron spikes that had stabbed out from the walls within his first ten steps, he slowed his pace considerably, cautious not to blunder into an untimely death. Every hundred steps or so, the stairs would even out to a platform. On each side was a large, intricately carved door. Every door he passed depicted some kind of historical event or symbol prevalent to the gods. "Which door holds what we're looking for?"

*Keep going. What we seek will be at the deepest part of these vaults.*

The further down Levy walked, the colder the air became. The torches on the walls began to flicker, changing from their typical orange to a deep purple, casting a sinister glow on the walls around him. After what felt like hours, he reached the final step. In front of him was a mammoth, obsidian doorway, embedded with little gems of every color and cast with silver filigree.

*Just a warning, lad; expect some kind of trouble.*

Channeling as much energy as he could into his leg, he pulled back and kicked out at the door. Even with the godly energy at his disposal, it felt like kicking a solid tree trunk. He did succeed, however, in opening it a fraction of the way, enough that he could slip inside.

The interior of the room was completely black, save a small glowing purple orb on a marble pedestal in the center of the room. Pale, white energy swirled around the interior of the orb, casting a dim light upon the pedestal and making a sound akin to a wailing soul. The orb made his skin crawl.

*There it is lad, the Orb of Hades. Grab that and get out of here. Hades creeps me out.*

Levy didn't need to be told twice. He wasn't overly fond of the chill in this room and wanted to leave it quickly. He moved toward the pedestal; taking cautious steps forward, careful to avoid any traps that may litter the floor.

Just as he reached out and grabbed orb, the hairs on the back of his neck stood straight up, sending a shiver shooting down his spine. From the darkness beyond the pillar came a low, earth shaking growl.

"Janus?" Levy asked.

*You're on your own with this one, kid.*

In the light of the orb, six giant, red eyes opened in front of him. As the growling increased in volume, so did the shaking of the ground. Following the eyes were three sets of razor-sharp teeth. Levy paled.

"Good doggy," he slowly backed away with his hands in the air. "Just gonna take this and go. You just go back to sleep."

*I don't think he's buying it, bud.*

"Yeah, no kidding," he said, feeling his back brush up against the door.

*Whatever you do, don't run.*

Janus' warning came too late. As soon as his back touched the door, he turned and sprinted back up the stairs.

*What did I JUST...ah dammit.*

# CHAPTER 26: Ashe

Flashes of fire lit up the night sky as waves of monsters crashed around her. Rain cascaded down from onyx clouds, plastering Ashe's hair to her head and turning the battlefield into a treacherous mess of mud and ichor. The forest acted as a natural barrier for the humans, forcing the monsters into lines if they wanted to reach their army.

However, even with that, the sheer number that attacked them was overwhelming. Normally it was the humans who made the first move into battle, crashing into the outer line of monsters as they fought to get closer to the tower.

Tonight however, the monsters had struck first, charging their way into her camp and catching them unawares. Ashe grimaced. The casualties with an attack like this were bound to be high, and with their already dwindling number, that was something they couldn't afford.

Beside her, Mallory was like a blur, cutting in and out of the monsters around Ashe, giving her time to work. Mallory was like her own personal body guard. Ashe needed time to gather her energy in such a heavy rain for her fire to have any chance of causing damage. In order for that to happen she needed to focus, which was nearly impossible when she had to stop every second to dispatch a centaur attempting to kick her head off.

She knew she was going to need to end this battle quickly if they wanted any chance of reaching the tower, so she was pooling all of her energy into one mighty attack. Monsters, being creatures of darkness, tended to fear fire. If she could scare them bad enough, this battle would end.

"I'm almost there," Ashe yelled to Mallory. "Keep them off of me for just a few more moments."

The swirling energy within her was reaching a crescendo, trying hard to burst forth. Just a little more pressure and she would unleash a spout of flame, engulfing the battlefield. Any monster it didn't kill would no doubt run with its tail tucked between its legs.

She didn't like to use her power in this manner, due to the burnout it would cause after. The last time she had consumed so much of her energy in one go was when she burned away the locked engravings on the door to the depths of the Citadel. The powerless feeling she had felt watching Quinn and Levy fight, barely able to even keep her head up, was a feeling she never wanted to experience again.

But the monsters seemed too organized for anything else. That was strange to her as well. Monsters were very much creatures of impulse. They were drawn to the tower due to the toxic magic it emitted.

Normally they were so busy fighting and crawling over each other to reach it, they were caught by surprise as the humans swept in behind, taking out their outer lines. However, this attack seemed almost planned.

They had attacked right as the soldiers had been settling in for the night. The scouts, of course, had seen the swarm approaching and had shouted out a warning, but the monsters had crashed down upon them so soon after, they had hardly had time to prepare. And then of course there was the rain.

It sluiced down from the sky, drowning out their fires and leaving the camp in darkness. Rain was typically sparse around these parts, and for the monsters to attack at just a time where the heaviest rains she had seen in her three years on the front lines had started pouring down upon them; it was too coincidental. Something was not right.

"I don't mean to hurry you," Mallory grunted through her teeth, catching a centaur seconds away from striking Ashe, "But they seem to be focusing in on you and whatever it is you're doing with your energy. It is becoming increasingly difficult to stop them. If you're going to do something, it would be best to do it now."

Her brown hair had come undone from its hold and was now plastered to her face. Mud and ichor were splattered all around her armor and dripped from her blade. If Ashe hadn't known any better, she would have assumed this woman was a goddess in disguise, reveling in the adrenaline pumping glory of battle.

"Just a few moments more," Ashe responded, feeling the warm energy push its way to the surface. "I need to be sure it's powerful enough not to fizzle in the rain."

"Not sure you're going to have a few minutes more," Mallory replied, staring at a hulking shadow lumbering toward them through the haze of the darkness. "I don't know what that is, but I would rather not find out. Any chance you could unleash whatever it is you're cooking up?"

The ground around them began to shake as the mountainous shadow moved closer, its giant, bloodshot eye glinting in the firelight. A deep rumble filled the night sky, vibrating through the air. "Like, now? Please?"

"Just a few moments more," Ashe said again, bringing the energy within to a boiling point.

"Oh, for gods' sake Ashe, that thing looks like it could use me as a toothpick. We don't HAVE a few moments."

"Just a little longer," Ashe replied, feeling the first few wisps of fire sneak their way through her clutches.

"ASHE!"

"NOW!" Ashe opened her eyes. A wave of fire spilled out of every pore of her body, accumulating in front of her into a giant golden orb. The light lit up the battlefield, drawing the attention of man and monster alike.

As the fire continued to pour out of her, the orb began to change shape, morphing into the shape of a phoenix. With a final push, Ashe drained the rest of her energy into, and pushed it out from her. The phoenix gave off an earsplitting cry and screeched up into the night sky, burning away any rain that would have tried to extinguish it. It climbed above the battlefield, lighting up the world around them.

Ashe grabbed the invisible strings of energy that attached her to the fire and pulled, splitting the phoenix into pieces and raining golden fire down upon the attacking horde. Monsters all around them began to screech as the first few globs of fire struck home. As one they turned, fighting over themselves in an attempt to escape.

Ashe knew they wouldn't have the time though. This was a technique she had practiced time and time again. It was meant for killing the masses of monsters between them and the tower. No monster would escape this battle.

As if to prove her point, the hulking shadow that had been coming their way roared out in pain. The fire had engulfed him, creating the largest bonfire Ashe had ever seen. With a final cry it fell to the ground, leaving only a charred husk behind.

"Yeah!" Mallory kicked the burnt corpse of what Ashe thought may have been the largest cyclops she had ever seen. "Try and eat me now!"

The battle was all but finished. Around them, soldiers were finishing off what was left of the monsters. As the light of her phoenix in the sky began to fade, Ashe's attention was pulled to the tops of a small plateau overlooking their camp. She squinted through the rain, trying to make out a small shadowy figure looking down at her. With a chill, she realized that staring back at her were two silver eyes, glowing in the fading fire.

"Mallory," she said, feeling the fatigue of what she had just done wash through her. "Help me up to that plateau. There's someone I think I need to speak with."

The walk up to the plateau was unpleasant to say the least. Movement was slow, largely in part to Ashe having drained nearly all of her energy with her last attack. Mallory had to help her along, hobbling next to her to support her weight.

Every few steps the charred corpse of a monster blocked their path, giving off a stink unlike Ashe had ever smelled. It was as if a skunk had sprayed a piece of rotten meat, and then that meat had been charred to oblivion. It was fortunate Ashe had as much control over her power as she did, or else the entire forest would likely be ablaze.

As they neared the plateau, the trees around them grew sparse, allowing Ashe a clear look at the back of the god atop the incline. From this height, they could see for leagues around them. Down below, their camp was in chaos; the small forms of the soldiers scrambled to recover bodies and shore up the defenses. Not far in the distance, the mountainous form of the tower climbed into the sky.

"Beautiful isn't it," Janus said, sensing their arrival. He turned as they drew closer, looking Ashe directly in the eye. "You've grown quite strong." A hint of a smile played across his handsome face.

"Save the pleasantries, Janus," Ashe replied, venom dripping into every word. "I have nothing nice to say to you."

"Then why come and meet me up here?" he smiled. Gods how she hated that smile. It dripped with smug superiority.

"Um, I don't mean to interrupt," Mallory said, staring back and forth between the two, "But did you just say Janus? As in the god?"

"Half a god now, actually." Ashe replied with a sneer. "He gave his other half away."

"And yet," Janus replied, coolly. "I am still god enough to destroy you, depleted as you are."

Mallory, sensing the threat, stepped in front of Ashe, sword at the ready. "Over my dead body," she replied.

Like so many other times she had begun to lose count, Ashe was grateful for the loyalty of her friend. Despite knowing she would be up against a god if he chose to attack; she was still willing to stand and fight.

"As much as I would love to do just that," Janus said, turning back away from her, "I am not here to kill you tonight."

"Oh?" Ashe replied with a confidence her drained body would not allow her to feel. "Could have fooled me. I assume that organized attack by a bunch of brainless monsters wasn't your doing then?"

"Oh, make no mistake, that was very much me. I wanted to see how strong you've become. Consider it a threat assessment. You are needed for my plans to come to fruition. I was curious at how much of a pain you would be in making that a reality."

He turned back to her and gave her another chilly smile. "I see now why the goddess chose you for this power. You are a fast learner."

Hearing that he intended to use her for whatever plans he was had made her skin crawl. If he chose to take her now, she wasn't sure there was much she could do. She had burnt herself out, and while Mallory was strong, she was only mortal.

Against a god like Janus, she doubted there was much she could do. As if reading her mind, Janus chuckled, showing genuine mirth.

"Relax, the time is not right. Only when the three of you have been brought together again can my plan come to light. Take the time to recover your energy. You're going to need it."

"Like Hades she is," Mallory yelled. "If you think I'm going to let you take the commander, you've got another think coming."

"Mallory, no," Ashe yelled as her friend began to charge Janus.

However, Janus just laughed, making no move to stop her. As Mallory's blade came down on him, he merely smiled at Ashe and said, "Soon," before disappearing; leaving Mallory to hit nothing but air.

With a relieved sigh, she pushed her way back to her feet. "Come on, Mallory, let's go check on the soldiers.

As they returned to the camp, the men were in a commotion, running around repairing defenses and checking the wounded. A few steps in, a soldier ran up to her, gasping for air.

"We have been looking all over for you." he said, eyes wide.

"Apologies," she replied, trying to settle the man's nerves. "We were tying up a loose end."

"Never mind that," the man responded, slightly more under control. "There is a messenger in your tent, says it's urgent. Wouldn't say what it was about but said to fetch you immediately. Something about an old friend of yours."

Ashe's heart leapt into her throat. Could Quinn be coming to help? It had been three years since things had ended between them. Ashe lived with constant guilt over how it happened.

At the time she had been overwhelmed with the feeling of betrayal. First from Levy, and then learning about the mask Quinn had gotten from his trial. She knew he felt horrible about it, but it had crushed her.

Perhaps it would be good to see him again and attempt to make amends. She hoped he would be willing to talk to her, though would not blame him if he were angry still. As she and Mallory entered her tent, her mood plummeted. The man in the tent was being worked on by a doctor, a vicious rend torn into his shoulder. The man looked up to her, fear etched across his face.

Swallowing her nerves, she said, "Report."

"We tried to stop him at the border," he apologized, eyes frozen onto hers. "But he was far too strong. It is only a matter of time before he reaches it and overwhelms us."

"Is he speaking in code or are you understanding any of this?" Mallory asked her.

Ashe felt numb hearing the words he spoke. "How long ago?"

"Days. By now, odds are he's scoping it out. Soon he will act. When he does, there is no telling how powerful he could become. There are many treasures down in that vault."

"Describe him to me," she said, already fearing she knew.

"Tall, muscular, brown hair and eyes like the moon."

"Mallory," Ashe's blood ran cold. "I need you to do me a favor. Normally I would take care of this, but I'm drained and can't leave the front lines."

"What is it?"

"Levy is going to attack the vaults the Masters left buried in the north. He cannot be allowed to get the treasure inside."

"You want me to go and stop him?"

"Absolutely not. He's too powerful for you. No offense. But there is someone who can stop him." Her heart fluttered at the thought.

"I need you to go as fast as you can to the Wastes. They will surely see you coming, but make it known that you are looking for Quinn with an urgent message from me. He will see that no harm comes to you. It may already be too late, but we need to try, or this war is over. Take him to the fortress in the north."

Mallory grinned. "I finally get to meet this Quinn you're always so tied up about? Count me in."

Ashe looked at her, eyes laced with concern. “This is no time to joke. That vault is filled with powerful artifacts we know nothing about. Convince him to help. Please.”

Mallory sobered. It was rare she saw such concern in her commander’s eyes. With a slight nod she said, “Understood.”

# CHAPTER 27: Quinn

Quinn was sitting in a dingy tavern, enjoying a drink while his young trio argued with one another. These were his favorite ways to spend his nights. He wasn't an alcoholic by any means, preferring to keep his wits sharp at all times, but a drink every now and then helped to take the edge off.

Andra on the other hand, sucked drinks down like there was no tomorrow. In fact, if she kept up the pace she was on tonight, he wasn't sure there would be a tomorrow for her at all. She said she liked the way the drinks tasted but based on the faces she made as she drank them, Quinn doubted that was true.

He figured it was more likely that she enjoyed feeling the courage it gave her, breaking her out of her shell. When she was drunk, she was an entirely different person. Though with her short stature, Quinn had no idea where the girl put all that drink.

Sen and Nes were in the middle of another of their drinking contests. Both boys were mad for the lone girl in their party and were constantly competing in silly contests to try and earn her affection.

"You...you're done" Sen slurred, finishing another drink, letting out a loud belch.

"Not a chanshe," Nes replied, wobbling in his seat.

Andra giggled, finishing one herself and pounding it onto the table before picking up another. She would drink them both under the table tonight. Quinn just smiled to himself, lightly sipping at his own.

These three had become more than trainees to him, though he hated to admit it. Watching them grow from bandits, barely capable of holding a blade correctly, to capable fighters under his tutelage had softened him a little.

Witnessing their friendship grow along the way made him long for his past. Whenever he thought of Ashe, his heart would still hammer in his chest. He missed her every day. It had been his own mistake that had led to that decision, and he knew from the second it was made that the split was inevitable.

There had been so many times over the last three years that he had wanted to reach out to her, but instead respected her wishes and left her alone. That didn't stop him from keeping a keen eye on the war effort. If he ever caught wind that she was in danger, he would not hesitate to go to her aid.

As he sunk deeper into memories of his past, the door opened, emitting a cool, refreshing breeze into the stuffy tavern. He snapped back to attention as he heard gasps around him. Making their way toward his table were two Abyssillian guards.

Clutched between them was a human woman. She had brown hair and striking brown eyes. Little flecks of gold sparkled in them when the light from the fire hit her a certain way. She was of medium height but toned with muscle.

Her hands were covered in callouses that only someone with knowledge of a sword would have. A warrior then. A small commotion was building in the tavern. It was very rare that a lone human wandered into the wastes.

With the exception of the odd trader every now and then, most humans avoided them as if they were plagued. "Monsters", they called them. As a result, the Abyssillians trust for humans was slim. Normally they would be turned away when they entered their territory. For this woman to have made it this far, something must have been amiss.

As the guards reached their table, Nes slammed down another empty mug. "Whas going on?" Quinn smirked at the boy's attempt at impressing Andra with leadership.

Sen quickly chimed in, "Yeah, whas the meanin o'this." Andra giggled into her mug.

"We caught this one attempting to gain entry to the village," a guard said to Quinn, ignoring the drunk slurs of his comrades.

Quinn raised an eyebrow. "And you brought her to me?"

The other guard shifted nervously. "She said she had an urgent message for you. Said it was imperative she speak with you immediately. Called you by your name, sir."

"Oh?" Quinn asked, looking back at the girl. She had not stopped staring at him since they first entered the tavern. She picked him out immediately, meaning she knew who she was looking for. "And how is it you know me, miss?"

The woman looked at him with a slight twinkle in her eye. "You're the famous Quinn Alesia. The hero that brought prosperity to a barren land. I see now why she seems so obsessed with you. The scar makes you look very dark and mysterious. The black clothing helps."

At the mention of a 'she', Quinn sat up in his chair. "Well then," he tried to hide his excitement. "Let's hear this urgent message."

"My name is Mallory, thanks for asking," she said, allowing a smirk to slip before shifting back to serious.

"Ashe has sent me to you specifically. Apparently, our vault in the north is going to be attacked by a mutual acquaintance of yours. I believe you know him as Levy."

Fire lit inside Quinn at the name. "She is currently unable to leave the front to go and stop him, so she sent me to beg your assistance. This vault contains many powerful, godly artifacts. We don't know what they do, but in the wrong hands we believe serious damage can be done."

"When was this information given to you?" Quinn tried to hide his eagerness. Mallory seemed to see right through it and smiled.

"We received the information that he was scoping things out and could make a move any day."

"I would love to help. I have a score to settle with him," Quinn replied. "But if he's already getting ready to make a move, there is no chance I'd be able to get there in time. Even with my methods of traveling around faster," he stroked the mask at this, "there is no way I'd make it."

OH!" Andra slammed down another empty mug. "Marilyn can help with that!"

Quinn considered that. It was true that with flight on their side, they might make it in time. It would be close, but he was willing to risk it if it meant getting a shot at Levy.

"Um," Mallory asked, separating herself from the guards. "What is a Marilyn?"

Quinn smiled. "Would you like a quick drink first?" He offered her his mug. "You may need it."

"As much as I'd normally love to drink with an attractive man, I don't think we have time. Let's go get this Marilyn and be off."

Quinn laughed, finishing his drink in one mighty gulp. "Suit yourself."

"I should have had that drink," Mallory gulped, as they stood in back of Andra's house. Standing in front of them, wings stretched out as far as they would go, was a large, scarlet drakon. Its serpent-like body was laid out in a straight line, inviting the would-be riders to climb on. Andra had just finished saddling her, and looked at Mallory with a smile, expecting praise.

"You named your drakon, Marilyn?" She paled.

"Of course," a gleeful Andra replied. "What else would I name her?"

"I don't know," Mallory shifted closer to Quinn, as though seeking shelter. "Apophis? Something, more...drakony?"

Andra stared back at her, considering. "Nah, that wouldn't be fitting. She's too docile for that. Marilyn is much better."

"If you say so." She looked at Quinn.

He only smiled back at her, enjoying the similar banter he'd had himself the first time he met the drakon.

"Well, let's be off then," he said, climbing into the front saddle. Mallory paled further.

"You're sure she won't, I don't know, eat me or something?"

Andra looked hurt. "Of course she won't! Marilyn is a good girl, aren't you?" She scratched the drakon under the chin. In response, Marilyn raised her head and roared, shooting a small burst of flame into the air.

"See?" Andra asked, as if that proved her point.

Quinn looked at his charges, all looking expectantly back at him. "Stay here and help guard the village," he said, looking each of them in the eye.

"And keep practicing. Don't kill each other while I'm gone. I'll be back soon. I have a feeling things are going to be lively for a bit."

They all looked disappointed to not be tagging along, but they nodded back. They were well trained, Quinn thought with a smile. As Mallory climbed onto the saddle behind him, he pressed his heels into the sides of the drakon, spurring the monster to life.

"Hold on," he called back to her. "Take off is the bumpiest part of the ride."

She shut her eyes tight and buried her head into his back as the drakon slithered, picking up enough speed before soaring into the air with a mighty flap of its leathery wings. When they had finally smoothed out enough for her liking, Mallory opened her eyes and gasped.

"Beautiful, isn't it?" Quinn asked, looking back at her. His red eyes twinkled in the moonlight, and an easy smile rested on his face. "I reacted the same way the first time I flew.

"Back at the Citadel, I used to climb the tallest buildings to look down at the capital. It was always my favorite place to be. Being up high relaxed me; helped me center myself when my emotions were in turmoil."

"Ashe always talks about how she liked it up there too." She regretted it as soon as she said it, seeing pain well up in his eyes.

"Yeah," he replied hoarsely. "How is she?"

Mallory gave an apologetic smile. "She's doing well. She's the most powerful person I've ever met. We've made good progress, you know. We'll reach the tower very soon, so long as we don't suffer any more surprise attacks."

They lapsed into silence for a while, Quinn's eyes having gone distant. After another hour or so, she said, "She still wears your pendant." She saw the slightest of smiles grace his lips.

Halfway through the journey they passed over the wreckage of Stormhaven. Where once a proud city stood; now all that remained were large piles of rubble and splintered timber. After rumors of Athena's revenge upon the Masters that held her leaked to the world around; nobody dared go near the fallen city, fearful of inciting the wrath of the immortals.

Not even looters dared venture inside the ravaged walls. It was a stark reminder for all that the gods were not to be trifled with. They rode the rest of the trip in quiet, both silently thinking about the fight that was sure to come.

As they flew over the snow-covered forest, they saw the first sign of combat. Sentries lined the frosty paths, bodies broken on the ground and blood pooling and freezing beneath them. They touched down just outside the fortress in a clearing.

Quinn patted the drakon, thanking her for getting them there quickly and telling her to wait for them to return. She curled into a ball, closing her eyes.

"She'll sleep until we come back so she has the energy to get us home," he explained. As they made their way toward the entrance to the vault, a large rumble shook the earth around them. Seconds later it was followed by a mighty roar.

"I am so sick of hearing that," Mallory said, drawing her weapon.

Quinn did the same, readying his energy to summon the mask should it be needed. From the darkness of the vault, a shape began to take form, sprinting at full speed through the entrance and sliding to a stop when he saw them.

The man was tall and muscular, built like an oak. "Hello, Quinn," he smiled, as if speaking to a friend.

"Levy," Quinn replied, an icy brittleness to his voice.

"I'd love to catch up, but I'm a bit preoccupied at the moment. How about a little help, for old time's sake?"

Quinn stepped back, careful not to drop his stance. He noticed the pulsing purple orb in Levy's hand. "Nah, I think you're on your own here." he smiled without joy. "You've made your bed, now sleep in it, as the saying goes."

Levy just shrugged, pocketing the orb. "How about you, pretty lady? Care to help a hero in need?"

As he asked, a monstrous black blur crashed through the fortress entrance, sending shards of debris flying out in all directions. Standing before them was the largest dog Quinn had ever seen.

Long black fur covered its body. Six red eyes stared back at him, drool falling in repulsive globs at its feet. Breath fogged from all three mouths as it panted, catching its breath from the chase up the vault steps.

"Is that…." Mallory began.

"Levy, what did you steal to cause Cerberus to chase you from the vault?" Quinn asked.

Levy looked at it, and then back to Quinn. "Is this your pet? It has your eyes."

Quinn growled, tensing at the jab. "Oh my, and apparently your temperament as well! Very well, if you don't want to help, I suppose I'll have to take care of it myself."

Levy smiled, cracking his neck and unsheathing his sword. Cerberus lunged forward, attempting to pin him to the ground, but Levy had grown much faster in the three years they'd been apart.

With speed so quick Quinn could only just follow it, he spun inside its outstretched paw, swinging his blade and taking the paw clean off. Cerberus let out a loud yelp, jumping back and slipping on the icy ground.

Not giving it any time to recover, Levy jumped in the air after it. The left head of Cerberus snapped at him, but Levy was faster. Using the monster as a springboard, he vaulted back to the packed earth.

The head that nipped at him missed completely; instead taking a large bite out of the center head. With a snarl, the center head snapped back, completely forgetting about the real threat. The right head, growled and barked, attempting to play peacemaker between the other two, leaving Levy free to strike.

With a patience Quinn wasn't sure he'd be able to feel, Levy walked behind the monster and ran up its back, raising his sword and stabbing down. The blade sunk into Cerberus' skull, spraying the snow around them with warm ichor.

As the middle head slumped, Levy pulled his sword free and

loosed a vicious horizontal strike, killing the other two heads at once.

Using Cerberus' fur, he wiped his blade clean. His eyes got distant for a second, as though listening to something Quinn couldn't hear before murmuring, "Because I needed space. That's why. You think I wanted to fight that thing with no room to move?"

"Talking to yourself, Levy?" Quinn asked. "Don't tell me your guilt has driven you mad."

"On the contrary, my friend, I am as sane as can be."

"Not sane enough if you think at this point, I'm still your friend," he said through gritted teeth.

"When I take the throne, and save humanity, all will be my friend," he smiled. "I saw you looking at my prize earlier. Care to know what it does?"

He held the orb up in the air. It wasn't large by any means, fitting easily in his palm, but the power Quinn could sense it giving off was astronomical.

"If I want to claim the throne, I need an army," he stared into the orb. "I had hoped you and Ashe would come to your senses and join me, but I see now that cannot be.

"So instead I've sought an alternative, thanks to the knowledge imparted to me by Janus. Allow me to introduce you to the Orb of Hades."

He smiled up at Quinn, resting the orb into the mouth of the snarling wolf on the pommel of is sword. "By trickling just a little bit of energy into it, I can call forth the power of the Underworld. Care to see how it works?"

Quinn sensed the danger before he finished saying the words. Not wanting to allow him time to finish his scheme, he summoned the mask onto his face, using its power to streak behind him and swing. With god-like reflexes, Levy whipped around, meeting his strike with his own, producing sparks with the impact. His eyes glowed silver, rivaling the red of his own.

"I see you've finally given in and allowed yourself to use the power of the mask. Unfortunately for you, I have power now too. I can track your movements through that other realm now, Quinn. Show me how strong you've become."

Quinn heard a scream from where he had left Mallory. The orb at the base of Levy's sword was glowing. All around them, the dead rose from where they lay. From the path leading into the forest, the broken bodies of the scouts they'd seen while flying in shambled toward Mallory. They moved in an unnatural way; as if they were marionettes, being controlled by invisible strings. Within moments they had surrounded her.

"Pay her no mind," Levy said, pulling his attention back with a quick strike. "Or you'll lose before the fun even begins."

He stepped back into the Realm of Night, swinging around to Levy's right before re-emerging and loosing another blow. This one he aimed for the base of Levy's sword, attempting to shatter the orb. Faster than he thought possible, Levy swung down, easily batting Quinn's blade aside.

"Come now, Quinn," he taunted. "You'll have to do better than that."

Quinn stepped back, taking a deep breath. Levy was playing with him and he was letting it get to his head. Centering himself, he crouched low, analyzing his opponent. Pulling the power of the Realm of Night into him, he stepped again, appearing just behind Levy.

As Levy swung around, he stepped a second time, ducking around to his unprotected side and striking. Levy, a step slow, was just able to deflect the blade, missing slightly and turning what would have been a kill shot into a shallow graze along his ribs.

Quinn narrowed his eyes in frustration and threw Levy's own taunt back at him. "Come now, Levy, you'll have to do better than that."

# CHAPTER 28:
# Levy

*HA*, Janus bellowed in his head. *He got you with your own taunt, lad.*

"Shut it," Levy muttered, livid. Quinn had never failed to be a thorn in his side at the worst times.

Time and time again Levy would better him in matches growing up. Yet every time, Quinn would always punctuate even his smallest victories with the perfect string of words to needle their way under Levy's skin.

They had been rivals to begin with. When Quinn first came to the Citadel, he had been enamored with Levy, following him around wherever he went. At the time Levy had wanted nothing to do with the boy the Masters called a monster.

As time went on, he began to grow more and more agitated. No matter where we went Quinn would follow, begging to fight. He was like a lost wolf pup. Eventually Levy had given in, pummeling the boy in the training yard.

Yet every day the boy came back, requesting another fight. It didn't matter how many times Levy beat him; he was there again the next day for another round. It had been after a solid few months of this beating that Levy noticed the change.

Quinn began moving faster, striking harder and thinking more critically. As the days went by, their matches became more and more even. What it had taken Levy years to learn, Quinn was picking up in months.

Then the fateful day came where Quinn had finally won his first match against him. After a swift kick to Levy's sword hand, Quinn had dropped in low, pushing the point of the practice sword into Levy's stomach with all his might.

Levy had felt the air fly out of his lungs as he fell to the ground. The next thing he knew, Quinn had been standing over him, a triumphant smile splitting his face from ear to ear. From then on out they had become fast friends, always challenging each other to be better.

The rivalry had been fun; that was, until their return from Hestia's realm. Seeing Quinn with power he not only had but didn't want infuriated Levy. Now, he wanted nothing more than to go back to those times where he could shove Quinn's face into the dirt and laugh. And they were coming soon.

*Snap out of it,* Janus barked. *He's coming again.*

Janus was right. With a quick step forward, Quinn flashed away, back into the realm of the mask. Levy wasn't exactly sure how the mask worked, but with half of Janus' essence within him, he could track his movements.

They appeared to him as a slim line of light, bouncing back and forth from point to point until Quinn emerged again. Even with that sight, he had to focus intently. The light moved incredibly fast, and if he was even a millisecond late in reacting the fight would be over.

*There,* Janus directed Levy's eyes to a spot partially behind him and in the air.

Sure enough, the light blinked to a stop and Quinn emerged; a shadowy wraith poised to strike. Levy brought his sword around in a wide swing, hoping to catch Quinn's blade and knock him back and off balance.

As their weapons clashed, lighting up the night, he felt a pressure in the air begin to grow. *He plans to use the momentum of your strike and fall back into the mask's realm. Stop him!*

Levy reached out and latched his hand around Quinn's ankle. With a mighty pull he turned his body, heaving Quinn over his shoulder and throwing him at the ground. He hit hard, trying to catch himself and failing.

Levy heard a loud crack and Quinn rolled to a stop just out of reach. He slowly got to his feet, panting, and holding a shoulder that was clearly dislocated. Unluckily for Levy, it hadn't been his sword arm. He sneered at Quinn, sending the man's earlier cockiness back at him full force.

"I hear you and Ashe split after the Citadel fell. What happened? Did she finally find out about that girl you let die? Does she know about your new girlfriend?" He asked, pointing toward Mallory.

Levy wasn't sure if it had been the verbal taunt that hit home, or the pain from his shoulder, but Quinn flinched.

"Really, Levy?" He was clearly in pain. "Taunting me with Ashe? Is that how far you've fallen? It wasn't so long ago that the three of us were inseparable. Now look at you, puppet to a god and killing the very humans you swore to protect."

Levy felt fire in his face. "How is it you still don't understand? These men were traitors. This fight isn't about saving the present. It's about building a better future. Look around you Quinn.

"Look at this very vault. The Masters have ancient artifacts of power hidden away all over this land of ours, and not once did they use them to help us win this war.

"They had the power of Athena at their very finger tips, and instead of using her to reach the tower, they used her to live in safety while underdefended villages all around the capital died daily. Meanwhile our forces on the front lines fought every day to give us a chance, waiting for the Masters to strike and save them from their never-ending battle.

"No, this world has become too corrupt. It is I who will breach the tower. It is I who will sit upon the throne, and it is I who will decide the future. With the Orb of Hades, I can summon an army that will cut through anything that stands against the salvation of humanity."

Quinn shook his head. "So, in order to change the future, you'll kill the soldiers currently fighting so that we can do just that. I was no fan of the Masters either, Levy; you know that.

"But you're currently no better than the very Masters you just condemned. In fact, Levy, you're worse. Because while the Masters may have been doing nothing, they did not go out and actively kill.

"You've become what you swore to destroy. You're Janus' puppet; his loyal lapdog doing whatever it is he asks. Going wherever he tells you to go.

"Did he lead you to this orb? I imagine he did. Do you truly think he'll allow you to sit on the throne Levy? If you do, you're not thinking. He's thrown a shiny thing in front of you and blinded you to the truth.

"If I had any inclination that there was any bit of the man I called my friend left in you, it's gone now. I don't like who you have become. But you know what? I think I pity you more than I hate you. You've become twisted by your lust for power."

"HA!" Levy spat, feeling rage at what his friend said building within him. "If that isn't the most hypocritical thing you have ever said. You want to talk about being blinded by power Quinn? Who put that mask in your hands?

"What right do you have to judge me when every day you rely on the power granted to you by Janus? We're the same, Quinn, whether you want to admit it or not."

Throughout his speech, the shadows around Quinn's body began to writhe and twist, enshrouding his body tightly.

*He's preparing for a powerful strike.* Janus spoke inside his mind. *If this hits us, we're dead. Hold out your hand and focus my essence into it until you begin to feel pressure, then release it all at once.*

Levy did as he was instructed, holding out his hand and aiming it at Quinn. With no warning, Quinn struck, blasting forward in a straight line toward Levy, leaving nothing but a shock wave and a spray of snow in his wake.

As he reached out a shadowy tendril, intending to spear Levy through the heart, Levy felt an immense pressure build in his hand. The pressure built until it felt as if all of the bones in his hand were going to shatter.

Then in one mighty push, the energy exploded out of him in a concentrated stream, blasting Quinn head on and sending him hurtling backwards into a tree. He hit with a loud crack, sending snow cascading down from the branches.

"Is he dead?" Levy asked Janus, staring at the still form on the ground.

*Unlikely,* he replied. *If you hit him with that while he had the mask off it would have splattered him. However, with how tightly he had the shadows wound about him, it's probable that they cushioned a lot of the impact. That being said, he shouldn't be getting up anytime soon.*

As if hearing him and wanting to prove him wrong, Quinn began to rise from the snow.

*That's one tough bastard.* Janus whistled in his head.

Levy held his hand out again, ready to deliver another blast should Quinn charge. Instead he just stood there, limbs hanging loosely in front of him, head cocked eerily to the side.

"Something's not right," Levy said to Janus. He could feel Janus' essence shiver within him.

*That's some cold energy pouring out of him.*

Quinn took a step away from him, toward the brown-haired girl he had arrived with. Though most of the undead had been vanquished, proven by the large mass of limbs at her feet, she still struggled against the remaining bodies attempting to tear her apart.

Pausing to look over his shoulder, a voice nothing like Quinn's rasped out from the mask.

*Another time, hero.*

With movements nearly too fast for Levy to see, he reached out and wrapped his hand around the girl's arm, before flashing away in the opposite direction of the vault.

"What just happened there?" Levy asked, feeling a cold creep down his spine that was unrelated to the winter air.

*Never mind that,* Janus deflected. *It's time to summon your army.*

Levy stared down at the Orb with a twinkle in his eye, relishing in the power thrumming through him.

"Let's get started then."

# CHAPTER 29: Quinn

Quinn awoke in the Realm of Night, groggy and dazed. As he began to sit up, the pressure of a hand on his shoulder pushed him back down.

"*Rest*," the voice of Chaos spoke in his mind. "*Or you will fall from the drakon.*"

For the first time since putting on the mask, Quinn could hear Chaos's voice clearly. There was no rasp, and no warble. It was strong and vibrant, and eerily similar to his own.

"What happened? he asked, looking down at the shadowed landscape beneath him. Mallory's face hovered over him, looking at him with clear concern.

"*You concentrated the shadows into a shell around you and struck at him like a spear. Had you hit; you would have no doubt impaled him. I have to admit, I have never seen the powers of this place used like that before. I was impressed.*"

"I take it by your words that I did not, in fact, hit him?"

"*Unfortunately, no. He summoned the power of the god within him, concentrating his essence and blasting it out at you. Had you not been wrapped in a cocoon of shadow it would have killed you. It seems you both narrowly escaped death this day."*

"If I was knocked unconscious, how is it I'm here? Did Mallory pull me back to the drakon? I can't imagine Levy would just allow us to leave."

Chaos shrunk back slightly, a war of thought fighting on his face. *That's funny,* he thought, *since when could he see Chaos' face so clearly?* The features were still not completely defined, but it was certain now that that Quinn could see the form of eyes, a nose and a mouth. He even had shadowy black hair falling from his head.

Finally, he said, "*I took control of your body while you were unconscious. It was the only way to ensure you escaped. I apologize.*"

Quinn's skin crawled at the admission. "You can do that?" he asked.

*"You are becoming one with the Realm of Night, as I warned would happen the more you accessed its power. The essence the goddess gave you erodes each time you use it, for a being of light such as her is not permitted in this realm. As she fades from within you, the darkness seeps in, merging with you. While it's risky to allow, it does come with certain benefits."*

Quinn concentrated on slowing his breathing. His heart rate had begun to pick up at Chaos' explanation. He had always known relying on the power of the mask was a risk, but after things had happened the way they had with Ashe and the Citadel, he stopped caring. Now however, the words he had heard from Hestia so long ago came unbidden, back to his mind.

*Be cautious of the creature within the mask.*

"What benefits might opening myself to this realm allow?" he asked, fishing for Chaos' intent.

*"As you assimilate with this realm, its powers become your own. In a fight, should you be in a pinch, you may call on me. I can infuse my essence, the essence of this realm, with your own for a brief period of time, as your friend did with Janus. It will add to your power, as well as to all of your physical traits."*

"And during that time, we will both have control of my body?" Quinn asked.

"*Yes and no,*" Chaos said. "*Should you will it, I will have access to control. During that time, I will be better able to use my power, making you even stronger. However, just merging with me for a brief amount of time will give you a boost. You are always in control. If you hand control over to me, and then change your mind, control will instantly be yours again so long as you have not lost yourself to this place."*

I see," Quinn said skeptically. "Thank you. You've given me much to think about. And thank you for getting Mallory and myself out safely. I owe you a debt of gratitude."

*"It was nothing. As I said, I exist to serve the master of this mask."*

Quinn reached up and waved his hand over his face, causing the mask to disappear. With a groan he sat up, feeling every single spot his body protested the movement. In the distance he could see Petram lit up among the cliffs of the Wastes.

"I thought you were dead." Mallory looked concerned. "When you pulled me back to the drakon, you spoke with such a raspy voice. And then as we took off you just laid down and stopped moving. I couldn't even feel you breathing. I was so sure…."

She cut off her words, shaking her head at the sky around them.

"Sorry." He patted her hand. "That last hit really took a lot out of me. I have to admit, I'm surprised to see you so worked up. I know a fight like that can tend to bring people closer but still, I'm just a stranger to you."

Mallory turned to him then, looking him in the eyes. "For the last three years, I have been Ashe's right hand. I've heard her talk in her sleep.

"I've seen her hold your crystal close while she stared off into the sky. Even the times she talked about you; I could see her feelings. I may not know a lot about you personally, but I know how you make Ashe feel. And anyone who can hold her attention for as long as you have is a good guy. She misses you Quinn."

Quinn looked away from her intense gaze toward the city he now called home.

"I betrayed her, Mallory. Not personally, but everything she believes in. I became the very thing she hated about our world. It wasn't me that left her. How can I just look her in the eye, after all of that, and expect her not to see a monster?"

Mallory shook her head. "I don't know, but you have to try. I've seen the way you look at those three kids you were with when I first arrived. I heard the speech you gave Levy during your fight. I see the way your heart hurts every time I mention Ashe's name. You may have made a mistake, but she still cares for you. Talk to her."

Quinn sighed as they touched down on the outskirts of Petram. "Thank you, Mallory. I will consider what you've told me. Now you should go back to her and warn her of what's to come. I'll provide you with enough provisions to make it back to her but travel quickly. We won't have much time."

"What will you do?" she asked, worried.

"I will do my best to rouse my people. Many of us have been mistreated by humans, but I will do what I can to make them see that this is the correct course of action. If we can successfully join forces against what Levy and Janus plan to unleash, we may begin to bridge the gaps between our people."

"And if they will not come?"

Quinn's eyes tightened, mentally debating his choices. Finally, he said, "If they will not come, then I will be their emissary. Tell Ashe to expect me."

Mallory's eyes lit up with a smile. "Aye, aye, sir!"

Quinn laughed. "I'm not your commanding officer."

"Not yet, you aren't." She winked back at him.

Shaking his head, Quinn smiled. "Come on, let's get you provisions for your trip back." Together, they entered the city.

# CHAPTER 30:
# Ashe

Ashe was sitting in her tent, circled by all of the top commanders. It had taken them a while to recover from the organized attack by the monsters. Their defenses had to be painstakingly rebuilt, many supplies had been lost or trampled, and they had far less hands to do it with.

She couldn't show it in front of the men, but she was beginning to worry. When she'd started pushing forward a few years ago, they had double the soldiers there were now. It was only natural that in war they would lose some along the way, but this last attack had decimated their numbers.

Now she wasn't sure if they would be able to reach the tower. She had sent a few messengers out to as many villages as she knew of, hoping they would be willing to send more men and women, but she wasn't hopeful of the outcome.

She didn't want to have to suspend the campaign, but she was beginning to not see another choice. They were so close to the tower now, but this was where the horde was thickest. She wondered if she could create another attack like the one she'd used in the last battle in order to open a lane for the soldiers to get through but decided that was a bad idea.

Mallory was the only one fast enough to take advantage, but she couldn't shake the feeling that the monsters wouldn't be the final hurdle. If Mallory made it through only to find Janus blocking her path, Ashe didn't like her chances.

Speaking of Mallory, it had been two weeks since she had sent her to find Quinn and had heard nothing from her in that time. Having grown impatient, she sent another up north to see what they could find at the vault, but they hadn't yet returned.

It had been a risk sending Mallory to the Wastes. The Abyssillians were wary of humans. She couldn't blame them, though. They had been outcast from human society and treated like outsiders just because of the gifts they were given through their bloodlines.

Making inroads with Quinn's people was one of the things she hoped to accomplish after this war, were she around to do so. She had seen firsthand the way Quinn had been treated by the people of Stormhaven. Even as a boy, when all he did was smile and show friendship, he was ostracized and spat on for what he was. It was one of the things that had pushed her to grow close with him. He had been desperate for a friend.

"All I'm saying," a gruff voice snapped her from her thoughts, "Is that at this point, we don't have enough men to push forward. We're better off pulling back and waiting for more troops."

Lend was a young man, recently promoted to the inner circle. He was eager to prove himself and liked to make his thoughts known in every discussion, whether it be about the war or about how the meat was seasoned for that night's dinner.

"There is no option for retreat," She explained, pointing at the map spread out upon the table. "If we move back from this location, the horde will move back in, and we may as well be starting over from the beginning."

"Is that so bad," Lend replied. "We could view this as a test run. We saw how far we made it, and we will know what worked and what didn't. In a few years' time, when we have regrouped and restocked, we can use this attempt as a road map and reach this spot much faster."

"HA!" The grizzled voice of Bartimaeus rang out. Old Bart had been the commanding officer when Ashe had first arrived on the scene. He was as much a veteran as a warrior can be, and half mad at this point in his life, Ashe suspected.

But he was as good a soldier as they came, and Ashe was happy to have his mind and his skills on their side. "I think the boy is scared! Wants to retreat to live another day!"

Red crept into Lend's face. He was constantly being provoked by the older soldiers. While he was a good fighter, his ego was large and the veterans in her group didn't take well to it.

"I'm not scared, old man. I just don't see a way forward from here. Moving forward will be difficult and staying here will get us killed. We do not have the supplies, nor the troops for continuous attacks on a stationary camp."

"And now we get to the point," Ashe interjected before the argument could persist. "Lend is absolutely right." All eyes turned to her.

"We cannot stay here. We will not survive another organized attack by the monsters. However, we cannot fall back either. We are on a time limit, my friends. Janus plans to make his move for the tower soon.

"If we fall back and allow him access, we have lost just the same as if we all die to the monsters around it. It will be difficult, and we may not succeed, but our only option is forward. We have fought long and hard, and now, one way or another, the end is in sight. The next few weeks will determine the outcome. Stay a little longer and see your duty to its end."

The tent was silent. All eyes stared back at her; determination mixed with fear on all of their faces. Finally, a loud "AYE!" burst from old Bart's mouth. Tentative smiles turned into raucous cheers. Ashe smiled back at the officers, proud of the men and women she fought alongside.

"Alright then," she began. "Let's break and start-"

There was a commotion outside the tent before the flap flew open. At once, all of the officers were on their feet, swords in hand. Ashe sat up straight, eyes wide, staring at the girl panting madly before her with hands up in a placating gesture.

"At ease," she commanded. "Mallory, it's good to see you. I had begun to fear the worst. Report."

"He still loves you!" She was half out of breath yet. All eyes in the room turned to Ashe, a mixture of confusion and amusement on their faces.

"Mallory," Ashe said, fighting the red from taking her face. "I meant report about the mission."

"Oh! Right. Sorry. We failed completely."

"Come again?" Ashe asked. She dismissed all but Bartimaeus so that they could speak in private, prompting a sullen look from Lend.

They all seemed very interested in who this man who loved her was, and even more interested in this mission they'd known nothing about. After leaving the tent in a grumble, Ashe poured Mallory some water. "Tell me everything."

"I found Quinn in a tavern in Petram like you said I would. Well, found him isn't exactly right. I was captured at the gates and they brought me to him, but same difference, really."

"You allowed yourself to be captured?" Ashe asked, raising an eyebrow. "I thought I told you to be careful."

"No, no, no, it's fine! They were perfectly friendly. They escorted me to him like true gentlemen. Speaking of gentlemen by the way, I can see what you like about him."

"Mallory," Ashe chided, getting her back on track.

"Right," she said. "So, I found Quinn in this tavern with a bunch of kids he's been training. Adorable, really. I told him about your request, and when I mentioned your name his eyes lit right up. I knew he was hooked."

Ashe sighed. Mallory was an incredible soldier, but she was still so young. On the battlefield she was as deadly as they come, but off of it she was just a young woman, eager to enjoy the non-violent parts of life. Ashe couldn't deny however, that at the mention of Quinn's interest her heart had begun to beat faster.

"So, then I get introduced to this drakon named Marilyn."

"Pardon?" Ashe asked, eyebrow climbing to the top of her head.

"Long story," she replied, continuing. "But yeah, so Quinn and I rode Marilyn the drakon to the northern vaults like you asked.

When we got there, we found a bunch of dead scouts and guards. It was grisly. Right as we landed, your other friend…."

"Not my friend," Ashe interjected.

"Right, so your other not your friend came running out of the vault with Cerberus hot on his trail. I thought we were going to have to fight it but you're not your friend did some cool flippy stuff and killed it. Also, quick side note here, but it's a shame that other guy isn't on our side because he is *fine*, Ashe."

Ashe knew better than to stop Mallory when she got excited like this. The words were coming a mile a minute, and her voice was steadily reaching a crescendo, indicating the climax was on its way.

"So, then he put this orb into the pommel of his sword, and it glowed purple and a bunch of dead dudes popped up from the ground and fought me.

"When I looked up, Quinn and Levy were fighting really fast. It was intense. They were both shrouded in this energy and it was hard for me to track, but eventually it looked like Quinn was going to win.

"Right before he killed him though some energy shot out of Levy, rocketing Quinn into a tree. He struggled to his feet, though he barely looked conscious, and we retreated."

When she finally finished her story, and Ashe had time to process the important parts of what she had told her, a pit had begun to settle in her stomach. "You said he attached an orb to his sword? What did this orb look like?"

"It glowed purple and had a bunch of white, wispy things floating around inside. He called it the Orb of Hades."

Ashe's eyes widened. "That's not good. That is really, really not good."

"Yeah, Quinn seemed pretty spooked by it too. He said to come and tell you right away to prepare because Levy would be marching with an army soon. He plans to wipe out both us and the monsters before claiming the throne."

"And what of Quinn?" she asked, trying not to give away the quiver in her voice.

Apparently, it didn't work, because Mallory gave her a knowing smile. "He said he would try and rally his people, though he wasn't sure they would listen. Either way, he plans to come here and fight."

Hope blossomed in Ashe's heart. The army was not prepared to fight Levy, Janus and another army, let alone the monsters still just in front of them. Pushing forward without help would be a suicide mission.

But with help from the Abyssillians, they stood a chance. With new determination, Ashe stood. "Spread the word that a battle is coming. Prepare our defenses and have the captains meet back here in an hour.

"Warn the soldiers ahead of time that the Abyssillians may be coming, and they are to be treated as allies, not enemies. They will be our best hope of survival."

"Aye, ma'am!" Mallory replied, far too gleeful for the situation they were in.

Mallory left the tent and Ashe sat, clutching Quinn's pendant. It had been three long years since they had least seen each other. Three years since things had ended the way they had.

Not a day went by where she didn't think back to that day and wonder if she'd made the right decision. And now he was coming back to her. A single tear made its way down her face as relief washed over her.

For the first time in a long time, she felt hope. Apprehension was prevalent within her as well. He'd been abandoned all of his life, and she had done the same. There was also the mask to consider.

She doubted he had gotten rid of it and she feared what emotions it would bring up in her. But more than anything, she was just excited to see her closest friend again.

"Don't go weepy on us now," Bartimaeus said, his voice soothing and supportive. "Whether this boy of yours shows or not, you are still our best hope at winning this. We all need you in top shape."

"Thanks, Bart." She said. "Your guidance these last few years has been invaluable."

With a deep breath, she gathered herself. It wouldn't do to sit here and cry while the army prepared for battle. With renewed vigor, she and Bartimaeus left her tent to see to the defenses. They had a war to win.

# CHAPTER 31: Levy

Levy relished the mayhem of battle. All around him, hordes of undead and monster alike clashed, littering the open fields surrounding the base of the volcano with broken bodies and monstrous limbs.

Swathes of land were carved from the ground as volcanic soil flew through the air, leaving craters the size of small meteors dotting the landscape. The shrill cries of the monsters battled the piercing wails of the undead, creating a horrific symphony befitting of the slaughter that was occurring.

For two weeks, Levy had marched endlessly, travelling south from the fortress where the Masters horded their godly treasures. Though he was tempted to explore further into the vaults after Quinn had run away, the likelihood of traps was great, and Levy saw no reason to risk it.

Once he took the throne, he would have no need of the other artifacts the vault contained. It was only a matter of time now. Along the way, he experimented with the orb, pushing more and more essence through it.

He found quickly that he could only rely on its power at night. When the sun rose in the sky, the dead would crumble to dust. That was fine, though. With an army as large as the orb provided, he wouldn't need much time.

The thick Mageia trees that made up the snowy northern forests began to thin out as he travelled further south, making way for the dark oaks that were numerous around the clearing surrounding the volcano in which the tower sat.

The closer he travelled, the louder the hordes that encircled it became. He knew that a few leagues beyond the opposite side of the clearing, deeper within the forest, the human army camped; slowly cutting their way through what remained of the monsters drawn by the tower's magic. They were likely preparing for what would be their final strike.

Levy smiled inwardly. *They have no idea what's coming.*

*Aye,* Janus chimed in. *But think about that later. Focus on the fight to come first.*

*Once the monsters are cleared, the tower will finally be mine.* He could already taste his triumph.

*Ours,* Janus interjected. *But that isn't quite true. You need the girl to open the doors.*

"Why would I need Ashe to open the doors?" Levy asked. He was getting annoyed at the amount of secrets Janus seemed to still possess. It further eroded his trust every time he was conveniently fed new information.

*Don't worry about that for now. Just clear out the rabble first. We can discuss it another time.*

*You're Janus' puppet, his loyal lapdog.*

Quinn's words had been eating at him the entire trip south. From the moment Levy had allowed the Citadel to be destroyed in return for Janus' power, he thought he was finally in control of his own fate.

Yet now, he continued to feel as though a power above him was stringing him along. It was as if no matter what choices he made, he ended up in the same position. It was something he decided he would need to think on; but first, he had a battle to win.

He picked a slightly elevated part of the forest overlooking the clearing. From here he could see the writhing masses below.

Cyclopes to drakons and everything between gathered at the base of the volcano, clawing over one another for a chance to move closer to the tower.

As the sun sank below the horizon, and the pale reds and purples of the sky transitioned to a deep midnight blue, Levy reached with his essence toward the orb nestled in the mouth of the wolf head pommel. Infusing it with his essence had become simple, and the more he had practiced with it along the way, the more he was able to feed it, fueling an obscenely large amount of the dead to rise.

They gathered in thick masses; blank sockets and pale, milky white eyes reflecting the moonlight back at him from amongst the trees for as far as he could see.

Growing up at the Citadel, he had always imagined this; the moment when he led his army into their final battle against the monsters that kept humanity from reaching the tower.

Though he never imagined it would be an army of the dead, he was still filled with adrenaline. There was absolutely no chance he would sit this battle out. After tonight, he would only have one more obstacle keeping him from his throne.

He looked down to the thrashing masses below and raised his sword high into the night. Channeling a small burst of essence into the orb, he dropped the point of his blade, commanding his army forward. The dead surged past him, tearing down from the incline at the unsuspecting monsters below. A cacophony of roars filled the air as the two groups made contact.

*Do you hear this Ashe? It's coming for you next.*

Levy rolled his shoulders, stretching the muscles in his back. He had held back long enough. It was time to join the fray.

Levy walked through the battlefield, taking in the sights as his army ripped the monsters to shreds. He watched with glee as a number of undead scaled a particularly large cyclops, jamming their bony fingers into its eye.

To his right a large group of them had a hydra pinned to the ground, stabbing gleefully with their crude shards of weaponry. Any time he felt as though the number of dead dwindled too far opposite his favor, he simply pumped more essence into the orb and fresh corpses would rise.

It was unfortunate most monsters were too stupid to form thoughts outside of their basic bestial instincts. He would have loved to see the fear in their eyes as they realized this battle was hopeless.

A corpse smashed into the ground a few meters in front of him, showering a wave of dirt into the air. Five centaurs came thundering through the spray, straight in his direction.

Wild, curly black hair hung low over their eyes. Their coats were matted with grime and ichor. With feral, beady eyes, they stared at Levy's blade, as if sensing the dreadful energy it gave off. Levy beamed a wicked smile, itching for the fight.

"You want some boys? Come get it!"

With a chorus of bellows, they charged him; crude clubs raised high in the air. As the first came within reach, Levy stepped aside, digging the point of his blade into the beast's body; dragging it along its flank as it ran by.

As he reached the end, he planted his foot in the dirt, whirling around and taking the next centaur's head off. The remaining three pulled up, wary of following in the steps of their brethren. Not wanting to give them a chance to regroup, he pointed at the middle one, letting loose a concussive blast that sent it flying into a group of undead, where it was promptly torn apart. As the other two took a step toward him, a large thump shook the ground.

Two colossal blue hands reached out from behind them and grabbed each centaur by the neck, lifting them into the air and hurling them into the distance.

Stepping out of the darkness was the scariest Gegenees, Levy had ever seen. It was at least ten feet tall with cobalt blue skin. Six arms, lined with hefty muscle, protruded from its torso; four of which were brandishing chipped, stone axes.

A ratty braid of hair started at a single point on the back of his skull, winding its way down its back. Levy recalled from his history lessons that the Gegenees were a race of giants thought to have been wiped out by the ancient hero Jason. *Apparently, he missed one.*

*Careful with this one, lad. The Gegenees are no pushovers.*

With a battle cry that Levy felt down to his bones, it charged forward; swiping down with two axes. Levy jumped backward, feeling the air of the axes ruffle his hair. Just as he landed, the

Gegenees swung the other two, attempting to cut Levy in half.

With hardly any time to react, Levy raised his blade, blocking the blow but getting knocked off his feet in the process. He hit the ground hard, feeling the air propel from his lungs. Panicking, he gave a command through the orb; watching as the undead in his vicinity stopped what they were doing and began to swarm the giant.

Though they succeeded in slowing it down, the Gegenees' arms went into overdrive, battering the corpses into dust as quickly as they reached it.

While it was distracted, Levy got back onto a knee, holding his wrist in one hand and gathering Janus' essence into his hand. As he felt the pressure begin to build Janus spoke in his mind.

*You're going to need more than that. Gegenees are resilient. It took Jason and Heracles together to defeat them. My essence may knock it off balance, but it will not harm it.*

Levy snorted. "Well, unless you have any other suggestions, this is all I have."

*Try to access the other gift you were given," Janus suggested. "You still have Hestia's essence inside of you.*

He shook his head, searching for the piece of Hestia within.

"I haven't ever been able to access that essence. When I reach for it, it runs away."

*Well then chase it boy. It's either that or get pounded like a stake into the dirt.*

As was normal, he located the warmth of her essence. Yet as he reached for it, it flittered just out of his reach, as if taunting him. Growing frustrated he tried again, lunging with his mind and attempting to force it to the surface.

Again, it danced just out of his grasp. The ground around him thudded, indicating the Gegenees had dispatched of the irritants and was making its way toward him.

*It's now or never.*

"I'm trying." Levy grit his teeth.

The thudding increased in intensity.

*Lad....*

"TRYING," He yelled, panic slipping into his voice.

*Come on, stupid essence.*

He grasped at it desperately. The pressure of Janus' essence in his hand was intense. Between that pain, the voice in his head yelling about his impending doom, and the increasingly thunderous footsteps getting nearer; Levy was struggling to stay focused.

*Please.* He thought, feeling foolish for thinking the swirling essence might understand him. *Aren't I one of your heroes?*

*"LAD!"* Janus yelled in his mind.

The Gegenees was standing directly over him; all four axes raised in the air. He had no choice left. Raising his hand, he released all of the pressure.

A powerful concussion shot forth, aimed directly at the giant's head. As the blast streamed from his palm, he felt a fiery warmth surge through his body, turning the concussive blast from its signature, silvery hue, to a vibrant gold.

As it hit the giant square in the jaw, the monster's head exploded in a shower of brain matter and ichor. Levy sat back in stunned silence; feeling all energy drain from his body.

*Nicely done,"* Janus said with a mix of joy and relief. *Now get yourself out of here and let the dead finish this off.*

Levy complied; limping back into the trees where he was free to safely regain his energy.

The sun rose at dawn to a peaceful silence. It hadn't taken long for the army of the dead to tear through the remaining monsters. Levy walked the battleground, surveying the carnage. The remains of corpses and monsters alike were strewn across the now open field.

With a satisfied smile, he looked up to the tower peeking over the top of the volcano. After recovering a bit of energy, he had tried to access the essence Hestia had given him again, but it was back to keeping just outside of his grasp.

*We're almost there, lad, Janus said, noticing where Levy was looking. "Just one more fight and the throne is ours. Soon, the gods will walk this realm again.*

"Yeah," Levy said. "About that. If I'm going to claim the throne for you, it's time you let me in on the rest of your plans. You can't keep deflecting every time I ask a question."

*Sorry, but that wasn't part of the deal,* Janus replied. *You just keep doing your part and everything will fall into place.*

*Lapdog.* He could picture a mocking smile on Quinn's face. *He throws a shiny thing in front of you and blinds you to the truth.*

"No," Levy said.

*Pardon?*

"We aren't doing things like that any longer. If you are going to keep me blind, then from now on we do things my way."

He focused on Janus' essence within him, pinpointing its match.

*This is a bad idea, lad. I understand what you're saying, but you don't know what you're getting into.*

"If you won't let me in on the full plan, then I already don't know." He rebutted. "Now let me concentrate. It's time we had a chat with your other half."

# CHAPTER 32: Quinn

After Quinn had seen Mallory off, he turned and made his way back through the city. The streets were quiet, with not a soul in sight. He made his way toward the center of town, thinking about what he might say to his people to bring them on board.

He would certainly not force any of them to partake in this war. They all had some sort of bad experience with discrimination from the humans. Many had lost family members to their prejudices, himself included.

If they chose to stay out in the Wastes, hiding from the dangers of the world outside, that was their choice to make. Though he had no doubt that one way or another, the war would come to them eventually.

Turning a corner, he began to hear a dull roar coming the direction he intended to go. Curious, he pressed on, closer to the noise. As he turned the corner, he stopped in his tracks, stunned. Every Abyssillian in the city stood there, gathered together.

When they saw him, the noise died suddenly. They stared at Quinn with a mixture of emotions. Some showed fear openly, while others showed determination. Others still showed a mix of confusion and excitement. As Quinn made his way to the front of the masses, Sen hopped down from the platform above.

"What's going on?" Quinn asked the boy.

"Suppose I'd better be asking you the same thing, boss. I couldn't help but overhear your conversation with the cutie that came to see you," he pointed to his abnormally large ears. "Sounds to me like you're going off to war. Figured I'd better gather the people to save you some time."

Quinn couldn't help but to laugh. Here he had been wondering how he was going to convince his people to go support a war they had no interest in, and this young man had gone out and gathered them all in one place for him.

"Good work Sen," he smiled. Sen's face lit up with the praise.

"For what it's worth, you have our support. Nes, Andra and I."

Quinn smiled again, grateful for their loyalty. "Make 'em listen, boss," Sen said, hopping back up on the platform and joining his comrades.

Collecting his thoughts, Quinn climbed up onto the platform. All eyes turned to him immediately, apprehension thick in the air.

"For many generations, our people have been forced to live a life of exile, isolated in this desolate landscape.

"While the humans built towns and cities on prosperous land, we scraped by, adapting to the climate of our new home. For years I lived among them; looked down upon for my heritage and despised for the color of my eyes.

"And yet, I stand before you today asking for your help with saving them. As we speak, an army of the dead is marching toward their army; led by a god who lusts for the power of the throne. Without our intervention, there will be nothing left."

"Why should we help them?" An older man screamed out from the crowd. His eyes were sunken behind heavy wrinkles. "They vilify us. They treat us as monsters and outcasts. What reason do we have to help them, when they have done nothing to help us? The gods granted us our gifts. I see no reason to help the humans lock them away."

Quinn knew this would be difficult. One could not easily wipe away centuries of discrimination and mistrust with words alone.

"I know the humans have given us no reason to help them. But do not blame the many for the crimes of the few. For every human who wishes us ill, there are ten more, ignorant to our plight.

They believe only what they are taught from the older generation. Last I checked, ignorance is not a crime. We must save them so that we may begin to educate and heal the wounds between our peoples.

"If you do not wish to do it for them, then do it for your loved ones. Like it or not, this war will reach us eventually. We cannot fight that threat alone."

"The gods will protect us, as they always have!" Another voice yelled out from the crowd.

Quinn could not pinpoint it, but he could tell he was losing them. They had spent too long isolated from civilization and did not see the threat for what it was.

"OI!" A voice yelled out from beside him.

Nes had stepped forward and looked out to the crowd, a scowl on his face. "In what world do you see the gods protecting us? Now I know I may be young compared to the lot of you, but even I can see the truth for what it is.

"The gods didn't give us our gifts. We got our gifts because our ancient ancestors got down and dirty with some snakes. It's no wonder the humans are skeeved out by us. It's a miracle we don't have gills!"

"That's fish, you idiot," Sen called from behind him.

"Whatever," Nes continued. "The point is it wasn't the gods that gave us these gifts. And when the humans pushed us out into these wastes, where food and water was scarce, and trade even scarcer, did the gods descend from their places of power and offer us the necessities we needed to get by?

"No. They abandoned us to our fate. At least there are humans out there who try to help. Not a great many, that's true. But there is sympathy out there for us. Since Quinn has returned to us, he has brought us all that we need to not only survive but survive comfortably.

"I think we owe him a debt for that. Change will not happen if we don't force the issue. If we let this god take the throne, we have no future. So, stay here if you want, and hide beneath this pile of rocks we call a city, but I am going with Quinn to fight.

"It's up to us to repair the bridge humanity burnt down. Let's show them we're more than the monsters they believe us to be."

As Nes finished, he stepped back to his friends, not taking his eyes off the people below. Quinn was stunned. The loyalty he had instilled in these three was touching.

As he looked out over the crowd, he saw the change in demeanor start slowly, but rapidly erupt. The initial apprehension had gone, and in its place was an outcry of determination. In the course of only a few moments, a nineteen-year-old boy had swayed his people to his cause. He smiled inwardly.

As the roar of the crowd died down, Quinn addressed them all again. "Thank you, my friends, for your support. This battle will not be easy, and many will die. But we will do this, not for ourselves, but for our futures. All who wish to join the fight are welcome. Take tonight to pack provisions and say goodbye to the loved ones you'll be leaving behind. In the morning, we march."

As he turned away from the crowd, nodding to the three young warriors at his back, he looked off toward the distant horizon, hoping he was not too late.

*Hold on Ashe, I'm coming.*

# CHAPTER 33: Levy

It wasn't hard for Levy to make his way into Janus' realm anymore thanks to the other half of him he now held inside.

*I'm warnin' ye lad, this is a mistake. Don't let the boy get under your skin like this.*

"Are you going to stop me?" he asked the bearded Janus.

*I couldn't if I wanted to. I'm just warning you against this. The other side o' me is ruthless. He will not take well to what you have planned, and you may see the end of your crusade if you go through with it.*

"But you'll help me if I request it?"

*Aye,* he said, resigned. *It is part of the agreement that fool made without me. I will help you complete whatever it is you set out to do, so long as you claim us the tower.*

Levy smiled a toothy grin. "Good. Then prepare yourself."

He opened a doorway and stepped into Janus' realm, popping out into a familiar silver room. Janus stood with his back turned, watching the pictures fly by on the wall.

"You shouldn't be here." Janus didn't turn around. "You have the orb, which means you have your army. Our plan is ready to be set in motion. The longer you delay, the longer our enemies have time to gather allies."

"All in good time Janus," Levy said softly, walking closer to the god. "But before that, I need to take what is rightfully mine."

Janus turned then, a cold fury in his eyes. "My, my, have we gotten brave. I suggest you reconsider this. I am a god. What you are hoping will not come to pass."

Levy smiled at him, tensing his muscles. "No, you are half a god. Whereas I have half of your power, as well as some of Hestia's. Tell me Janus, do you think you can so easily beat me, despite having less godly essence within you?"

For the first time since he had wormed his way into Levy's life, he saw panic in Janus' face. "I have created a monster." He laughed to himself.

"No," Levy responded. "You have created a god. Now will you come willingly, or do we have to do this the hard way?"

Janus met his eyes then, defiance written on his face. He raised his hand and shot a concussion of energy directly at Levy's chest. Levy reacted quickly, raising his own hand and deflected the energy with a blast of his own.

"Hard way it is then." He slid the sword Janus had given him from the scabbard on his back and held it in front of him. The silver of the blade matched the silver of the room perfectly. Without hesitation he leapt forward, stabbing at Janus. The god spun deftly to the side, unleashing another bolt of force at Levy, taking him off his feet.

"You may have more essence in you, but you still lack experience. I have walked this earth for millennia. You are nothing but an upstart pup."

"Any advice here?" Levy asked the Janus residing within him.

*Don't die?* He responded sarcastically. *Look kid, he's right. You are far inferior to him in actual fighting experience. I don't see a way for you to win this.*

*I warned you not to do it. We see all choices on the walls of this room. He undoubtedly saw this decision as a possibility and was ready for it.*

*The best chance you have is to catch him by surprise and stick him with that blade. It's made from the same energy that makes up this realm. But he is aware of that as well, so I would not expect it to be easy.*

Another blast hit him square in the chest, launching Levy back into the wall. Had he been fully mortal, it would have done a lot more than just daze him.

"Face it, kid, it's over," Janus taunted. "You had your chance at glory, and you blew it. I gave you everything, and you have thrown it back in my face. But it matters not. Now that you have procured the orb for me, I can kill you and take my essence back, along with the essence of that traitor of a goddess'.

"It should provide me just enough energy to walk your mortal realm for an extended period of time and claim the throne for myself."

Levy shook his head clear. This had not gone according to plan, but he wasn't ready to give up just yet. He knew exactly what he needed to do to claim the throne, he just needed the power to do it.

With all of Janus' essence, there was nothing Quinn or Ashe could do to stop him. And with Janus out of the way, he would be in complete control. He raised his palm at the slowly approaching Janus. As it stood, with half of Janus within him, their concussion blasts were likely to be equal, even at full strength.

*But it isn't only his essence within you,* the bearded Janus whispered in his mind. *Try to access Hestia's power again. It's your only chance at victory.*

Levy focused the energy into his palm. First came the power of Janus, feeling the familiar pressure tighten. Janus scoffed at him, moving ever closer.

"Please," he sneered. "Your power and mine are matched. No matter what you throw at me I can deflect. This fight is over Mr. Sylva. Our contract, null and void. Beg for mercy and I may yet let you live."

Levy ignored him, continuing to focus on the energy pouring into his palm. As he began to feel the painful pressure build, he closed his eyes and searched deep down within him. Again, he felt Hestia's essence tickling the edge of his consciousness.

*I'm going to die if you don't help me.* He no longer felt foolish talking to the essence. This was life or death, and he was willing to do whatever it took to survive this encounter.

*Do you not have a plan for me? Why give me your essence only to hide when I need it most?*

He thought he felt a brief moment of hesitancy before the warmth of her essence flooded into him. Pulling on it as hard as he could, he yanked it to the surface of his mind, mixing it with Janus' power.

As Janus came within steps of him, he opened his eyes and let out a mighty roar, pushing the energy forward and unleashing a torrent of golden force at the god. Janus' eyes bulged from his head as the blast knocked into him, violently sending him crashing across the room into the opposite wall. The god's body crumpled onto the floor, twitching.

*Well, I'd say you found it. That sure got the job done*, Janus sounded stunned in his mind.

With shaky steps, Levy made his way over to the fallen form of the god. Wasting no time, he pointed the sword at him, and plunged it into his chest, siphoning the essence from the immortal into himself.

An intense wave of powerful energy washed through him, sharpening his senses. His body felt like it was going to explode from the amount of power that was coursing through him. It was like the adrenaline he felt after a sparring match, only magnified tenfold.

As it finally settled, he couldn't stop a smile from settling upon his face.

*Well, crap.* A begrudging voice sounded in his head. *Guess you're running the show now.*

With a newfound confidence, Levy opened a portal back to the mortal realm; emerging back within the forest between the clearing leading to the volcano and the human army. The tower stood tall in the background, watching his every move.

Holding his sword in the air, he pumped his new energy into the blade, lighting the Orb of Hades. All around him, corpses rose from the forest floor, clawing their way out of the leaf litter and dirt. Masses of putrid, decaying limbs surrounded him, awaiting their orders. With eyes set on the tower, he addressed his army of the dead.

"And so, the end begins."

# CHAPTER 34: Ashe

Tensions were running high throughout the camp. Ashe had a heated war council after Mallory had delivered the news of the intended attack. All of the commanders, save Bartimaeus, counseled pulling back and retreating.

In their eyes, there was no way they had the manpower to face down the army of the dead the scouts said were marching on them. It was likely they were right, but Ashe knew that if she pulled back now, the war was lost.

Levy and Janus, without any opposition, would easily reach the tower, casting the world into another millennia of darkness and pain. No, pulling back was not an option.

"This is what you don't seem to understand," Ashe had said to her commanders that afternoon. "You heard the battle that took place last night. You read the reports from our scouts who went to find out more.

"We don't have two more battles to win, we only have the one. Levy's army eliminated the monsters in our way. If we win this fight, we have a straight shot to the tower."

She didn't know what Levy was up to, but it was the truth. He had decimated what remained of the monsters blocking their way. If what Mallory said was true, he intended to wipe them all out before reaching the tower. If they won this fight, they still had a chance. Everything hinged on the battle that was to come.

The sun sank in the western sky, painting the world crimson. It cast a beautiful red light upon the land around them. A gentle breeze blew through the air, stirring the loose dirt around her feet into action. The smell of forest and campfire mingled together, wrapping Ashe in a warm embrace.

To any unseasoned warrior, this would calm the nerves; a reminder that not all is bad in the world. But Ashe knew better. This was the calm before the storm. They stood in the eye of the hurricane, and all they could do was wait until the chaos of the storm enveloped them again.

Ashe knew, logically, they didn't have the numbers to win this fight. The troops that remained were all battle-hardened, seasoned soldiers who had been through Hades and come out the other side. But even then, what chance did they stand against a god and a horde of mindless soldiers?

She had hoped Quinn would arrive with an army, but he had yet to show up at all.

"He'll be here." Mallory's calming voice came from behind her. He gave me his word he would come. I believe him."

Ashe smiled sadly at her friend as she stepped up beside her, staring off at the tower no longer very far in the distance. "I just can't help but think about how things ended." A far off look in her eyes.

"If I hadn't lost faith in him when he told me about his trials, he would have stayed with me. Together, we may have already reached the tower and ended this war. I can't help but wonder if my fear has cost us lives, as well as our only chance at victory."

"This army does not fight with yesterday's orders," Mallory replied.

Ashe looked at her, eyebrow quirked. "Was that supposed to be some profound words of wisdom?"

Mallory smiled, shaking her head. "I never was one for the whole 'encouraging speech' thing. All I'm trying to say is, don't get stuck in the past.

"Every decision you have made up until this point has brought us to where we are. Three years ago, this army was stagnant. We made no progress in this war, and would not have, had you not come along.

"You have led us here now, and it's like we've reached this cliff. On this side we stand, facing what seems like insurmountable odds. Across the abyss stands the tower, and within it the throne that will change the world for the better.

"Without you at your best, we cannot span that darkness. Maybe things would be better had you and Quinn not split. Maybe they wouldn't. Fate works in ways nobody understands. But none of that matters now. Keep your mind here in the present, so that you can lead us into the future."

Ashe gave a genuine smile then, filled with the warmth her friend had instilled within her. She was right. She had followed her ideals, and she had to believe it had been the right thing to do.

Whether Quinn arrived or not, the war had reached its climax. She had led the army this far and had only one more obstacle to overcome. With renewed vigor, she turned to the camp and yelled, "BART!"

"Aye, ma'am!" The grizzled man appeared next to her.

"Get the men ready and in position. Tonight, we send a message to the gods that their time in this world is over. We have a war to win!"

He responded with a wicked smile. "AYE MA'AM!"

Ashe turned back to the tower; eyes hard with determination. *Come at me, Levy. We're ready.*

# CHAPTER 35:
# Levy

The full moon bathed the world in its silvery hue. Levy stood upon a plateau, looking at the campfires that dotted distance like little fireflies, flickering between the trees. Behind him stood the entrance to the volcano, and within it the tower.

From here he could just see the peak of the tower rising out from the crater. The monsters had posed little threat to his army. How could they, when all Levy had to do was pump some essence into the orb and replenish what he had lost.

This war was all but won. But claiming that victory now wasn't good enough. No, the tower could wait. Come morning it would still be there. First, he had to wipe out his opposition. With Janus' essence now firmly ensconced within him, he could feel Ashe's presence.

*She has grown quite powerful*, Janus spoke within his mind.

"I'm a god now," He replied, bitterly. "She will not be able to stand up to my might."

*You have all of my essence within you, but that does not make you a god. You are still just a mortal man who possesses an enormous amount of power. A sword will still sever, and fire will still burn.*

Levy shook his head. "It doesn't matter. She doesn't have the energy to defeat me. Her fate is sealed. Come morning her army will be decimated, and she will be brought to her knees."

*You had better hope that happens before morning. You know the orb's power. But remember, do not kill her. You need her alive.*

Levy narrowed his eyes. "I will do my best, but if push comes to shove, there is always another. Now enough of this."

He stepped forward, raising his sword high into the air. The purple haze of the orb swirled out, pulsing and wrapping around him in response to the energy he poured into it, before sinking into the ground.

Sweat lined his brow as his energy was leeched away. Behind him, more desiccated bodies rose from the earth, clawing their way to the surface, joining his already vast army. The corpses stood silent save the ominous creaking their bodies gave off as bone scraped against bone. Panting, Levy lowered his blade, pointing it at the fires in the distance.

*Do it,* both Janus' said in unison, excitement dripping from their voices.

Levy smiled. "Go."

With that one command, the army of the dead surged to life, groaning and screeching as they sprinted toward the lights scattered amongst the trees.

# CHAPTER 36:
# Ashe

The silence of the night was deafening, save for the crackle of the fires set up around the perimeter. Ashe had felt the presence of Levy's immense power hours ago and prepared the troops accordingly. She didn't know when the attack would come, only that it would come tonight.

The soldiers stood around her, swords at the ready. A nervous tension filled the air, knowing that for many of them, this would be their final night. But instilled in each of them was a sense of duty.

They knew the future they fought for. It was a future of prosperity, not just for their families but for all of mankind. If it meant laying down their lives, they would gladly do it to accomplish that dream. Ashe could not have asked for a more loyal group of men and women to fight at her side.

Mallory stood beside her; long brown hair tied back into a braid. A fierce determination lit her eyes. Ever since she had returned from her mission north, she had been muttering about paying Levy back. Though she had been successful at gathering critical intel, she had failed overall at stopping him from stealing the treasure he had sought. She took that rather personally.

"It won't be long now," Ashe said, staring off into the trees in the direction she felt Levy. They took position around the inner perimeter of the camp, keeping enough distance from the tree line to see what shambled out from between them.

"Before this begins, let me just say, thank you for your valuable friendship these last three years. I don't think I would have succeeded without you encouraging me along the way."

Mallory chuckled. "Ain't that the truth. You were a sobbing wreck when you first came to us. 'Oh, my precious Quinn,'" she mocked.

Ashe smiled.

"But for real," Mallory sobered up. "You don't need to thank me. You don't even need to thank the soldiers. You've been a guiding light for us. Without you, we had no hope of making it as far as we have. So, save the mushy stuff for after we've won."

"Aye, ma'am," Ashe saluted smiling. "I…."

A surge of power unlike anything she had ever felt before ripped through the trees, frying her senses and nearly taking her off of her feet. "Brace yourselves," she called out. "They're coming!"

An otherworldly wail rent the air, echoing off the trees. The ground shook as the pounding of feet encroached swiftly upon their location.

Ashe hated fighting at night, because it was nearly impossible to see anything outside of the ring of torches and campfires. Gathering energy into her palm, she unleashed a ball of fire, hurling it up into the night sky.

What she saw made her stomach drop. Charging toward them through the trees was a vast wave of undead in a mixed array of decay. Their limbs flailed madly as they ran, screeching every step of the way.

As their beady, decaying eyes locked onto her and her men, the hunger in them drove them ever faster. It was horrifying.

"Stand strong," she yelled at the soldiers with a confidence she didn't feel. "They are many, but they are weak! Do not let them swarm us and we stand a chance!"

Reaching for the energy within her, she summoned fire and lit the ground in front of them, creating a wall of flame. She hoped it would slow them down and funnel them into a formation they could handle.

Had they been alive, it may have worked. However, these creatures were unthinking, following a simple order. Kill. So as the wave reached the fire, they sprinted right through it. The first line caught aflame, dropping them to the ground. The waves after continued to run, smashing into the front guard of soldiers.

The world around Ashe was a blur as bodies around her were in motion. The time for planning and thinking was over. Ashe now moved strictly on instinct and reflex.

Her knives were in her hands, fire extending from the ends in whip-like fashion. To her, battle was like a dance. She moved fluidly from step to step, spinning, striking, ducking and lashing out as she had been taught at the Citadel.

The flame was an extension of her body, reaching out and engulfing every enemy in her path. Wave after wave of undead crashed around her, meeting a fiery demise. Any that got within the reach of her fire crumpled at the end of Mallory's blade.

They were a duo of death in the eye of a maelstrom. Fire had spread swiftly during the attack, as the undead caught flame, lighting up the carnage around her. Men and women fought desperately, hacking down the deceased enemies in front of them.

Yet they just kept spilling into the clearing. Every few moments, a human scream would sound in the air, signaling another loss. There seemed no end to Levy's undead, while Ashe's army was sickeningly finite.

As Ashe dispatched a particularly gruesome corpse, the others of the horde attacking her began to back away, forming a loose ring around her. She could hear the battle continuing on in the background, as more shouts rang out amidst the crackling flame.

Ashe stood, still, taking the opportunity to gather her breath. Mallory nudged her, pointing to where the ring of corpses began to part. Sauntering toward her, cocky grin plastered on his wickedly handsome face, was Levy.

He held his silver blade at his side, the orb of Hades glowing purple in the mouth of the wolf-head pommel.

"Hello, Fire Queen," he taunted. "Lovely night, isn't it?"

Ashe gave him a scorching look. "Hello traitor. Did your master send you my way to die?"

Levy sneered. "I am my own master. Janus is no longer a player in this game."

As if to prove his point, he held out his hand, letting a silver energy fill his palm before blasting it at one of the nearby corpses, ripping it apart.

Ashe paled. "You absorbed his essence."

"That's right, Ashe. I have the full essence of a god within me. Nobody can stop me now from claiming the throne. Your campaign is over."

"So, you came here to mock me?" Gold lit the irises of her eyes. Anger had been building within her since he had first arrived. Now, after seeing Levy's display of power, it mixed with a desperate hopelessness, surging unevenly throughout her body.

"On the contrary," he replied coolly. "I came here to bargain. Come with me Ashe. Quinn isn't here anymore. Maybe there's a reason for that."

Ashe narrowed her eyes, disbelief plastered to her face.

"Your forces are outnumbered. Look around you, Ashe. Even now the last of your men are surrounded by my army. Lay down your weapons. Lay down your claim to the throne, and I will spare what remains. After all, everything I do, I do for the good of our kind. Give me the throne willingly, and I will spare you."

Ashe could hardly hold back the fire within her. She couldn't believe what she was hearing. "You do *nothing* for the good of our kind." she seethed.

"You have killed *thousands* of humans in your mad quest for power. You joined forces with a god intent on a world with the unequal distribution of power.

"Asking me to allow you the throne is the same as asking me to allow humanity to once again live under the boot of the gods. How dare you try and bargain with me.

"You want me lay down my weapons and give up the fight? I will not. Even if it means my death, I will fight for the only future I believe in."

Levy shook his head, shooting her a pitying look. “Then you will die for nothing.”

Ashe let go of the tumultuous energy, allowing it to seep through her every fiber, pouring out into the world around them. Her eyes shone a brilliant gold, lighting up the anger on her face. With a roar, she lashed out at Levy, whipping the molten flame at his face. With wide eyes, Levy raised his blade, knocking the fire away.

He stepped in closer, swinging a strike at her open side, but a blade swooped in, knocking it aside. Taking advantage of Levy’s surprise, Mallory stepped inside his guard and delivered a punch, right across his jaw.

“YEAH, SKÝLA,” Mallory cried as he stumbled back, blood running down his chin. With a seething anger he raised his hand, shooting a quick concussive blast directly into her chest piece.

“No,” Ashe cried out as she was launched backward, out over the circle of undead and into the battle raging beyond.

“The weak should not get in the way of a god.” A warped voice escaped from Levy’s mouth.

Hearing the way Levy’s voice distorted, mingling with Janus’ gave her an idea.

Ashe looked at him and laughed, mockingly. “What’s wrong Levy? Too much godly essence for you to contain? Do you even have control of that twisted little god within you, or are you just calling yourself a god now?”

Levy roared and swung a wild vertical strike at her, attempting to split her in half. “Enough!” his voice roared out, halfway between Janus’ and his own. “I have had enough mockery from you.”

He continued striking wildly at her. She swerved away from each strike, finding small openings each time to open small gashes along his body. Even with the power he had now, he was still easy to rile up, causing him to make dumb mistakes.

Realizing he was bleeding from multiple wounds, he started to rely more on the essence within him, sending small bursts of concentrated force at her. Each time she felt them build, she would send a ball of flame to meet it half way. As the forces met, they would explode, sending showers of fire streaking down around them.

“What’s the matter, Levy?” she taunted further. “All that power and you can only match my strength? I thought you were a god!”

Ashe knew she was pushing her luck. All it would take was one good hit on her and it would all be over. But the more unhinged he got, the more off balance he became, allowing her chances to get inside his guard.

"You are NOTHING," he screamed back at her in his distorted voice. "I am the one who will claim the throne. I will usher in a new world." Spittle flew from his lips as he screamed, his eyes growing deranged in the flickering light.

Taking a chance, she flung her left knife out, hoping he would allow the fiery, whip-like energy to wrap around his blade. Fortunately for her, he did just that. As soon as it was wrapped tight, he gave a mighty pull, wrenching her forward, toward him.

With his left hand he formed a fist, aiming a mighty punch directly at her oncoming face. A few paces before she would have made contact, she let go of her knife, dropping herself onto the ground. Using her momentum, she rolled under his fist and sprang back up, planting her other knife right in the open spot of his armor beneath his arm.

He let out a bellow of pain, pulling his arm back and unleashing a wave of raw power slamming into her and sending her sprawling into the dirt, dazed. He stalked toward her, murder in his eyes. His chest heaved with his rage.

In a calm, sinister voice he said, "Look around you Ashe. This battle is mine. What remains of your troops are far too few to stop me. And you, their beacon of hope, will be extinguished before their very eyes."

He raised his sword, readying the tip to plunge into her heart. "I'd offer you some last words, but quite frankly I can't be bothered to care what you have to say."

Without another thought, he pushed his blade forward.

A silver flash flitted across her vision, meeting Levy's blade with a metallic clang that reverberated over the chaos of the battlefield. A familiar, writhing cloak of shadow stood over her, protecting her from further harm.

"I've got some last words for you," said Quinn.

# CHAPTER 37: Quinn

The trek across the wastes had taken longer than Quinn had hoped for. Moving a couple hundred Abyssillians at once through a barren land was a slog to say the least. Though he was in a hurry, Quinn knew he had to stop and let his troops rest.

It would do no good for them to reach the battlefield only to be dehydrated and exhausted. Above the party circled Andra on her drakon. She would constantly scout ahead, reporting anything she felt was useful information to Quinn.

Anxiety over bringing the three young warriors with him on this fight ate away at him the entire journey. It wasn't that he didn't think they were all capable fighters.

He had trained them himself, after all, and knew first hand just how good they were. However, outside of a few skirmishes as bandits, they had yet to see real combat. He couldn't hold them back forever though.

This was the future that they chose for themselves, and it wasn't his job to stand in the way of that. They had been some of the most vocal in rallying the Abyssillians to battle. He had a strong sense of pride in them for being willing to try and bridge the gap between their generation and the humans. They were in for a tough fight in that regard but allying with them in this fight would go a long way.

As the terrain changed around them from dusty, packed ground to the earthy soil of the forest, visibility began to decrease. Quinn had to rely on Andra, flying overhead, to keep them travelling in the right direction.

On his own, Quinn would have been able to find the army just fine, but with such a large group behind him, he didn't want to risk losing some along the way. They would travel by day, doing their best to stick to the paths of the wood.

Eventually, there became a clear trail of burnt out fires and the shells and corpses of slain monsters, leading them along the path the human army had left in their wake. Quinn was impressed at the amount of carnage.

At first there were mainly monsters littering the paths, but the closer they got to the tower in the distance, the more frequent the hastily made graves of soldiers would pop up. To Quinn's horror, some of the graves appeared to be empty. Fresh soil was piled to either side as if something had dug its way out.

As night fell, they camped beneath the stars, surrounded by the fresh scent of forest. It delighted Quinn to see the smiles on his people's faces, as for many of them, it was their first time outside of the Wastes.

They were experiencing earthy scents and vibrant colors unlike anything they had ever seen before. Suddenly, a herd of deer burst through the trees, startling everyone, as they made a hasty escape in the opposite direction.

Andra came streaking into view above on her drakon. "QUINN!" she called; desperation laced her voice. "The forest is on fire a few leagues ahead! The humans are being overrun by corpses. If we wait until morning it will be too late!"

Quinn bolted to his feet, hollering for Nes. The bleary-eyed youth crawled out of his sleeping furs and came to attention. "There is a battle being waged to the north of us and the humans are running out of time. I'm going on ahead with Andra. Gather our people and make haste, as fast as you can possibly go."

"What's the plan when we get there?" The youth was wide-eyed.

Quinn gave him a smile, attempting to instill the young man with courage. "Send them back to Hades."

~~~

Andra and Quinn sped along through the air. The treetops raced by below them in a shadowed blur. Up ahead Quinn could see the orange glow of a blaze, lighting up where the battle was taking place. Even from this distance he could hear the blood-curdling screeches of the dead.

"When we arrive, I don't want you to directly engage." He ordered Andra. "If you see stragglers, feel free to use Marilyn to pick them off. Otherwise look for humans in need of help.

"Transport the injured back to our base so our healers can tend to them. The more humans we can save, the better chances we have of being welcomed when this is over."

The girl nodded; determination set upon her face. Quinn was impressed with her lack of fear. For such a small girl, she had a steel spine.

As they reached the clearing where the battle was ongoing, Quinn's heart dropped. Piles of undead bodies lay scattered around the earth, yet even more heaved their way toward the living. Only pockets of troops remained, small clusters in a sea of writhing corpses.

Over near the edge of the battle, he saw a ring of undead, standing still around a pair of fighters. Quinn's eyes widened as he realized who the fighters were. Sitting up against a tree, just outside of the ring sat a familiar woman, clutching her arm to her chest. Despite being seriously wounded, her eyes reached him.

A bright smile was plastered to her face. Before he could do anything else, a large force of energy burst out of the ring, nearly knocking him from the drakon. He looked back and saw Ashe on the ground, dazed and unmoving. Stalking toward her, sword raised for the kill was Levy.

Quinn pointed at the woman leaning against the tree.
~~~

"I'm going," he said. "Save her first. Then come back and save as many others as you can. Point our troops in the right direction on your way back, and tell them to hurry."

Catching a quick nod in response, he slipped the mask on his face and jumped, praying he was in time to stop Levy's blade.

*You won't make it in time,* Chaos spoke, traveling alongside him through the Realm of Night. *Despite moving faster here, it won't make a difference. The blade will strike just before you reach her.*

"I have to try," Quinn said, panic in his voice. "What other choice do I have?" He was streaking toward her now, as fast as the power would allow.

*Let me in.* Chaos offered his hand. *As I told you before, should you allow it, I can temporarily take control, lending you the full energy of this realm, alongside your own. With it, you can reach her.*

Quinn was hesitant. "If I let you in, what are the chances I lose myself to this realm?"

*That is entirely up to your power of will. Assimilation has already begun, as I'm sure you are aware. You are able to reach the power of this place so easily now. However, I assure you that if you do not allow me to help, the girl will die.*

A wide range of emotions waged a war inside Quinn within a fraction of a second, but in the end, his love for Ashe won out.

"Very well," he said, taking Chaos' hand. Pure black power arched out of him, enshrouding Quinn. So much energy entered him then, it felt as though he was going to explode. Time slowed down even more before his very eyes.

*Very good.* The voice of Chaos spoke from within. *Now watch and learn the depths of the power of a Primordial at work.*

With a burst of power unlike anything he had ever felt, Quinn's body rocketed forward. Just as the point of Levy's blade was about to strike home, Quinn streaked out of the Realm of Night, inserting his blade between the Levy's own and Ashe.

"How about me?" Chaos spoke through Quinn's voice. "I've got some last words for you."

Levy's eyes narrowed suspiciously, listening to the voices in his head. "They say you aren't Quinn."

Chaos answered again showing his teeth. "I am as much Quinn

as you are Levy."

Levy's eyes flashed silver, a wicked smile lighting his face. "Your time is long past, Primordial. Go back to your slumber."

Chaos cackled then, jarring Quinn to hear such a sound come from his own throat. "My time began again when you pulled me from my slumber into your scheme. Beware Janus, you are messing with a power you do not understand.

"Do not think that because you are a god you can control me. I will have my time again." His voice strained near the end, as Quinn began to feel Chaos' power fade from him.

"Sounds like your time is just about up," Janus taunted.

"For now," Chaos replied, fading back into the recesses of the mask.

The silver light faded from Levy's eyes leaving a dull grey in its place. "Never do that again," he heard Levy mutter before turning his attention back on Quinn. "As for you, you're too late. Her army is surrounded, and you alone will not change that fact. After I slaughter the remainder, the throne will be mine."

Quinn smiled back at him, pushing the fear of what had just happened to the back of his mind. "Who says I'm alone?"

A large rumble shook the earth, knocking human and undead alike to the ground. With a battle cry that would make his ancestors proud, Nes charged through the tree line, leading the Abyssillian force behind him.

They crashed into the walls of undead, crushing through their brittle bodies. Andra swooped back and forth through the air, picking off stragglers while pulling confused humans to safety.

Levy screamed in frustration, raising his sword and pumping more energy into the orb. It shone weakly, as hands began to claw their way out of the dirt, but as the corpses reached the surface, they crumbled away into dust.

With a start, Levy swiveled his head to the sky. The sun was beginning to rise in the east, casting the first, early rays of light upon the earth.

"Tch." Levy shook his head. "It doesn't matter anyway. You win tonight, but you know you won't win again. Your troops are too few and too wounded, whereas I can replenish mine every night. This battle is meaningless.

"Come to the tower tomorrow when you've had a chance to replenish your energy and let's end this the way it was meant to be, just the three of us." A portal opened up behind him, showing a silver room on the other side. With one last glare at each of them, he stepped through it, snapping it closed behind him.

# CHAPTER 38: Levy

"What WAS that?!" Levy stormed around the room, staring at the portrait on the walls. Ever since he had taken in all of Janus, he had gained control over them.

He had immediately stopped the scrolling feed, leaving only one portrait on the wall at all times. It was himself, in front of the throne, sword raised in victory. It was the only one that mattered.

*That was a Primordial,* Janus replied. Ever since they had reunited inside his head, the clean-shaven version had taken over the prominent role. *He is a being I had enlisted to ensure your success, though it seems he has gone rogue.*

"Did you feel the power that thing gave off? There is no way he should have been able to stop my blade in time."

*Be thankful he did, lad.* The bearded Janus spoke up. *In your anger, you had forgotten that we need her alive.*

Levy shook his head. "I told you we could have used Quinn."

*After seeing the power of a Primordial firsthand, do you really still think that?*

Levy seethed again. "How am I expected to stop that thing then? If it shows up again at the tower, we're done for." Levy felt amusement tickle his mind, before an image popped into his head. "Ashe?" he asked, perplexed.

*The Primordial is unlikely to show up again. Having your body possessed tends to be a jarring experience. It would not surprise me if the boy locked him away far into the recesses of the mask.*

*However, if he does show up, who do you think it will affect most? Whose heart would be most affected by seeing someone they love consumed by darkness?*

Levy began to put the pieces together. "You're saying that if it shows up again, Ashe will likely help fight it."

*A one versus two becomes a free for all. And while the Primordial wields tremendous power, it is the power of shadows and darkness. What cuts through darkness better than fire?*

*Hestia was craftier than I gave her credit for. She saw what I was up to and decided this was the best way to counter me. But never mind that for now. We can still work together in this.*

A slow smile began to creep across Levy's face as Janus flashed images of a plan in his mind.

"And one way or another, I get what I need out of it to access the throne. Brilliant."

He looked back at the portrait one last time, soaking in his victory.

# CHAPTER 39: Ashe

The aftermath of the battle was a macabre affair. The undead had all turned to ash and crumbled, leaving a battlefield of the wounded and the dead. The stench of death was heavy in the air, and blood soaked the slick grass.

Smoke left over from the fire rose high into the sky, blocking out the rays of the sun and creating a haze. The Abyssillians had moved their makeshift camp as close to the field as could be stomached.

Quinn had left her almost as soon as the battle had ended, being called over by a short girl with multicolored hair. Laying at her feet was a young man with overly large ears. In any other situation it would have been slightly comical, however there was nothing funny about the angle at which his neck had been twisted.

The muscular man, *boy really*, she thought, who had led the Abyssillian charge knelt next to them, sobbing into the young man's corpse. She could see the pain on Quinn's face as he gently closed the young man's glossy eyes.

He held his arm around the girl, comforting her as she quietly cried. She wanted nothing more than to run over to him, but it would have to wait. She had her own wounded to tend to. She just had to find her first.

As she entered the medical tent the Abyssillians had provided, she saw the subject of her query sitting up with her arm in a sling. Her bright, brown eyes met hers and she smiled, slurring her words slightly. "I told you he would come! Did you guys *talk* yet?"

Ashe felt the heat of embarrassment creep into her face as all eyes in the tent turned to her. Ignoring her question, she replied, "I came to see how you were faring, though I see my worries were unfounded. Are you behaving for the healers?" She asked, making eye contact with a grey haired Abyssillian woman. The woman smiled back at her, a tentative humor in her eye.

"Of course!" Mallory sounded hurt. "These people are great. They have so many uses for monster parts. Did you know they can make a tonic out of manticore venom that numbs pain and makes your head feel like it's flying? You should try some of this!"

Ashe couldn't help but giggle at her friend, clearly high off her ass. "I'm glad you're feeling well. I need to go meet with the commanders and talk with Quinn. I'll come back to check on you before I go."

"Where are you going?" Mallory asked, sobering up for a moment.

"Never mind for now. Just rest up and I'll be back to check on you later."

"Ok!" Her face lit back up. "Have fun with your council. Have more fun with Quinn," she winked.

As Ashe left the tent, she heard Mallory belt out "Ashe and Quinn sitting in a tent." she giggled to herself. Ashe buried her face in her hands, certain her face was bright red.

~~~

"WE NEED TO RETREAT," Lend yelled, showering Bartimaeus in spittle.
~~~

"Bugger that," he replied, not rising to the young man's bait. "We have fresh troops now thanks to Spooky over there."

He pointed to Quinn in the corner, who quirked his eyebrow.

Her tent was in an uproar over plans of how to proceed. Ashe and Quinn both knew, of course, that what they decided didn't matter. But she figured it best to let the commotion die down before giving the men the bad, or good depending on how they looked at it, news.

"With all due respect," Lend began, glancing over at Quinn. "We just spent three years fending off monsters in an attempt to reach this bloody tower, and now you wish to enlist more of them to fight WITH us?"

Quinn chimed in from the corner, cool amusement in his tone. "By 'with all due respect' did you mean no respect at all? Because my 'monsters'" he flashed air quotes as he said the words, "Just saved your lives."

Lend bristled. "Apologies, but you saw what happened when the sun rose. We had but to hold out for moments more."

Quinn narrowed his eyes at the man. "With all due respect," he mimicked, "you and yours did not have moments more. My people came to your aid, despite years of forced isolation and mistreatment.

"We lost many of our own as well in those 'mere moments' so that you could go back to your loved ones. If you wish to throw your false bravado around, I couldn't care less, but don't you dare do it in my presence or in the presence of my people."

As he finished, he was nearly nose to nose with the man. With a pale face, Lend slowly regained his seat. "Yes of course. My apologies."

"HA, Bartimaeus crowed. "That'll teach ya to try and run with the big dogs, boy!"

Quinn returned to his corner, shooting a quick glance over at Ashe. She covered a smile as their gazes lingered.

"Anyways," Bartimaeus continued. "With this new blood, and the two of you," he pointed between Ashe and Quinn. "We may actually be able to take the tower."

Ashe stood, finally ready to deliver her orders. "Sorry Bartimaeus, but for once I agree with Lend."

"You do?" he asked, bushy eyebrows shooting to the top of his head.

"You do?" Lend's mouth was agape.

"I do," she said with a sad grin. She was going to miss the chaos of these councils. "There is no point in continuing to throw bodies at a constantly respawning army. It will only lead to all of our deaths. Levy has offered Quinn and me a chance to meet with him at the base of the tower, and end things between the three of us. We're going to take it."

"You can't be serious," Lend said. "Look, I am ecstatic, truly, that for once you are willing to listen to my council. But you can't honestly think he would make such an offer and not have a trap ready for you."

"He most assuredly does," She replied. "But at this point in time, we don't really have a choice. Like I said, I doubt we will last another night against a renewed army of his dead. And even if we do, we will suffer heavy losses. We certainly won't survive a third."

"Wouldn't it make more sense to take what's left of this army into the crater with you?" Bartimaeus asked. "Surely he can't stand up to the combined might of all of us." Ashe looked to Quinn for help.

"Your army and mine, it makes no difference," Quinn told the group. "For starters, the path leading to the crater of the volcano that houses the tower is narrow. We would need to march almost single file.

"If Levy got even a hint of us trying to pull something like that, he could easily shoot a concussive blast at the walls, showering you all in thousands of tons of rock. Even if we were to somehow get through that, you all are only mortal.

"Have you ever gone up against the might of a god before? For that matter, have you ever tried to stand so close to molten lava without the essence of a goddess to protect you?

"It will not end well for you. Your numbers will mean nothing to him. One blast the likes of which he sent out last night, and you're all plummeting into the lava below. It has to be us."

"Don't your people have gifts that can help?" Lend asked, avoiding eye contact.

"Most of my people have very thin bloodlines. The amount of ichor that runs through their veins is almost non-existent. The ones who do have stronger gifts must strain to use them. Overuse causes great pain and damage to their bodies and minds.

"After the battle last night, I will not ask that of them again. I have brought most of my people here with me, leaving only the extremely old and young behind with a few guards to watch over in the unlikely event of an attack. I will not sacrifice the futures of my people for a doomed cause.

"They will be sent back tonight. I would recommend you take your wounded and do the same. Only Ashe and I can make it to the tower alive, and that's what we will do. I know it's frustrating, since this has been your whole lives, but now you must put your faith in us."

Their eyes connected again, and Ashe felt a familiar warmth spread throughout her.

"I'm sorry it has to end this way," she said to the men around the room. "But I swear to you we will not lose. Go home happy, knowing that because of you, and the sacrifices of your fellow men and women, we may finally have the peace and freedom we have desperately craved."

At this point she locked eyes with Quinn. "Spread the stories of our victories far, to every town you visit along the way. Tell them how in our greatest hour of need, the Abyssillians came to our aid."

Quinn smiled back at her, gratitude in his eyes. With a final word she said, "It has been an honor to fight with you all. Truly, I could not have asked for more loyal men. When this is over, I pray we meet again. For the final time, dismissed."

As her commanders left the tent to spread the news, she called out. "Quinn." He paused, his hand on the flap of the tent.

# CHAPTER 40: Quinn

He had been about to go out and speak with his people when she said his name. “Quinn.”

It stopped him in his tracks, sending electricity jolting through his body. Her mouth was pressed to his before either of them knew what was happening.

Their tongues found each other a moment later, dancing with one another to a melody known only to them. Heat and passion enveloped them, feeding off of each of each other’s hunger and desperation.

Wisps of golden flame twisted out of Ashe, entwining them both. The fire didn’t burn Quinn, but instead held him closer to her like a warm embrace. Quinn placed his hands on either side of her face and stared into her eyes, glowing golden with the essence.

“Quinn I’m so sorry I….” she said, a tear falling down the corner of her eye.

“Shhhh.” He cut her off, catching the tear on his thumb. “You have nothing to be sorry for. We both knew what would happen when you found out the truth. Your passion for your ideals is one of the things that makes me love you as much as I do."

He met her lips again, soft and passionate. "Besides, I'm the one that should be apologizing. What I did…."

This time it was her turn to shush him. "We all make mistakes Quinn. I should have reacted better. I saw the guilt eating you up. But with Levy, and the Citadel and then I just hit my breaking point. I'm so sorry for abandoning you like that."

Quinn just shook his head. "It doesn't matter. Like I said, you have nothing to apologize for. All that matters is that we're here now, together again," at this he looked to the ground, embarrassed. "That is, if you'll have me."

Ashe tilted his chin back up so his eyes met hers. "Until the end," she whispered, leading him over to her sleeping mat. She kissed him again, long and deep.

Quinn lay there sometime later, Ashe's arms wrapped around him; his head nestled on her shoulder. Neither of them had spoken for a while, relaxing in the comfort of their embrace.

As Quinn began to wonder if she had fallen asleep, she whispered, "You still have the mask."

It wasn't a question, nor an accusation. It was just a simple statement.

"I do," he replied, knowing what she was getting at.

"Does it affect you still?" She asked, carefully. "The pull of power from the other realm?"

"It does," he replied hoarsely. "Last night, I think I nearly lost myself to it. When I saw you in trouble, I allowed its spirit to take control of my body, granting me the power I needed to reach you in time.

"I wasn't sure I was going to come back from that. But if I hadn't…." He trailed off.

They both knew if he hadn't allowed Chaos to possess him, Ashe would have been dead at the end of Levy's blade.

"Do you think there's a chance of it happening again?"

"I still feel its presence in the back of my mind," he answered honestly. "Even now, the Realm of Night calls to me. I'm afraid that if I put the mask back on, I'll never come back from it." He felt her stroke his hair, calming his nerves.

"Then don't," she said soothingly. "Rely on me, like I used to do with you all those years ago. Let me use my power against Levy, and you can back me up. Even without the mask you have the essence of Hestia within you. You are still fast and good with your blade.

"Let me be the spear, and you be the shield." Quinn nodded, relieved. The truth was, he had dreaded putting the mask on again. Chaos terrified him. If he could make it through this final fight without relying on its power, he would be happy to. However, he didn't believe for a second he would get off that easily.

"What do you think he's planning?" Quinn changed the subject.

"Probably to kill us," Ashe replied, dryly.

Quinn chortled. "Seriously though, he is definitely up to something. If he only wanted us dead, there would be no reason for the invite to the tower. It's like you said, he could have just waited for tonight and sent his legion of the dead to finish us off. Even you and I wouldn't last more than a night against a mindless, replenishing army."

"True," Ashe replied in thought. "Besides, if he already has access to the tower in the first place, why has he not already taken the throne? There would be no reason for him to wait for us to get there. You don't think he's so petty as to want to take it in front of us, do you?"

"Yes," Quin rolled his eyes. "I do think he's that petty. But I don't think Janus is. And if last night is any indication, Janus is still very much present in this."

They lapsed into silence again, both deep in thought. Finally, Quinn untangled himself and rolled over.

"I should probably go give the marching orders to my people. They're eager to return home. You should go say your final goodbyes as well. We get one more night together before everything goes to Hades.

"I'd like to spend it without hundreds of ears around to hear it." He smiled and kissed her one more time as he got up to find his clothes, afraid that when he left this tent she would disappear, and he would find that it had all been a dream.

As he exited the tent, he bumped into a familiar grinning face. "Hello Mallory," he greeted her with a smile. "Shouldn't you be in bed resting? Manticore venom is potent stuff."

"Shouldn't you be in bed not resting?" She shot back with a wink. "Oh wait, never mind. Everyone already heard that happening."

Quinn felt the red creep up his neck. Mallory let out a loud bellow, drawing looks from around the camp. "I swear you two are such prudes."

Quinn chuckled, shaking his head. "Thank you, Mallory," he pulled her into a hug, careful not to bump her wounded arm. "Without you, I'm not sure I would have ever had a chance to set things right with her."

Mallory looked back at him with warmth in her eyes. "Ashe deserves to be happy."

Quinn smiled at the compliment before seeing a familiar, mischievous twinkle light up her eye, "But if things ever end poorly again, give me a call."

With a light, playful squeeze of his arm she tore open the flap of the tent and yelled, "HOPE YOU HAVE YOUR CLOTHES ON CAUSE I'M COMING IN!"

Quinn found Nes and Andra standing together off to the side of the camp. Nes had a few minor cuts along the surface of his arms, indicating the overuse of his power. Though his clothing was ripped and dirty, he didn't seem to have any major wounds.

Andra had come out of the battle completely fine; though with the protection of a fully grown drakon, Quinn didn't find that surprising. Marilyn had her tail wrapped around them, as if shielding them from their sorrow. They had burned Sen in a funeral pyre as was the Abyssillian way, along with the others of his people who had been lost in the fight.

"I'm so sorry," Quinn said, putting a hand on each of their shoulders. He noticed they were holding hands, likely pushed together by the bond the loss brought. It was a bittersweet feeling.

"Don't be," Nes replied, eyes rimmed with red. "Sen died fighting for a future we can believe in. You'd be surprised how accepting these people have been of us.

"We still get some dirty looks and some muttering, but most of the soldiers have thanked us and invited us to their fires. I know it's only a small step forward in the grand scheme of things. Most of humanity isn't here to witness it. But it's a start."

"Sen would be proud to know he died for such a thing," the usually quiet Andra chimed in. Quinn could only smile.

They had only been children when he had first bumped into them, but now they stood in front of him, forced to age before their years. Nes was only nineteen, but in his eyes, Quinn could see the wisdom and determination this had instilled in him. He couldn't think of anybody better to lead his people.

"Take them home, Nes." He drew both of their stares. "Share what happened here along the way. Lead them to a brighter tomorrow."

"What about you?" he asked. "When you've finished all this tower business, won't you be coming back?" Quinn wasn't so sure. Time and time again, Hestia's words had been coming back to him.

*Two of you must reach the throne room together. Ashe will be the guiding light for all of humanity.*

If only one could sit on the throne, then why did two have to reach it together? Combine those words with Levy's unwillingness to outright overpower them and kill them, despite having the ability to do so, and something didn't sit right with him. He knew something that they didn't.

"Perhaps I'll be able to make it back, but perhaps not. Either way, I think once this task is over, my time in the spotlight is done." He had serious doubts it would matter, but he didn't want to verbalize them.

"I don't suppose you'll let us come with you, will you?" Nes asked.

"Marilyn can eat him," Andra added, quietly.

Quinn smiled. "I will not let you throw away your lives. You said it yourself, be proud of what you did here. Lead the Abyssillians and help bridge the divide between our people and the humans. Change is slow, but it will come."

Nes sighed but nodded, resigned to his role. "Come back when this is over," he said looking Quinn in the eye. "Even if it isn't to stay. You've spent the last three years providing for us. Let me do the same for you."

Quinn smiled, shaking his hand. "It's a deal." He leaned down and hugged Andra before turning back toward the clearing. "Lead them well, Nes."

"Aye, sir!" He saluted, proudly. Andra smiled at the ground.

Finding a quiet spot among the trees, a ways from the clearing, Quinn sat, folding his hands together and channeling his energy. The fog was heavy, creating an ethereal environment in the forest around him. The air was damp and cool on his face, causing the smells of the vegetation to come to life. He sat the mask on his lap, afraid to put it on, but needing to have contact with it so he could ask his questions.

*I'm surprised to feel you reach out to me so soon.* Chaos said, appearing in his mind. *I would have thought that last night would have scared you worse than that.*

*It terrified me*, Quinn answered honestly. Since having allowed Chaos access to his mind and body, he had felt the constant connection to the Realm of Night, trying desperately to pull him back to it. Even worse was the desire to do just that.

*Then why reach out?* the voice asked.

*I assume I already know the answer,* Quinn began, *But I want to know for sure. What are you?*

*I am Chaos,* the voice proclaimed, crystal clear in his mind. The rasp he once spoke with had long gone from him. *A Primordial god who has slumbered for eons. Since before gods, humans or monsters walked the earth.*

*Janus pushed the mask to fall into my hands. Did he know the power he gave me?*

*Of course he did,* Chaos replied. *The mask was his second attempt to get you to lose yourself to my power.*

Quinn scrunched his brows together in confusion. *His second?*

He saw the image of a snowy landscape in his mind. Around the edge, a dark abyss fell away into black nothingness.

*You're sick of always fighting a losing battle. Humanity is on its last legs. Jump into the darkness and end your suffering. Any of these thoughts ringing a bell?* Quinn's eyes widened.

*You were influencing me in my fight with Perseus,* Quinn stated. *You almost convinced me to jump into the abyss.*

*And you would have, had Hestia not allowed the girl to interfere. After that Janus had to rely on plan B and I allowed him to infuse my essence into the mask.*

*What do you get out of all this?* Quinn asked.

*A body with which to walk the earth again,* Chaos replied, matter-of-factly. *Had you fallen into the abyss, I would have been able to possess you right there, surrounded by my essence. Instead I have had to rely on the mask, allowing you to grasp at fractions of it, pulling them within you.*

Quinn shivered. *And Janus is just okay with you having a physical form? He seemed to believe last night that you were not supposed to be a player in this game.*

*Janus thinks he is far more clever than he actually is,* Chaos spat. *He believed he could control power that he does not understand. Had I gotten you in Hestia's domain, he would have tried to collapse it down upon me.*

*With the mask, he believed the possession would take far too long, and his plan would reach fruition before I had the chance to stop him. With the throne in his possession, he would have silenced the threat that I posed, before I ever posed it.*

Quinn shook his head. *I don't understand. If this is your whole master plan, why would you tell it all to me. You are a foe, yet you act as a friend.*

*You are human. A creature that would normally be too far beneath my notice. I do not think of you as neither friend, nor foe.*

*Still, by telling me this, you have doomed your plan. What makes you think I would ever put this mask on again, knowing that if I do, I'll lose myself to your power and you will own me?*

*Because, little hero, what makes you think that without my power, you can stop a god? You'll fight your hardest, I'm sure. But in the end, when all seems lost, you'll think of me.*

*You'll think, 'maybe I can control it one more time. It's either that or I let Janus end the world as I know it.' and you'll slip the mask back onto your face. And when you do, you will be mine.*

The mask fell to the forest floor as Quinn snapped to his feet. Sweat drenched his shirt, sticking it to his back. He was breathing hard, struggling to get his pulse back under control. In the back of his mind he heard the calm, monotonous voice of Chaos. *See you soon, little hero.*

# CHAPTER 41: Ashe & Quinn

Ashe sat outside by the fire she'd started, waiting for Quinn to come back from the woods. She knew he had gone off to meditate and didn't want to intrude upon him. Normally around this time, fires would be roaring to life all around the camp.

Raucous drinking songs were a common sound; used to combat the days labors or sorrows. Now however, she sat at the lone fire, quietly stoking it so Quinn would have some comfort when he returned. The remainder of the soldiers had left just earlier, saying their goodbyes and wishing her well.

It was clear that leaving after having come this far didn't sit right with them, but there was no argument they could make to her as to why they should stay. They knew that they were all outmatched in this the rest of the way.

While she could see the argument and guilt written all over their faces, she could also see their relief. It had been many years since they had been able to see their families, and many of their brethren would never get to again. Ashe was sad, knowing how many she led to their deaths, but she knew that was just a part of war.

Having to say goodbye to Mallory had been the hardest part.

Her closest friend had burst into her tent just after Quinn had left. She didn't poke any fun at Ashe, but she wore her signature, knowing smile. The two had become like sisters over the years, and Ashe was going to miss her horribly.

As she had sat there, partially clothed and trying to think of what to say, her friend had wrapped her in a big hug and said, "I know."

"Help them, Mallory. Promise me you will. You have had more contact with the Abyssillians than any of our people have had in ages."

"You have my word," She replied. "Between that Nes kid and I, we can probably manage something. Things won't go back to how they were so long as I live."

They sat together for some time after that, reminiscing about battles past. By the end of it they were both fighting tears. When it was time for her to go, Ashe stood, pulling Mallory into one last hug.

"I don't know where I would be without you," she said, not wanting to let go.

"You'd be right where you are now, only much skinnier. I doubt anybody else would have saved you bacon every time you overslept."

Ashe laughed. "You're probably right."

"I know I'm right." She grinned. "Kick his ass, Ashe."

"I will."

As she poked at the fire, with crickets playing their symphonies in the surrounding woods, her mind wandered back to her time at the Citadel. It had been a long time since she'd thought of that place. Before Levy had betrayed them to Janus, it had held some of the happiest days of her life.

The three of them were always going on adventures together when they were young, getting up to all sorts of trouble. Their favorite game to play was to see how long they could stay outside before the Masters came looking for them. When one would get close, they would all split up, giggling as an angry master would curse and try to chase them down.

As they had gotten older, their training became more intense.

That kinship grew from a friendship to a bond. They each knew the others would have their back. Even through all of the distance and betrayals, that bond had always existed in the back of Ashe's mind.

She pitied Levy. She hated him for the thousands of people he had murdered. She hated him for breaking that trust they'd had, and for losing himself to the siren call of power. And yet, she couldn't help but feel sorrow for him as well: Sad for the good he could have been for the world.

There was also a sense of bittersweet excitement for the next day. Even though their friendship was no longer there, finishing this between the three of them just felt right. Their entire lives had been spent preparing for this very moment, as if the strings of fate had guided them to this very spot. No matter what happened tomorrow, this chapter of their lives would finally be ending.

She felt Quinn returning before she saw him. Ever since they had reconnected with one another, their energies had mingled. It felt as though a tether now existed between them. As one got further away from the other, that string of energy would stretch and thin, but never break. It didn't put any kind of pressure on her, but she was constantly aware of it. It comforted her.

He walked into the clearing; distress written all over his face. It was clear he was trying to hide it from her, but there was no longer the possibility for secrets to exist between them. He glanced her way, and must have come to the same realization, because he sat down, took her hands and looked deep into her eyes.

"I spoke to Chaos today as I was meditating."

The admission didn't surprise her. She hated the mask, and he did as well. She could tell. But she had realized, once their energies had connected, that the power of the mask was now a part of him. Despite the fear he felt, he could not just let it go.

"I need you to promise me something."

She listened as he told her all about what he and Chaos had spoken about.

As he finished, he let out a sigh. "I know it sounds stupid, but I think I still need to bring it with me tomorrow. No matter what happens, we can't let Levy take the throne. If we need to rely on the power of the mask, I think we should."

"But…." she began to protest but he held up his hand.

"I know. I won't use it if I can help it. It scares me. But I think it is naive of us to assume we can defeat Levy, who holds the full power of a god, without any assistance.

"Which is why I want you to make me a promise. If the time comes that I need to use the mask, I need you to promise me that you will kill me when it's done. Even with Chaos in control of me, my body is flesh. That golden fire of yours should be enough to cut through the cloak of shadows and kill me."

Ashe was speechless hearing his request. It was cruel to reconnect in such an intimate way, only to be forced to consider killing him. She shook her head, tears spilling down her face.

"Ashe," he said gently. "I promise you; I will do everything in my power to make sure I don't have to use it. But it's a possibility we need to consider. Janus cannot have control of the throne, even through Levy.

"Chaos would be even worse. He's old Ashe. I can feel his thirst for that power. Even if we don't use the mask and manage to defeat Levy, his influence is in me. It has tainted me. I'm not even touching the mask right now and I can feel the Realm of Night pulling on me.

"You have to be the one to take the throne in the end. It's the only way we can ensure that tomorrow is a brighter day. Hestia once told me that you would be the guiding light for humanity.

"At the time I didn't know what she meant. But I do now." He kissed her hands, so gently. There were tears on his cheeks now as well. "You are the only one of the three of us who has never been corrupted by the powers in this world."

Ashe leaned forward resting her forehead against his. She was so tired of the twists life continued to throw at her. Thinking back to that fateful day the three of them had entered that cursed cavern, she wondered how different their lives would be now if they had never entered it.

She knew why it had been necessary for them to go. Humanity was facing an extinction crisis with the gods locked away in their realms and the monsters running wild. Had they never met Hestia and had this responsibility thrust upon them, she imagined how happy her life could have been.

She and Quinn would have settled down in Stormhaven and had

kids. They could have lived a happy life together, never knowing the horrors they had faced. She knew it was a selfish thought, but she just wanted to be selfish.

She could feel Quinn, running his thumb in little circles over her hand. He knew what he was asking was a lot. He hated having to ask it. But she could feel how much he felt it was necessary. With a sigh, she raised her eyes to his. "I promise." she whispered.

Relief flooded his face. Slowly he leaned in, meeting her lips with his own. Tomorrow, their lives, and the lives of the world would change forever. Tomorrow, they had a responsibility to fulfill. Tomorrow, their story would come to an end. But tonight, she was determined to enjoy one more night of bliss.

# CHAPTER 42: Levy

*You remember the plan, lad?*

"For the millionth time, yes," Levy replied. "Just because I'm mortal doesn't mean I'm stupid."

He stood on a stone platform, overlooking the burning magma below. A small bridge connected the platform to an opening in the wall, the only way in or out of the volcano. The tower was just behind him; its ornately carved doors depicting the ancient history it had witnessed over the many millennia of its existence.

Though he wanted nothing more than to stare at the beautiful carvings upon the door, he needed to focus. The war had finally reached its end. It was only a matter of time now before the throne would be his, and he wanted his smiling face to be the first thing his former friends saw.

*Everything comes down to this,* Janus said in his mind, barely able to contain his glee.

Levy had spent all night formulating this plan with Janus. He was still hesitant to trust the god, especially after turning on him, but he knew that without Janus' support, he would be unlikely to succeed. He may have overpowered Quinn and Ashe, but what needed to happen would take time; and if he had to fend of constant attacks from one while he dealt with the other, he wasn't sure time would be something he had.

*It's all water under the bridge, kid. We still have the same goals as before; despite how we got here. So long as you hold up your end of the bargain, I'm still happy to support you.*

"I swear upon your essence, I'll do just that," Levy joked, trying to lighten the mood.

*Smart-ass,"* Bearded Janus replied, snickering.

Between his fight with the monsters and his fight with Ashe, Levy's armor had seen better days. The once shiny onyx had dulled; covered with scratches and dents. His brown hair had grown shaggy, matching the patchy stubble he just hadn't had time to deal with. Yet through it all, his sword stayed shining, a beacon leading him into the future.

He thought back to Hestia's domain; the first time he'd come into contact with Janus. At the time he had been so resentful that his friends had gained such power while he had nothing but a sword to show for it. Yet now, he stood only feet away from claiming the throne, as was his fate.

For a brief second, he felt a moment of sadness. His old friends had no place in his future with their way of thinking. He'd offered Ashe an out the previous night, only to have it spat back in his face. That was twice in his life she had turned him down. Then there was Quinn; the one person he thought he would have in his corner no matter what.

*There is no such thing as friends when it comes to the tower. That is the very nature of it. Only one may sit upon the throne. The moment the three of you were fated for this future, your friendships were over.*

"Hestia was aware of that, wasn't she?" he asked. "That's why we were not allowed to walk the same path. The moment we were split, this fate was sealed."

*Aye,* Bearded Janus confirmed. *It's best you throw that sentiment away. It has no purpose other than to get you killed. Focus on the task at hand. Forget your past and claim your future, as is your right.*

Levy took a deep breath. Janus was right. If that was the way of the tower, it would do no good to dwell on what could have been. It was him or them. There was no alternative. Their friendship would be their downfall.

Janus began to hum in anticipation, snapping Levy from his thoughts.

*They're coming,* he buzzed. *Don't let them know we're working together. It'll hit them all the harder.*

Levy cracked his neck, readying himself for a fight.

"Showtime, boys."

# CHAPTER 43: Quinn

The path into the volcano was narrow and steep. All around them black, jagged obsidian dug into their feet. The closer they got to the entrance, the more the power of the tower bled into his conscious. It was no wonder the ancient structure attracted so many monsters to it.

The energy that assaulted his senses was grotesque and overwhelming. It was clear to him that when the Masters had fired their massive chains from the ancient cannons, anchoring the tower in place, they had been unaware of the damage the toxic essence would cause to their world around them.

Feeling his pain, Ashe reached out and grabbed his hand, sharing in the burden.

Higher and higher they climbed, feeling the air grow thinner around them. The view from this height was beautiful. He could see miles of verdant, green forest stretching away into the distance, disappearing under a cloud of dust, marking the border of the wastes.

He felt a pang of sorrow, hoping Nes was able to lead his people home okay. They would be in good hands with him, especially if Andra stuck around to guide him. Ashe squeezed his hand, surely feeling similar feelings herself. It was too bad they couldn't stick around and enjoy the scenery for longer. It would have made a great place to spend a day.

As they crested the top of a particularly steep climb, the ground before them leveled out. They had climbed in relative silence, both thinking about the task to come. With the bond between them as strong as it was, they hadn't had to say much to each other anyways. Now however, as they stared at the cave leading into the caldera of the volcano, they both had a similar thought.

"Kinda reminds me of…." Quinn began.

"Yeah," Ashe replied quietly. "Hopefully there's no alternate paths we have to take this time. Imagine if after all this time, it turns out we had already died, and our eternal punishment was facing a cycle of these absurd godly trials."

Quinn couldn't hold back the nervous laugh that escaped his lips. "Wouldn't that be something. Look at us," he said. "All we want is to be done with this, and yet here we are, standing outside stalling."

He had intended to start walking after saying that but found his legs still rooted to the spot. He looked at Ashe, somehow knowing that while both would enter, they wouldn't both leave. She must have felt something similar, because she looked back at him with sadness in her eyes.

"It'll be alright," she said, as though trying to convince herself.

"Yeah," he agreed, hollowly.

"Oh, this is ridiculous!" With a sharp tug she began to walk towards the entrance, pulling Quinn along behind her. He couldn't help but smile, as he watched the strongest person he had ever known, lead them into the end.

The heat increased dramatically has they made their way into the interior of the volcano. Passing through an archway, they found themselves on a narrow bridge, suspended above the bubbling lava below. The long walkway led to a large circular platform. Resting on the platform was the tower.

Sleek, white marble made its way into the sky, towering out of the volcano and casting its presence over the land below. It was bigger than he had ever imagined it would be. At the base of the tower, two enormous, ornately carved stone doors formed a barrier between the outside and the interior. The doors depicted many carvings from the annals of history.

On one quadrant it showed Zeus, thunderbolt in hand aimed at his father Kronos. Another image depicted a young maiden reaching up to pluck a pomegranate, a sinister shadow rising up behind her in waiting. Yet it was not these images that really caught Quinn's eye. It was instead, the very center that drew his attention.

Larger than all of the other carvings were three figures. A muscular man stood at the forefront with his arms folded behind his back. He wore a proud look upon his face. To the left of him was a girl, her eyes and hands lit ablaze. To his right was another man, wreathed in shadows, a half skull mask upon his face.

"Beautiful, isn't it?" Levy stood at the base of the doors, hands folded behind his back, mimicking the carving. "Every time the tower appears, it records those who vie for its power. This time it's us."

He walked forward until he was standing in the center of the circular platform. "When we began this journey, who could have thought we would end up like this? I mean, it was certainly meant to be based on what I see here.

"Who really could have known? Hestia had plans of course, though they were disrupted by Janus. Even Janus had schemes. He believed he was driving this forward. And yet when we arrive here, at the end of our road, we find out that it was recorded as such all along. Anybody who denies the fates exist are not paying attention."

"You done?" Quinn asked, eager to get this over with. "If it's all the same to you, I'd rather not sit here and listen to you drivel on about power you only pretend to understand. You said it yourself, we began this together, and we'll end it together. No more needs to be said."

"And you agree?" he asked, turning to Ashe. "You're usually the sentimental one after all. No eloquently thought out speeches about the power of friendship in an attempt to turn me back to the light?"

Ashe stepped up beside Quinn, fire already burning in her hands. “You chose your side a long time ago, Levy. There is nothing I wish to say to you now.”

Levy reached back and slid the sword from his scabbard. “Well then,” he shrugged. “That makes things easier.” Without warning he lunged forward, directly at Quinn.

# CHAPTER 44: Levy

*Remember, try not to let him put that mask on,*" Janus repeated for the thirtieth time that day.

"Obviously," Levy replied. "That's why I'm attacking him. He'll be too busy trying to defend my strikes to have the time." He swung at Quinn, feeling the first shower of hot sparks fall over him as his blade deflected the blow. Before he had time to strike again, he heard Janus yell, *Watch out!*

A glob of fire shot just past him, pulling his attention away from Quinn long enough to see Ashe relight her hand.

*Two at once is going to be tough lad."*

"It will be even harder if I have a voice in my head distracting me every time they attack." He raised his blade just in time to block Quinn's oncoming strike, before rolling backwards to escape another ball of fire. Just as he got back to his feet Quinn was there again, jabbing at his chest.

With a flourish of his blade he swept the attack away, pivoting so that he positioned himself on the other side. The plan would be to keep Quinn between himself and Ashe at all times.

*Smart!* Bearded Janus roared in approval.

"No. More. Commentary," Levy gritted keeping all of his concentration on blocking Quinn's swift strikes. The two of them were working together in perfect harmony, keeping him constantly on the defensive.

Any time Quinn slipped up and left him an opening, a ball of fire would appear, pushing him back and giving Quinn time to recover. It was as if they were reading each other's minds.

"Come on, Levy," Quinn taunted, pushing him closer to the edge of the platform. "I thought you were a god, now? Why are you being pushed back by us two measly mortals?"

He gritted his teeth. Quinn really knew what to say to get under his skin.

*Are you ready?* Janus asked.

"Just about," he muttered, watching his feet scrape the edge. "As soon as he attacks again."

Quinn, thinking he had Levy right where he wanted him, feinted a stab at his chest before sweeping his blade around and striking at his neck. Had Levy really been in a precarious position, it would have been a good strike.

Even if the feint hadn't worked, the impact of his blade on Levy's would have sent him over the edge. Instead, as his blade swept out, Levy ducked, sweeping his leg around the back of Quinn and kicking, sending his friend tumbling over the side.

"NO," Ashe yelled, sprinting forward to try and catch him. Before she could even get halfway Levy raised his hand and yelled, "NOW!"

A concussive force ripped forth, striking her hard and sending her crashing into the doors of the tower. A force began to build in his skull, feeling as though his head was ripping apart. Janus' essence tore itself free of his body, causing a scream to erupt from his throat.

Silvery essence coalesced at the base of the tower, starting to take shape. As the last of the god's energy left him, Levy fell to his knees, breathing hard. Behind him, he saw Quinn, clutching the side of the platform, staring in disbelief. It was hard to resist kicking him over the edge, but he wanted Quinn to see what came next.

# CHAPTER 45: Ashe

Ashe lay at the foot of the tower, curled up in pain. The blast Levy shot at her had sent her careening into the stone doors, breaking a few ribs on impact. Around the tower the ground was indented. Hollow channels of stone ran from the ground where she lay into the base of the door, before climbing up the sides and meeting at the top.

In front of her, a silvery blob of energy began to form. She forced herself up onto her knees, turning to look at where Quinn had tumbled. Her eyes widened as she saw him hanging off the edge, trying frantically to kick his way back on. Next to him, slowly fighting his way back to his feet was Levy, a triumphant grin lighting his face.

"Quinn," she cried out, clutching at her side.

"Oh my," a voice so sour it could curdle milk, spoke softly in her ear. "I don't think it's Quinn you should be worried about right now my dear."

Ashe turned her head to find Janus standing before her. The

blood drained from her face. "How are you here?" she asked. "I thought Levy had taken your essence."

He smiled a poisonous smile, gently caressing her face. "He got the drop on me, that's true. But he and I have since come to an understanding of sorts."

Ashe tried to scoot away, repulsed by his touch, but every movement she made sent waves of pain stabbing down her side.

"I wouldn't do that if I were you," he cooed. "You hit this door awfully hard. Those ribs are surely shattered. Move too much and you might puncture a lung."

He let out a gleeful little giggle. "Now just sit tight, I have someone who wants to talk to you."

He straightened his body as his head spun around so the bearded Janus faced her. He let out a sigh, as if seeing her this way pained him.

"I tried ta warn ye lass," he said, looking down at her with pity in his eyes. "If you'd have just married me, you could have avoided all this pain. Alas, it's too late now. No amount of begging can save you. You know what we gods say, 'There'r plenty o' maidens in the sea.'"

He laughed to himself as if he had just told the world's funniest joke. "Anyway lass, that's it from me. I'll let the big boss talk to you again."

His head spun back around, leaving the cold silver eyes of the clean-shaven Janus staring back at her.

"Alright, then," he said, looking past her at Levy. "Let's get this show on the road. These doors gotta open and the blood of a hero ain't gonna spill itself."

Ashe's eyes widened in horror. "That's why…."

"Ooooo dat's why," Janus mocked, sneering down at her. "Of course that's why, stupid girl. You think we'd allow you to stay alive just for fun? These doors are sealed tight so that any random being can't just come and sit on the throne. Now honestly, I don't have time for this. Levy, do the thing please."

Ashe glared up and Janus, eyes glowing bright. "I will not allow you to sit on this throne. Even if it burns me up in the process, I will unleash everything I have."

Janus' eyes grew wide at the power she was beginning to display.

"I will…."

A sword burst through, sending blood spurting from her mouth. Her energy died off around her, causing her eyes to revert back to their typical blue-green. She felt herself collapse, all of the fight draining out of her, as her blood pooled into the stone channels, running up the sides of the door.

"Sorry," Janus cupped his ear, leaning down to her. "You'll what?"

The last thing she saw before her eyes closed was a blast of darkness, smacking into the doorway of the tower.

# CHAPTER 46: Quinn

Quinn felt entirely helpless as he was left dangling off the edge of the platform, completely ignored. At the base of the tower, Ashe sat on her knees, holding her side. Janus leaned down into her face, mocking her. Quinn felt fury like he had never felt before, kicking wildly to try and get back up.

If the platform hadn't been so damn smooth, he may have been able to, but as it was, he was stuck there, not quite slippery enough to fall, but not rough enough for his foot to find purchase.

*Use me Quinn.* The voice of Chaos tickled the back of his mind.

Quinn refused, seeing Ashe begin to glow. Janus was in for a world of pain if he thought she was helpless just because she couldn't move. It was then that he saw Levy, slowly walking up behind her, his sword pointed at her back. An image flashed into his mind. He had seen this exact scene before.

*Yes,* Chaos cooed again, almost sadly. *You have seen this very image play out. You know what's going to happen. Janus told you that without the mask you would be unable to save her. But you have it now. Use my power. Allow me to have you, and I shall save her.*

Quinn shook his head, tears pooling in his eyes. He remembered their talk at the fire the night before, but he feared that now she wouldn't be in any position to stop him if Chaos took him over.

"Levy!" He hoped beyond hope to talk sense into his friend, but he never once looked back as he rose his sword to strike.

"Fine," Quinn yelled, summoning its power and bringing the mask to his face. There was a flash of light followed by immense darkness. As Quinn's awareness came back, he found himself on his knees in the Realm of Night. Next to him was an exact copy of himself. But when it spoke, it had Chaos' voice.

"Welcome to your final resting place," he said, staring out at the scene in front of them. Quinn looked on, watching Levy's blade inch toward Ashe's back.

"What are you doing?" he asked, fighting through the fog that had begun to settle on his mind. "Stop him!"

Chaos shook his head. "No."

"What? You promised!"

Chaos smiled, looking back at him. "I promised you nothing other than that when the time came, you would use my power. And here we are. I SAID I would stop this, but I never promised. Humans are so easy to coerce."

Quinn looked on, helpless as he watched Levy plunge his blade directly through Ashe's back. He saw every excruciating detail as the blade pierced her. The confusion slowly worked its way across her face, before it was replaced by pain. Finally, it ended as the light left her eyes and she collapsed.

Quinn felt completely numb. Everything they had been through had led to this moment. And in the end, he had let himself be tricked by the promise of power, as he watched the love of his life die to its hands.

"If it is any consolation, I promise you that Janus will not reach the throne."

Quinn shook his head, utterly defeated. "I don't care anymore," he said, empty. "Do what you will. I am powerless to stop you."

"That's the spirit!" Chaos patted him on the cheek. "Now close your eyes and rest. The Realm shall claim you, as it has claimed so many before. It really isn't that bad of an existence you know, floating around in the nothingness.

With no fight left in his body, Quinn sat back and watched, as the Primordial god wearing his skin stepped out of the Realm of Night.

# CHAPTER 47: Levy

The seams of the doorway ran red with Ashe's blood. As the cracks filled completely, the blood was replaced with a shimmering white light. Slow as can be, the doors began to rumble, loosing debris that had settled between the cracks from the century of lying dormant.

"Yes," Janus said, transfixed by the light. "For many millennia I have waited for this moment. Finally, I will claim the throne. This world is mine!"

Something black streaked past Levy, slamming into the stone. A writhing mass of shadowy tendrils was plastered to the door, slowly spreading over everything it touched. It appeared as though it were alive, crawling over the surface of the stone until it covered the entirety of the doorway, halting it in its progress.

"Sorry about that," came a silky voice from behind. Levy spun around, seeing Quinn back on his feet, head tilted to the side at an impossible angle. "Alas, I'm going to have to ask that you step away from the tower."

Levy complied, seeing the fight that was about to unfold and thinking better than to get involved with the two powerful forces. There was no way in Hades he planned on giving up his claim to the throne, but he wasn't going to stop these two from tearing each other apart first.

"That's a good boy," Chaos said to him.

"What's gotten into you, Quinn?" Levy asked, annoyed at the dismissive tone he had thrown his way.

Janus stepped forward, eyes glowing a dangerously bright silver. "That's no longer Quinn, lad," Bearded Janus said.

"Your godly patron is right," the shadow confirmed. "Quinn is no longer with us I'm afraid. You may call me Chaos. Now if you wouldn't mind stepping aside Janus, I'll be taking over from here."

"Like Hades you will," Janus said. "I've worked far too hard to let you swoop in at the last minute and steal my glory."

"Come now Janus, be reasonable," the silky voice hummed.

Levy couldn't help but feel like his eyes were getting heavier with each word he spoke. "You are but a god. You can't honestly hope to defeat me."

"You may be powerful, but you're still trapped in a mortal body. I can beat you."

Chaos smiled. "Shall we test that theory?"

# CHAPTER 48: Ashe

*"Wake..."*

*Ashe slept so peacefully, floating through the warm darkness.*

*"Wake up."*

*She couldn't remember the last time she had slept so soundly. There had been a time, she was sure, wrapped in the arms of a man she loved. But that felt like such a long time ago.*

*"Wake up!"*

*Ashe's eyes fluttered open, meeting a pair of warm, amber eyes peering directly back at her.*

*"Hestia?" she asked, trying to remember where she was. Had she just completed her trials? That also felt like it had been a lifetime ago. "Where am I?"*

*"You are at the edge of life and death." She said, settling across from her. They sat in a room of blackness. The only light came from the tiny fire Hestia was tending to.*

*"What happened?" she asked. She remembered confronting Levy in front of the tower, but everything was hazy.*

*"It is not time for you to be here. You need to wake up. You made a promise. Humanity depends on you to keep it."*

*None of this was making any sense to Ashe. "What promise are you talking about?"*

*Hestia moved closer to her, grabbing her hands within her own and staring into her eyes. With a flash of recollection, Quinn came to her mind.*

*"Is he okay?" she asked Hestia.*

*She turned back to her flames. "That is up to you." she began fading into the blackness around her. "You need to wake up."*

Ashe opened her eyes, peering at the flickering orange glow of the volcanic walls. As consciousness slowly returned to her, she could hear a commotion echoing off the stone. Levy sat a little way away from her, his back resting against the tower, eyes widened in awe. Turning her head toward the sound, she saw a nightmare.

Janus darted around the cavern, faster than Ashe thought possible. His body was glowing with a silver outline so bright it made spots dance before her eyes. Standing in the center was Quinn.

Her heart dropped when she saw the mask resting on his face. Long tendrils of shadow burst out from every part of his body, reaching for and swatting at the god that flitted around him.

Janus streaked back and forth, lunging in and swiping a jagged knife at his foe before deftly bounding away, just out of reach of the shadowy tendrils. Whenever one got too close to him, he'd blast it with a concussion of force before ducking inside and swiping again at Chaos.

Chaos, for his part, was howling a sinister, crackling laugh. Power unlike Ashe had ever felt before was pouring out of him, drowning out the light and slowly turning the cavern to shadow.

Yet despite all of his power, he had yet to truly hit Janus. Every time the room got darker, Janus would let his silver energy flare, fighting toe to toe with the shadows.

Just when it looked like Janus had the upper hand, a shadowy tentacle shot from the floor, punching the jagged knife from his hand and skewering him through his stomach. It raised him into the air, immobilizing him. Ichor shot out of his mouth, as he stared wide eyed at the monstrous shadow before him.

Chaos smiled a toothy grin. "I'll give you this at least," he said in a silky voice that was entirely not his own. "You gave it a good effort."

Tendrils shot forward from all around him, piercing Janus repeatedly, inducing an agonized screech from the god. Chaos raised two fists out in front of him, and with a mighty pull, the tendrils burst in all different directions, tearing Janus into pieces. Ichor sprayed across the room, drenching both herself and Levy. With slow, methodical steps, Chaos began moving toward the doors of the tower.

Ashe knew she could not allow whatever being possessed him to enter through those doors. She summoned all of the remaining strength left within her and raised her hand, pumping all of her essence into it.

A flickering golden flame sprang to life, fighting the darkness of the shadow that had taken over the cavern. As if sensing its anathema, Quinn's head whipped around staring directly at her outstretched hand.

With a quick flick of his wrist, he sent the shadowy tendrils racing toward her. Putting every last bit of her strength into it, she unleashed the fireball toward her lover. The shadows wilted under the golden heat of her fire, shredding them.

The flaming mass of energy smashed into the cloak that had wrapped itself tightly around him, burning away the darkness until the glistening white mask was revealed. With one final burst, the flame collided with the mask, shattering the alabaster into pieces.

# CHAPTER 49: Quinn

Quinn sat, alone in the darkness of the Realm of Night, watching the events play out before him with a glassy stare. The amount of power Chaos was channeling through his body was incredible.

Tendrils of shadow thrashed about in a combination of lethal force and impregnable defense. Janus was a silver blur, striking in close before bounding back, just out of the tendril's reach. The power of the Realm had begun to envelop him, pulling him down into nothingness just as Chaos had said it would, but Quinn no longer cared.

He thought that all of the pain and heartbreak he had gone through up to this point had been worth it after reuniting with Ashe, but now he realized just how cruel fate was. He had failed Hestia. He had failed humanity and his people.

What stung more than anything else, was that he had failed Ashe. His journey, his true journey, had started the moment he chose to grab the mask over saving the life of a child. He wondered if this fate had been sealed from that moment on.

Would things be the same if he had chosen differently? Would Ashe still be alive? He couldn't find it in him to care anymore. His emotions bled out of him as the realm pulled him further down. Soon his consciousness would cease to exist all together, and he would finally be free.

A small movement in the corner of the room drew his attention. Ashe's head had turned, her stare no longer blank, but filled with clarity. A tear ran down her face as she took in what had become of Quinn. But she was alive!

Hope poured back into him, filling his body with an energy he thought he had already lost to the nothingness. He fought to his feet, pulling against the tendrils that tried to hold him captive. A scream lit the air as Janus was held aloft, pierced repeatedly by shadowy tendrils.

A second later, warm ichor washed over his body. Even though he was no longer in control of himself, he could feel the sensation as the blood slapped his skin. But none of that mattered. Ashe. He had to get to Ashe.

As he took a couple steps her way, a familiar, warm energy began to fill the air. Chaos must have felt it as well because his head snapped toward her, malicious intent washing through his awareness.

Quinn saw a golden orb of fire form in her hand and smiled. So, this was it then. She planned to keep their promise. Chaos tried to make his way to her so he could snuff out the flame, but Quinn fought him every step of the way with everything he had left.

This pure, godly fire seemed to be the one thing he feared. And Quinn could sense that fear. It was almost animalistic. He fought against the Primordial god's will, doing his best to hinder each step he took toward her from within his prison.

It must have had some affect, because in a panic Chaos stopped, instead sending tendrils of his power lashing out toward her. He smiled, seeing the orb of fire release from her hand, knowing Chaos was too late.

The fire shredded his shadows, increasing in speed until it lit his vision with a brilliant golden glow. As it made contact, Quinn's vision flashed to white. He basked in the warmth of her energy, ready to move on from this world knowing that Chaos had been stopped.

The mask shattered from his face, falling into large fragments upon the warm volcanic rock of the platform. Quinn was on his hands and knees. The eye of the mask, being the only whole piece left, staring back at him. He ran his finger down the scar marking on the mask, feeling only a trickle of the otherworldly energy respond. With a start, he snapped his head up, staring into the relieved eyes of Ashe.

He ran to her, cradling her head in his lap as she reached up, stroking the side of his face. He winced at her touch.

"I'm sorry," she said weakly. "You're still handsome."

He reached up to where her hand had touched and felt his skin. It was hot to the touch and tender, scarred from the effect of the flame.

He shook his head, tears forming in his eyes. "How many times are you going to make me tell you," he cried with a sad smile. "You don't have anything to apologize for."

The doors to the tower rumbled, cracking the globs of shadow that held it in place. Ashe's eyes never left his. She looked into his soul, seemingly happy with what she saw.

"Finish this," she gasped weakly. "Finish this and change the world."

The light began to fade from her eyes as her head slowly rocked back, losing its strength. With a sob, he gently removed it from his lap, rising up and facing the doorway to the tower.

Standing in his path was Levy, looking back at him with fierce determination. "Stand aside Levy," he growled. "You've done enough."

Levy just shook his head, for once not smiling back at him. "This is how it ends, Quinn. Just you and me. No essence, no gods or powers, just us and our swords. Just like back at the Citadel when we used to spar. If you want to take this throne, you'll have to take it from my corpse."

Quinn looked down at Ashe. "I'm okay with that."

They moved to the center of what would be their final arena and drew their blades, facing each other for the last time. Both were extremely fatigued thanks to the effect of their immortal patrons having separated from them.

Levy looked around the cavern at the flickering shadows dancing along the walls. "Seems a shame nobody is here to witness this. The soldiers at the Citadel would have loved it."

Quinn looked around as well, imagining the stands of soldiers that used to line the bleachers of the training pit during one of their fights. He turned back to Levy, cold determination running through him. "I'm sorry it had to turn out this way," he said, staring into eyes that had once been friendly.

"I'm not," Levy growled before springing toward him.

Their swords met, sending a loud clang reverberating around the cavern. As they fought, their shadows joined the dance upon the walls, graceful in their movements.

Over and over again the blades clashed, neither fighter gaining the upper hand, as if they were destined to spend eternity locked in fateful combat. Levy struck first, opening a gash along Quinn's shoulder.

Quinn responded with a nick across his ribs. Back and forth they traded blows, each man slowly bleeding the other out. Sweat poured into the wounds, setting their bodies on fire in the heat. But still neither warrior backed down. The only sounds in the cavern were the ringing of their blades and their grunts of exertion. Nothing more needed to be said between them.

Levy roared, swinging a vicious vertical strike down upon Quinn. He made himself skinny, allowing the blade to swing past him, before stepping inside Levy's guard and throwing a strong punch into the man's muscular jaw. Levy rocked back, giving Quinn time to grab his wrist and twist, wrenching the sword, all that remained of Janus, free from his grasp.

As it fell to the ground, Quinn threw his aside as well, losing himself to his rage, and tackled Levy, landing on top of him and raining blow after blow down upon him. Levy's guard broke after the first few hits.

No longer wishing to take the brunt of Quinn's rage, he bucked his hips, sending Quinn over the top of him. Then it was Quinn who was on the defensive, blocking the blows that fell from the stone fists of his former friend.

With a roar of frustration, he lashed out, landing a hard hit to

Levy's stomach, blasting the air out from his lungs. He took advantage of the momentary weakness and swung a punch in a wide arc, clocking Levy in the temple.

Levy's body fell off of him instantly, tumbling toward the edge of the platform. Quinn struggled to his feet, fighting to catch his breath. Blood dripped from his nose, falling upon the volcanic rock and sizzling. With a quick lunge he reached out, grabbing Levy by the collar; barely stopping him from falling into the lava below.

"When we were younger," Quinn rasped. "All I wanted was to be your friend. You were everything I looked up to; strong, smart, brave. But now when I look at you, all I see is a spiteful coward, chasing after power because you fear you are too weak to accomplish anything on your own."

Levy laughed, showing his bloody teeth. "You and I are birds of a feather, my friend. You proved it when you took that mask. You'll prove it again when you take the throne."

Quinn shook his head; his eyes filled with regret. "You're right. Which is why I never intended to take the throne."

Confusion flashed across Levy's face. "But I see no way forward for you either, Levy. You're just a shell of the man you once were, too twisted by Janus to allow you to take its power for yourself.

"I don't see any other alternative. I am truly sorry it had to end this way between us." Levy's eyes widened as he realized what Quinn was saying. "Goodbye Levy."

Quinn let go of him, letting the weight of his choices pull him from the edge of the platform and down toward the lava below. For the first time ever, Quinn saw fear in his old friend's eyes, and he knew it would haunt him for the rest of his life.

The shadow blocking the doors to the tower had mostly gone now. As the stone slowly scraped open, flooding the chamber with pure, white light Quinn stooped down to Ashe, taking her up in his arms. He stood in front of the doors, waiting for them to fully open.

As they finally ground to a stop, Quinn waited for his eyes to adjust to the harsh light emanating from within. The tower consisted of a circular chamber which rose high enough into the air that Quinn could not see its ceiling.

The walls of the chamber were bare and white. In the center of the room sat the throne. It was a simple chair which sat upon a raised dais. Both the dais and the throne were made out of the same exact white as the inner chamber walls.

With slow and deliberate steps, Quinn crossed the threshold, immediately feeling the familiar pop of pressure that indicated they were no longer in the mortal realm. The power that flooded into Quinn then was overwhelming, nearly knocking him off of his feet.

It took all of his concentration just to keep hold of Ashe. It was clear that the tower was fighting him, telling him only one was to enter at a time. But Quinn pushed forward towards the throne, fighting the waves of energy that assaulted him.

As he climbed the dais, the pressure became nearly a physical barrier. Quinn reached down deep within himself, calling on his last dregs of energy and pushed out, creating a hole in the barrier just long enough for him to place Ashe's body on the throne, before blacking out.

# CHAPTER 50: Ashe

Ashe awoke to a brilliant white light. She was floating, but in what she could not tell. There was no ceiling or floor and no walls surrounding her. All around her, millions of orbs floated in place, each with string attaching them to another. Inside the orbs were pictures, some of places, some of people. A few she recognized, though most she did not.

"Welcome, hero, to the Tower of Fates." An elderly crone floated in the air above her. "My name is Clotho, the last hero of prophecy to have successfully reached the tower, over a millennia ago."

"I know that name," Ashe said, staring at the woman in wonder. "You're known as the Weaver of Fates."

"All who take the throne are known as the Weavers, my dear," the woman replied. "Until our millennium of service is up, and a new weaver takes their place.

"That is the secret of this place. Fate is what moves this world forward. There must always be a weaver, lest the nothingness devour all life."

Ashe looked around again at all of the strings which attached the orbs to one another, telling an elaborate story. "So, the rumors that whoever sits here can change the world are true."

"Yes and no," the woman replied. "The Weaver spins the string and sets the story, however she may only influence, never direct."

"I don't understand," Ashe said.

The woman smiled at her. "In time you will. For now, all I can describe it as is this: creatures have a will of their own. You can push them toward a certain fate, but if their will is strong enough, they can deviate from your path."

At this she pointed to an orb that held a picture of Quinn. "Take your friend for example. He was never meant to reach this place. In my weaving, the mask would have consumed him, you would have died, and Chaos would have ascended the throne."

Ashe looked up at her, aghast. "But Chaos would have destroyed our world. How could you have chosen that to be our fate?"

Clotho smiled sadly. "Fate is a fickle thing, as you will learn. Sometimes the world is going in a direction you cannot control, and you must choose the best of the worst in the hopes that from the ashes, new light will rise."

"So, you're saying there is something out there worse than Chaos?" Ashe paled.

Clotho's eyes became distant. "There is always something worse, dear."

Ashe looked at the shriveled woman feeling a burning passion begin to blossom within her. "I will not allow something like that to hurt this world."

Clotho smiled a knowing smile back at her. "I hope you're right. Now my time as weaver is up and I must go. Say goodbye to your friend." She pointed to Quinn, curled up and unconscious at her feet. "Your watch begins, and he may not stay here for it."

Sadness blossomed in Ashe's chest. She wasn't sure how, but she knew Clotho was right. The moment she was sat on the throne, it had changed her.

She had ascended into a higher state of being. This was no longer a place for him. She found his orb and could see that his string was no longer entwined with her own. She had evolved past the small range of human being, and understood that her new duty was more important, yet she couldn't stop the tears from spilling down her cheeks.

*Remember dear, those with strong wills don't always follow the strings of fate. You may yet meet again.*

Clotho's weak voice echoed around the chamber. Ashe doubted it were true, but she held hope in her heart. With a resigned sigh, she used her newfound power, and woke him from his slumber.

# CHAPTER 51: Quinn

Quinn awoke to find Ashe smiling down at him, lit by the white light of the tower. Sitting on the throne, she was radiant. And yet, as he looked at her, he realized he felt a distance that he had not felt since they had reconnected.

With a start, he realized he could no longer feel a connection to her. Though he could feel power wafting off of her, he could not interact with it as he once could. It was then that he knew that he'd lost her. He shouldn't be surprised.

He had a feeling that he or she who claimed the throne would be unable to return from it, but he'd hoped there might yet be a way. As if reading his thoughts, she descended the dais and wrapped him in a mighty hug.

"I'm sorry it ended up this way," she spoke into his chest. "I want you to know that you made me happier than anything else in life."

Quinn felt the tears cascade from his eyes, unable to hold them back, knowing he had to say goodbye. "I know you can feel it as well, this distance between us now."

"You are a part of the tower now," he said, words barely escaping his mouth in more than whisper.

She nodded, before turning around and reclaiming her seat upon the throne. Her eyes grew distant for a moment, before locking back onto his.

"I promise you I will do what I can for your people. I will do my best to lead this world to prosperity, but I am afraid it's time for you to go. If you stay any longer, you will be unable to fulfill the destiny I have planned for you.

"But before you do, I must ask for one more favor."

Their eyes locked, and Quinn knew immediately what she requested. With a sigh, he nodded to her.

Hestia had warned him they were on a path of separation. He had assumed she'd meant the three years they were apart, but he realized now that she'd intended for this to be the outcome all along. It broke his heart to leave Ashe here, but some part of him had been preparing for it all along.

As he looked up to her again, he saw that her eyes were already distant; her consciousness no longer in the room with him. With a longing he could do nothing about, he turned to leave and fulfill her last request. Just before he walked across the threshold that led back out into the volcanic crater he heard, "Quinn!"

He whipped around, seeing her eyes once again locked onto his.

"I love you," she said with a sad smile.

"I love you, too."

He stepped out of the tower, watching the doors slowly close behind him. He watched her until the doors had shut completely, burning the image of her beautiful blue-green eyes into his mind.

Quinn stood at the top of the volcano, staring down at the last chain that tethered the tower to this realm. He had already snapped the other three, each time fighting the urge to leave them in place and find a way back into the tower.

He could feel the eagerness of the energy that radiated from it. The tower had been trapped in this realm for a century now, far too long for its liking. He knew that when he broke this last chain, it would disappear, likely for the rest of his life, taking Ashe with it.

For the fourth time, he considered leaving it and dedicating his life to finding a way to reopen the doors. An image of Levy flashed in his mind at that thought, and he shook his head, knowing where that path would lead. With a sigh, he drew his blade and steeled his resolve.

Breathing out he swung down, severing the links of the chain. Immediately the tower responded, releasing a brilliant white light before shooting out of the volcano and disappearing, back to its own realm. Quinn looked out over the land.

He knew he could return to the wastes if he wished, but despite the knowledge, he just couldn't help but feel that without Ashe, there was nowhere he belonged.

Footsteps behind him alerted him to the presence of someone coming up the trail. Unsure if it would be friend or foe, he grabbed the handle of his blade. Despite not knowing what to do now with his life, he didn't plan to let some random monster take him out here.

*Old habits die hard.*

A bald head crested the hill, followed by a surly face. The man's brown, unkempt beard travelled all the way down to his chest. Unbelievably, he wore the tattered robes of one of the Masters back from his time at the Citadel.

"At ease Quinn," the man said, raising his hands in a placating gesture.

"How do you know my name?" Quinn asked. "I see your robes, but I've never seen you at the Citadel."

"And you wouldn't have," the man kept his hands in the air. "I was responsible for your training, but I never showed myself to you or your friends. I was ordered not to."

"Ordered by whom?" he asked; his face rife with skepticism.

"Hestia," the man replied. "My name is Talius. We need to talk."

# Epilogue

Ashe was hard at work weaving the strings of Fate between the floating orbs around her. Most of the time the connections were mundane, having no great impact on the world. Though these connections bored her, they were a part of the job she couldn't ignore as weaver.

Every so often she would find a particular connection that sent reverberations though the yarn connecting one orb to another. Those were the ones she knew meant something.

Fate was fickle, as she had soon found out. Sometimes she would connect a person to an event, only to have the yarn snap. Those were the people Clotho had talked about, with wills strong enough to fight their fate.

She found it more annoying than anything. She did her best to keep her promise to Quinn, connecting the fates of humans and Abyssillians alike, hoping it would help create a blossoming friendship between the peoples.

Every so often she would check on her friend's orb. She tried not to mess with it unnecessarily, knowing his will was stronger than most. A couple of times she had tried to reconnect it to her own, only to have the connection fail immediately.

She did notice however, that yarn had been woven between his and a bearded man. The yarn was thick, indicating a strong connection between the two. From there the yarn rose high into the tower. With her interest piqued, she followed it, floating ever higher. She rarely came to this part of the tower.

Most of the orbs here were ancient and she feared the ripples she may cause for her world by messing with them. However, the yarn that had connected Quinn with the man named Talius had found its way here, wrapping around many of the ancient orbs in the process.

As she climbed higher, she noticed the string had connected to a large, sky blue orb. Though she couldn't see the image inside of it, she felt the power it exuded, crackling around its surface like electricity.

Peering closer, she caught a glimpse of the entity within. With a gasp, she realized what she was looking at. She flew back down to Quinn's orb, following the other strings attached to it. Each string was like a path; a potential future he may create for himself.

However, each of them always ended up back at the large, blue orb. Another war was coming, one that Quinn would be heavily involved in. She began furiously weaving strings, attaching them to his orb, trying to make a connection with those who may be able to assist. Having done what she could, she sat back, terrified.

*Good luck Quinn,* she thought. *You're going to need it.*

The last thing Levy remembered was the resolve in Quinn's eyes as he released his hold on Levy's collar, allowing him to fall over the ledge toward the lava below. Just before impact, he felt a strong snap of power, followed by a flash so bright, he had to close his eyes so as not to be blinded.

He felt the atmosphere enveloping him change from the burning sensation of the lava to a warm breeze. The air around him smelled of ozone, and he opened his eyes to see himself standing on a smooth surface which reflected the sky around him.

Sensing an immense power, he turned, meeting the piercing blue gaze of a man who could only be described as godly. He wore a purple toga underneath bright bronze armor. A long, white beard cascaded down his chest, ending just above his stomach. Power flashed in his eyes, reflected by the clouds around him.

"Welcome to my Realm," his voice boomed like thunder.

Levy stared back in awe, fear creeping into him.

"You failed to secure the throne, however, thanks to your snagging my brother's orb, you have released a powerful bit of godly energy back into the mortal realm. Soon, we will uncover more, and your realm will once again be flooded with our power. When that happens, I will have use of you."

Levy smiled, hearing the implication in the man's voice. Bending to a knee, he dropped his head. "Whatever you need, Lord

Zeus. I am yours to command."

He looked past the god to where the form of an old lady was bound; body haggard and face bloodied.

Following his eyes, Zeus warned, "Do not think you can overwhelm me as you did Janus. Use Clotho here as an example of what happens following betrayal."

His face paled as he felt the threat in the god's voice. "Understood, my lord."

A brilliant white smile split the god's face. "Ready yourself. Now the real war begins."

# About the Author

Brian has dreamed of being an author since his early days of high school. He used to sit in the school library whenever he had the chance, soaking up as many tales from Greek Mythology as he could get his hands on; fascinated by the stories of gods and heroes. After stumbling upon the Percy Jackson series in his school's library, he began reading at a feverish pace and never looked back. Fate Weaver marks his debut as an author, as well as the first book of an Epic Series; Wrath of Olympus.

Printed in Great Britain
by Amazon

51958662R00170